GRAHAM STRUGNELL

Graham Strugnell was born in Wallington, Surrey, in 1961. In a life filled with adventure and mishap, he failed his 11+, faked his way into grammar school and blundered through his teenage years. After a bureaucratic oversight, he found himself at Oxford University in the 1980s. He then turned his hand to journalism, working briefly for a free newspaper and as a freelancer, where his stories of life as a hapless bachelor met with some acclaim. Later, he succumbed to the lure of abroad, living and teaching for many years in Japan.

On his return to the UK, he became a teacher, journalist, musician and playwright, mainly of school plays that baffled audiences with their scale and ambition. He now lives quietly with his wife and son in deepest Devon where he teaches on zoom. As he seldom meets people who do not appear in pixelated form on his computer screen, his greatest ambition is to turn himself into a meme. *Becoming Henry* is his first novel.

BECOMING HENRY

BECOMING HENRY

GRAHAM STRUGNELL

Constellations Press

First published in 2025

Typesetting by Constellations Press
Printed and bound in the UK through Xpedient Book Print

A CIP record for this book is available from the British Library

ISBN 978-1-917000-09-3
e-ISBN 978-1-917000-15-4

MIX
Paper | Supporting responsible forestry
FSC® C013604

For Ros and John Strugnell,
without whom Henry would not have happened.

Home is where you're always wrong
Too fat or too thin
Home's an endless argument
You never can win.

Home
Fran Landesman

I believe the power of observation in very young children to be quite wonderful for its closeness and accuracy. If it should appear from anything I set down in this narrative that I was a child of close observation, or that as a man I have a strong memory of my childhood, I undoubtedly lay claim to both these characteristics.

David Copperfield
Charles Dickens

Prologue

Brave New World

There was something wrong with Henry Truffle. The black-and-white snaps and washed-out Polaroids revealed a child large of head and short of limb, with a pair of pale eyes that were trained on the camera. It was as if he knew, even at that age, what was being done to him — that his image and soul were being snatched from him without so much as a by-your-leave — and heartily disapproved of it.

He was born at home on Tuesday, October 31st, a day when the membrane between one world and the next grows thin: a day when the spirits of the dead return to Earth to wreak vengeance on those who have done them harm. Whether Henry was one of those vengeful ghosts had yet to be determined, but as he lay there in a puddle of warm excrement, dolefully flailing his limbs, it certainly seemed that way.

After the unpleasant business of delivery, his mother lay back on the pillows and averted her gaze from the biological disaster below. It had been a difficult birth, and the suppository, administered by an inexperienced midwife, had had predictable consequences. Birth was a humiliation as well as bitter agony. Still, the baby had been slapped and was mewing like a kitten, so at least her little child was alive. Fortunately, there was a plentiful supply of hot water and towels, so the thing the midwife finally passed her was clean if a trifle odd — a raw, red creature with a scruff of pale hair. 'Hello,' she whispered, when he was lying in the crook of her arm. She was loath to startle so small and vulnerable a being, one whose ears, moreover — so delicate, so crumpled — would be tender from lack of use. 'Hello, you,' she said. She couldn't bring herself to call him 'Henry' just yet. He looked, somehow, as though he would object to a name being imposed on him without his consent. Still, she could at least feed him. 'Now, little one,' she said tenderly, 'let's have some milk, shall we?'

The 'little one' gazed blindly upwards and aimed a vague punch at the breast that loomed above him. He appeared to have no idea what a breast was, and to be mildly affronted that one had been so rudely thrust in his face. Still, with some encouragement, he finally settled onto the nipple and did what was expected of him. Yet it seemed to the mother, as her baby drew life from her in snuffly little gulps and then pulled away to bring it up again in a spasm of vomit, that he was somewhat indifferent to the process of survival.

Chapter 1

The Truth About Triangles

Henry was informed that he must go to school. Gone were the days when he could sit watching his mother at her domestic chores in the warm fug of the kitchen, Henry making sausage shapes in the pastry that she rolled out, or using coloured plastic moulds to create faces which he starred with raisins and currants and bits of peel, pressing the fruit into the mix to make eyes and noses and mouths. These faces went into the oven on a metal tray and emerged as biscuits — and then he could eat them, these little men he had made, now hard and crunchy and warm and sweet. They looked at him with mild reproach when he bit into them and left them with one eye or a broken skull or a severed smile, but what else could he do?

At school, he learned other things, things that weren't cooking and getting dressed and tying his shoelaces and eating pastry faces in a way that upset him. He learned about words. He learned how to shape his letters properly and make them sit on the line, or trail a leg under it, or stretch on tiptoe to reach a line pencilled above. He learned how to make a letter all shouty and big, and how to make dots and tadpoles to break up the words. Then there were maths lessons he didn't understand, and a girl who sat next to him who had a pretty face but mischievous eyes. Once, she pulled down her knickers and showed him, under the desk, the different thing she had. It was a thing with a split in it like the entrance to a padlock, and this was also learning, but of another kind. Her thing smelled musty, like something that had been kept in a cupboard for a long time. He'd seen his sisters naked in the bath, but this wasn't the same. He asked if he could touch it. He wanted to tease it gently with the tip of his pencil, because he was a little afraid of it. It looked alive and independent of the girl who had it, like a small, untrustworthy animal that might bite you if it caught you unawares. But no, she said. Just look: no touching. So, he looked. And then, suddenly and without any explanation, she covered it up, as if she had grown bored with this act of showing, or as if he had cheapened himself by asking. He felt ashamed then, although she had been the one to pull her knickers down, not him.

School was full of strange people who did unexpected things. Often, they were girls or women that didn't behave as his sisters or mother would have done. There was a dinner lady he liked, and once he did a special wave as she walked away to indicate his love for her, even though she couldn't see him do it. A teacher spotted him and said he was making a 'vile, insulting sign,' and that he was 'a disgusting little boy to do such a thing.' She pulled him roughly from his chair and made him stand beside a curtain whose stiff and velvety folds went up to the ceiling. He stayed there as the hall emptied and everyone forgot about him. He heard the distant echoey sound of the kitchens and of people washing up and banging saucepans together, and then, when it was quiet, the murmur of lessons: the teachers' voices, calm and clear; the children's voices in a chant or chorus. The children in those classes were in the present, but he was in the past. He had been left behind, merging with the curtain and the dust in its folds and the empty room where the tables were bare except for a lake of spilled water and few bits of cooked carrot. He did not dare to move because he had not been given permission. At school you had to do what you were told; you must accept a punishment even if you were innocent.

After a while there were footsteps and his teacher came. She wanted to know what on earth he was doing, standing there like that, when lessons had already started? He wept, and his explanation got all tangled up, and then the teacher said, well, never mind, Henry, come to class, I expect it was all some silly misunderstanding. And it was. Because Henry didn't know how a little wriggly finger-wave, which he'd invented as a secret sign of his undying affection, could be considered disgusting and wrong. Why couldn't people understand what was in his head, that his thoughts were innocent and good? Why couldn't they see his heart? He would never make bad signs at people he loved. He didn't even know what bad signs were.

It wasn't always like this, because there were good things about school, too. Going home was a good thing. In summer, when you came out, there was ice-cream, and this was the best thing of all. The van with its chugging engine was always there, parked near the school gate. It sold pink ice cream on a stick, and soft, white ice cream in a cone and topped with a flake and sauce dripped from a red plastic bottle. There were ice-creams shaped like faces, lollies like rockets with fins and coloured sections, and ones that were supposed to taste like cola but didn't. Sometimes there were jokes on the wooden sticks that went through the lollies. When he sucked the stick, he got a woody taste in his mouth, and after a while the stick started to go thready, and he had to throw it away or risk a splinter.

It was summer, and summer smelled of things like cut grass in gardens and cucumber in sandwiches and curdled milk in corridors. There were red ants to avoid and earwigs to be afraid of because they could crawl into your ear and pull out your brains with their pincers. But it was fun to play with his toy car in the dirt at school breaktime, shrinking himself down to the size of a tiny man and racing through blades of grass that were really trees, and past stones that were great boulders in a canyon.

Sometimes a boy or girl would laugh at him, saying he had a head shaped like a triangle, coming up to tell him this as if he were ignorant of it and they were doing him a favour. He didn't want to be a triangle. He wanted to be normal. But now they had told him, he couldn't forget.

Triangles were funny because they could be tents and teepees and musical instruments and abstract shapes. Sometimes they played triangles in assembly, and anyone could do it; you just struck them with a little metal wand and listened to the chiming. They sounded like they looked: silvery and bright, like the edge of a star. When you played them, all you needed was rhythm, which meant timing. Timing was important in life, his teacher said, like when you made a joke, which wasn't funny without it. His teacher didn't explain what she meant because she never made jokes. Nor did she explain how a triangle could be your head, and how people could use a shape to hurt you, and to make a joke out of you.

He told his mother what the others had said about his head being a triangle. 'You have a high forehead,' she said quietly, as if it were a secret she should have explained before. 'When you were born, the bones in your skull were very soft, and your poor head got squashed when you came out. If we're careful with your hair, and don't cut it too short at the back, no-one will notice.'

But his mother was wrong. They did notice. Henry's head was a triangle, they said, and they laughed, and it was his fault. He didn't cry, but when he got home, he banged his head with his fist to see what would happen, and it didn't ring like the side of a star. It hurt, and made lights come on behind his eyes. But that was all right, because it made the other hurt go away.

At night, in bed, he counted to a hundred, not because he wanted to, but because a voice told him to. The voice was both outside and inside. 'Count to a hundred,' it commanded. It was a bullying voice, gruff and jeering. Henry wasn't allowed to go to sleep, the voice said, until he'd finished counting. But when he got to a hundred, the voice tricked him and acted as if Henry had made a mistake when he hadn't. 'Count to *two* hundred!' it demanded. 'I said *two* hundred! Start again, Henry!' So, he did, counting until the numbers got very big and his head had to expand to hold them all.

If his head kept getting bigger the triangle would turn into a trapezium. His dad had taught him that word; it sounded better than triangle because it didn't have 'angle' in it to remind him of his pointy head. It sounded like a trapeze in a big top where you could fly through the air while another person flew towards you and you caught them, and the audience applauded wildly. He wanted to be a boy on a trapeze and be applauded, so he kept counting. Then he felt dizzy and lost his way, because he was thinking about circuses and safety nets and putting chalk on his hands. The voice told him to start again, because he was a stupid little boy who got distracted too easily. He agreed that he was and started at the beginning. In the end, exhausted by numbers, he fell asleep.

God was a number, so there was good counting as well as bad counting. God was number one, but He was also three. That didn't happen in maths, because numbers couldn't mean more than one thing at once. Only words could do that, which was why Henry preferred them. *In the beginning was the Word,* the Bible said. It didn't say, *In the beginning was the Number.*

Henry believed in God and said the Lord's Prayer along with all the other children in school, chanting the words, his and their voices blending and becoming one murmuring sound, sleepy and warm. Henry had a friend who sat beside him and said the Lord's Prayer too. His name was John. Their mothers knew each other, and sometimes they would share lifts, John's mother driving them in her funny black car with indicators that stuck out at the side when you turned left or right. John was nice, but he didn't speak much on account of his stutter, which meant some words came out wrong, or stuck in his throat as if they had spikes, or awkward edges, or were shaped like triangles that no-one could stand. John looked different too, but Henry liked him anyway. He was thin and dusty and angular, as if there wasn't quite enough skin to cover his body. The bones poked through in places such as his knees and elbows, where he always had a scab that he picked at and afterwards ate. He had a comfortable smell of washing-powder and the liniment his mother rubbed on his chest, and he breathed with a whine, as if he had a tiny mosquito trapped inside. But when John chanted the Lord's Prayer, his wheezy voice blended in with all the others, and everyone forgot that he couldn't speak properly.

Henry liked the Lord's Prayer. He liked the rhythm of the words: 'Forgive us our trespasses as we forgive those who trespass against us and lead us not into temptation but deliver us from evil for thine is the kingdom the power and the glory forever and ever *Amen*.' He knew God was in that rhythm and in those words. Maybe that's what the teacher had meant about the importance of rhythm and timing. Although he didn't know what trespasses were or how he could be trespassed against, it didn't matter. The words were a spell that would keep him safe.

Henry believed in Father Christmas, who was a bit like God. Father Christmas came once a year, at the same time that baby Jesus, who was the son of God but also God, had been born. God and Father Christmas were kind but strict. Henry's father was strict but not kind, and his mummy was kind but not strict. If you were naughty, Father Christmas wouldn't bring you any presents. And if you were bad, God wouldn't let you into heaven. Heaven was a place his grandma had been to, but only once. It was in a story she told. When she was a child, she'd tripped while skipping and hit her head on a kerbstone, waking up in an orchard. She had never seen such amazingly red apples, she said. She was happy and never wanted to leave, even though there was nothing there, just apples and trees and empty space. And then she'd heard a voice telling her it was time to go back, so she went down a long, dark tunnel and woke up in the playground with blood coming out of her head and a circle of children looking down at her. So, Henry knew that heaven was real and knew what it was: a garden full of beautiful red apples but no people. And that was a relief, because he wasn't sure he liked other people very much; he loved apples, and the colour red, and his grandma. If they were in heaven when he died, he would be happy.

Father Christmas was red too, and his face was a bit like an apple. Henry had heard him once on Christmas Eve, moving along the landing when Henry was safely in bed, his long robes rustling and his great boots creaking. Henry had been careful to close his eyes tightly, otherwise Father Christmas would give his gifts to another child. For a reason that no-one had explained, you couldn't look at him. You couldn't look at God either. God was so bright He would blind you, so, if you were ever in His presence, you had to look away. Pinching his eyes shut and knowing Father Christmas hadn't forsaken him, Henry felt a wave of joy move through his body; and then he felt all soft and floaty and he fell asleep, carried by that wave. And in the morning, the gifts were there in a stocking at the foot of the bed. At the very bottom of his stocking was a polished red apple, so Henry knew then that God and Father Christmas were the same.

The Devil was the opposite of God. Once, Henry had challenged the Devil to appear, because it wasn't easy to believe in him in the daytime. And when he looked down, he saw a wasp sitting on his finger, its long, yellow-black body throbbing and pulsating. He knew it was the devil in insect form, and that he had manifested it. He shook his hand, and the wasp flew away, and it didn't sting him. Even so, it was a warning, a sign that the Devil was also real. Like God, Satan's name was not to be taken in vain. If you challenged him, he would come to you.

But there was good magic in the world as well as evil magic.

When his mother got one of her headaches and lay for days in the dark, Henry crept into her room and asked what was wrong. 'Migraine,' she said. Migraine was a special kind of headache that no-one could cure. Some people said '*me-grain*' and others '*my-grain*'. Either way, it belonged to you and you belonged to it. You could never get away from it.

Henry stood there, wanting to help, wanting to use his powers in the room where his mother lay in her single bed. The room had the sour, sickly smell of illness and it was strange in the half-light: the sun making long shadows that moved because a window was open; the air breathing the curtain in and out like a lung. His mother lay with her head turned away as if disgusted with the world, her long, bony arm over her eyes. Henry drew closer. There were green-blue veins branching in the pale skin of her temple where the pain lived. Without being invited, but knowing it was the right thing to do, Henry put his hands on his mother's head and began to rub softly. Her hair felt dry when he pushed it aside. His mother's eyes were shut and her face hot. 'That's nice, dear,' she said, her voice dreamy and faraway. Silver snail-water leaked from the corner of one of her eyes. Henry prayed to the God who lived in the Lord's Prayer. He asked for the pain to come out of the forked vein in his mother's head and to go into his fingers. He didn't care if her agony became his; he wanted it to. He didn't care if his head swelled into a trapezium or a rhombus or a dodecahedron, or if he had to spend days like this, lying in a darkened room with a look of nausea on his face. It would be worth it, to sacrifice his life for hers.

After a while, his hand grew tired. His mother thanked him and said he could stop now; she wanted to sleep. 'Thank you, dear,' she said, the way adults did when they thanked you for something that hadn't really helped and that they hadn't really wanted.

'All right, Mum,' he said, and went away.

Later that day, his mother came downstairs and said her headache had completely disappeared. 'It's a miracle!' she added, smiling at him. 'You have healing hands, Henry, I'm sure of it.' And when he looked at them — his dirty, ordinary hands — he knew he had. And he knew then that he would be a priest one day, or a doctor. He would heal the sick. He would take their suffering into his own body and end it.

Most of all, Henry determined that he would keep his mother alive. He would do this by kindness, and by touch, and by prayer. His father got angry when his mother was ill, so it would fall to Henry to do it. He would spend his life mastering the art of healing, and in that way his mother would never die.

Chapter 2

Two Sisters

Henry had two sisters. Alice was ten and Henry was seven and Chloe was four. Alice was like the girl in the story by Lewis Carroll. She had a long sheet of hair that hung down her back, although sometimes she plaited it, and then it was a rope. She was tall and serious and had long, thin legs with large, red, awkward knees. Chloe was short and chubby. She had curly, russet hair and looked like the picture of a cherub Henry had once seen in a book.

They were playing on the swing that had been hung from a bough of the great horse-chestnut, the one they called 'the conker tree'. Looking up at the tree was like looking under a wide skirt, or into the roof of a ribbed tent. Sunlight strained green through the leaves and it was cool even on a hot day, so that goosepimples rose on the white skin of your arms. The smell was of sap and the chlorine that came over the fence from next door's swimming pool.

Sometimes the neighbours would let them go in the pool. Mrs Shroeder was a short, fat woman who had once walked on top of a ball in a circus. She was kind. After the swim in the freezing water, she gave them chocolate cornflake-cakes that were sweet and crunchy. Instead of a back door, she had a curtain of plastic strips that hung down like coloured rain, and she came through it with a swish and a plate of cakes in her hand, like a performer in a show. And because she came through that curtain and appeared like magic just when you wanted her, Henry knew the story of her walking on the ball in the circus was true.

It was funny, because she looked like a ball herself. Henry's mum said Mrs Shroeder probably gave the children cakes because her own son had grown up, so she missed having someone to mother and be kind to. This meant that mother was also a verb. It meant a woman whose child had grown up and moved away would try to mother someone who wasn't her child because she felt empty inside. Henry wasn't sure if fathers felt the same way when their children grew up. It wasn't the sort of thing he could ask, especially of his father, who was often angry and told him he was 'impertinent.' And then one day his mum said fathering just meant planting a seed in a woman's baby and that was all.

Henry imagined that Mr Shroeder had gone to the circus and had sat eating peanuts and been smitten by the little woman trundling around on her ball. Ball-walking was a unique talent that would attract admiration, so it was natural that Mr Shroeder had fallen in love with Mrs Shroeder, who wasn't called that then. And maybe she had been impressed with him because, although he was very short and had a funny accent, he owned a jeweller's shop. Henry knew that women loved jewels. His mother had a box full of pearl earrings and bracelets that she called her family heirlooms. She said she would be lost without them. So, no wonder the woman on the ball had married the jeweller, and no wonder he had married a ball-walking woman.

Henry and his sisters often played under the tree. Sometimes conkers fell in their prickly casings, and they prised them from the pithy caves. Each conker gleamed like the wood of the dining table. Their mother polished the table with a stained cloth that had beeswax on it and a smell that burned Henry's throat and eyes.

'Push me higher!' cried Chloe. She was too small for the swing and wasn't allowed on it unless an adult was present, but their mum was inside and would never know. Chloe couldn't swing herself very high because her legs were too short and she couldn't build up any momentum, so Henry pushed and Alice just stood there, watching. Alice always watched. It was like she was waiting for someone to make a mistake and not doing anything to stop them. When things went wrong, it had nothing to do with her.

Alice and Henry were playing the twisting game. This was where you sat on the swing and walked your legs in circles, twisting the rope until it tightened and shortened, hoisting your legs off the ground. Then you let go and spun round and round until the garden became a blur and you felt dizzy and sick but in a good way. When the creaking rope slowed and lost its power, you stumbled off and staggered about, falling in a heap and laughing, like Dad when he got drunk.

They also played a game where they swung themselves as high as they could, and then, at the top of the arc, launched themselves from the wooden seat, letting go of the rope to see how far they could fly. Alice called it swing-assisted long-jump. Chloe was too small for these games, but she whined and whined to join in, and in the end they had let her. She couldn't jump off, they said, but they would push her on the swing, as long as she promised to hold on tightly to the ropes. When she promised, they lifted her onto the seat and Henry pushed her. The skin of her back was warm and living through the thin fabric of her dress. As she flew back and forth he felt how small she was, and how tiny her ribcage, like a little bird's.

Chloe soared on an upward line — up, up — then plunged back towards him, getting bigger as she came closer, her body pausing at the bottom of the arc as if waiting for him. 'Higher!' she cried, laughing. He pushed her again, watching her sail away with the momentum he had given her. *'Higher!'* she screamed. Henry pushed harder, and this time he shoved too hard, and she flew clean off the seat. She sailed through the air and landed in a crumpled heap on the ground. Then there was a different kind of scream, and Mum came out in her pinafore. 'What happened?' she asked, wiping flour from her hands.

'She fell off the swing,' said Henry, breathing hard because he was in trouble.

Alice watched and said nothing.

'You *know* she's too young for the swing, Henry. I *told* you.'

Henry looked at his sandals. There were little holes in the toes. 'I know. But she kept on and on.'

His mother picked Chloe up. Henry was sorry he'd hurt her because he'd felt her tiny bones through her dress and realised how easy it would be to break her; but now he wanted to hurt her again for making such a silly fuss.

'Never mind that,' his mum said. 'Who pushed her?'

Henry looked at Alice, who moved a piece of hair out of her eye.

'No-one,' Henry said. 'She swung herself.'

'I didn't!' wailed Chloe. 'Henry pushed me! He pushed me *really* hard!'

Henry stared at Chloe's dark, sobbing face. One day he would shove her so high that she would fly off the swing and land on her head and break her stupid neck. 'I pushed her a *little* bit,' he said. 'She kept on nagging me, Mum.'

Their mother was cuddling Chloe and inspecting the damage. Chloe had scraped skin from her knee. It was pink and shiny under the surface, like the flesh under the skin of a peach. 'You shouldn't lie to me, Henry,' his mother said. 'You mustn't play roughly with your sister. She's only small. I've told you I don't know how many times.'

'I'm sorry,' Henry said, kicking at a daisy. 'It was an accident.'

His mother shook her head. 'It takes two to make an accident, Henry.'

He didn't know what that meant. Sometimes it was one person, sometimes many. His mother's statements didn't always make sense.

'You should look after your little sister, not hurt her,' his mother added, lifting Chloe, who'd gone all limp and floppy, into her arms. His mother gave him a meaningful look. 'I think it's because you're jealous.'

She turned and began carrying his sister towards the house. Chloe glared at him over his mother's shoulder, her face swollen and ugly with tears. She stuck out her tongue and he clenched his fists. How could he be jealous of a stupid, snivelling little baby like that?

But when his mother and Chloe had gone inside, and Alice had drifted off to wherever she went to be alone with her thoughts, Henry realised his mum was right. When he'd pushed Chloe on the swing, he'd half-known what would happen. It was an experiment, because a younger sister was a convenient person to try things out on, to see what effect a particular action might have. Chinese burns. Wrestling moves. Swing experiments. Just to find out if something hurt as much as you thought it would, but with someone else feeling the pain instead of you.

He liked playing with Chloe when she didn't cry, but she always cried in the end. In one of their games, the green settee was the sea. The rug, which was round and had warm colours in the centre and a white cotton fringe, was the sun, or sometimes their raft; and when it was a raft, Chloe would be thrown overboard by a great wave.

Henry was the wave. His arms were as mighty as the sea when he picked up her small body, which smelled slightly of wee and her own spicy, toasted-popcorn smell. Then he threw her, bouncing and laughing, onto the settee. Again and again, he threw her, and she flew, splashing and shrieking, into the cold sea, the white antimacassar the lacy foam on the wave's curling lip. After a while he was out of breath, because she was heavier than she looked. He told Chloe she must dive by herself now; she must plunge into the back of the settee that was an incoming wave as clear as glass. She laughed, her teeth small and white, her brown eyes seeing it as he described it, the little fishes under the wave's translucent skin. She stood with hands together like a man on a diving board, tensing herself. Then she launched into the oncoming wave. She disappeared into the fabric that bowed and yielded under her weight. There was a crack — the hard, dry sound of a cricket ball on a bat — and she rebounded and fell onto the carpet. There was a pause and then Chloe sat up slowly and carefully, her face all squashed. Blood came from her nostrils, two bright streams running down and drawing lines around her mouth. She started to scream, her red face like a devil's. His mother came in and began dabbing and staunching and cooing and mopping. 'Why, Henry, do you play such stupid games with your sister? Don't you see what you've done?'

Henry stood, pale and shaking and indignant, because how was he to know their spongy sofa had a rock-hard board behind the padding? That was the sofa's fault, not his. That was his parents' fault for not telling him. He couldn't be expected to know what lay beneath the surface of things. He didn't have X-ray eyes.

Nonetheless, accidents often seemed to happen around him. He didn't know why, but his mother implied he did. She suggested he did them deliberately, meaning they weren't accidents at all.

His father tended the boiler each morning. That was the first thing they heard when they woke up: the clinking of the poker in the grate. It made an echo in the house but also in Henry's head and bones. Soon he would hear the rattling sound of coal being poured. His father was giving the fire its breakfast, because he was the keeper of the furnace. It was always his father who performed this feat.

His father's world was smoke and fire and subterranean banging noises. It was the same ritual every day, winter and summer, because they must have hot water. That was what a father did: snapping the kindling to make a nest; making a circle of coal; stuffing in the balled-up newspaper. Lighting the flame and shutting the little door with the brown glass pane. Crouching to watch the flame lick the paper and spread wider. Then listening to hear the pipes creak and expand. Finally, lighting a cigarette, the hot ember at the end glowing red and burning to grey ash which he tapped into the fluted glass dish, tap tap tap, while sipping his scalding tea.

When the scuttle was empty, he went into the coalhole to fill it. The coal was sometimes called coke, but it wasn't the dark, fizzy stuff that went up your nose when you had it in a bottle as a treat. This coke existed behind the battered wooden door of the coal cellar and lay in a great mound like a black snowdrift. It breathed out cold, as if it was not really an overground thing at all and should never have been brought to the surface. Henry shovelled it sometimes with the little metal scoop, the higher pieces of coal trickling down at him like a slowly rattling landslide. It wanted to bury him alive if it could. Coal was evil like that. His dad said it was made of the compressed bodies of things that had died millions of years ago when dinosaurs were alive. Henry could imagine an avalanche of dark stuff falling on him and flattening him and turning him, through the slow crushing of the ages, into more coal, his bones preserved as a fossil that another small boy might find in a piece of coal millions of years later when he scooped it into a scuttle.

It was strange that something that cold could have fire inside it. Those little sooty grenades were so hard, so dense, so staining to the hand when he picked one up and threw it to see how far it would go.

'Dad, what's that hard stuff?' he asked, one day. His father had been raking out the grey ash that was left in the metal tray under the boiler. The tray was full of sharp, jagged things and a soft feathery dust. 'That's clinker,' his father said.

Clinker was a funny word. It clinked in your head with a high, sharp ring. Clink was the sound of one key knocking against another, which was why prison was sometimes called that. Clinker was funny because it rhymed with tinker, which was a man in ragged clothes who came knocking at the door and asked if you had knives to be sharpened, or any old iron, which Henry's mother certainly didn't, thank you very much, and good day to you. But tinker was also to play with or adjust, because words could mean several things at once, and you had to be careful when you used them. Dad sometimes tinkered with Henry's bike when it had a flat tyre, holding the inner tube underwater and inflating it and looking for the stream of bubbles.

'Is it metal?' Henry asked, looking at the strange stuff the fire had left behind.

'No,' said his father. 'It's the vitreous matter the coal burns down to.' Vitreous was a word Henry didn't know. 'Like glass,' his father explained, because sometimes his dad told him things.

Henry examined it. It wasn't glass like window glass that you could look through. It was opaque, like stone or dark crystal. It was glassy and rocky and metallic all at once. Who would have thought the black bullets of coal contained glass and metal as well as heat?

'What do we do with it?' he asked.

'*Do* with it?' his father laughed. 'Nothing. Put it in a black bag. The bin men take it away.'

Henry imagined them, those silent, dirty men who came loping up the drive, and who resembled the silent, grimy ones who brought the coal, the bags slung over their shoulders like dark Father Christmases. 'I see,' he said, because he did, in his mind's eye.

The bin men didn't always take the clinker away. Sometimes it was left in pinky-grey piles in the back yard, in the place where they kept the mangle, a strange thing that looked alive and sad and whose rubber lips were chapped and perished. This was the place where the concrete was cracked and there was an outside toilet and a wooden gate to the side passage. The gate was ragged on its underside as if rats had gnawed it. Henry had seen a rat once: big and brown and fat and nasty. It had come out of their shed and his dad had had to put the poison down. Then there were no more rats, just tooth-marks on the underside of the gate.

Henry was playing a game of chase with Alice, who didn't usually play with him. She had followed him down the side alley towards the gate. She was gaining on him because she was taller, and her legs were longer. She would catch him and tickle his ribs. He mustn't let this happen, because tickling was a thing that felt good but also hurt, because it made you squirm and made your legs go all powerless and wobbly. He stopped beside a pile of the soft, grey dust. The ash lay against a wall and was mixed with clinker, the clinker standing out like bright bits of shrapnel, which was what they'd had in the war when a bomb blew apart. An idea came to him, something that would keep him safe from Alice's terrible tickling. At the last minute, just as Alice bore down on him, he stooped, grabbed a handful of the flinty, flaky stuff, and flung it at her. It plumed up in a grey cloud and his sister covered her face. She stopped running, and then she screamed.

When his parents and Alice came back from the hospital, Henry was told never to do that again. The doctors had had to use long tweezer-things to get the pieces of grit out of Alice's eyes. She could have lost her sight, they said, and that was his fault. He didn't understand, because in cartoons like *Desperate Dan* and *Tom and Jerry* no-one ever got hurt. A heavy iron would be dropped on Tom's head and squash it flat, and he would get up with a head shaped like the iron, shake himself while watching the chirping birdies that circled him, then carry on as if nothing had happened. So how was Henry to know his sister wouldn't wave the ash away with her hand, dispersing it like smoke, then carry on running? Why had she let it get into her eyes? That was a stupid thing to do. But no, they said, it was *his* fault, and he should have known better. He must not hurt other people, especially his sisters.

He couldn't help himself, however. Sometimes he even hurt his mother. Once he tied a string to all the saucepans stacked on the stand in the scullery and attached it to a chair leg, so his mother would walk through his invisible tripwire and all the pans would fall down, clatter-bang-crash. That would be funny, and she would laugh, and love him for his brilliant ingenuity. But when his mother walked through it, her foot snagged and she fell, hitting herself on the counter. She held her side and her eyes went watery because she'd hurt her ribs.

How could he have known that would happen? He was only playing a game. But it wasn't a game, they said, and he would be punished if it happened again. He had been warned.

Chapter 3

Dog Years

The black Labrador, Anna, was pregnant, but Henry's mum didn't like him to use that word. 'Expecting' was what she said. Expecting was when a baby was growing inside something, and now that had happened to Anna. She had run off, deep into the woods, and perhaps it was then that some other dog had mounted her. Mounted was the word they used. She had been 'in season' and dripping blood on the kitchen floor, and already some dogs had come sniffing at her hind quarters, so that their mother had had to drive them off with her walking stick. Anna had only been gone for five minutes, but she came slinking back, her body near the ground, her tail wagging low, her lips wrinkled back over black-purple gums in a strange grin, as if she knew she had done a bad thing, which she had. She had another dog's slobber on her coat; and then, a few weeks later, she began to swell.

'Anna will have puppies soon,' their mother announced. The children were excited, because one dog would become many little ones in a miracle of multiplication. Henry asked how this could be, because he had never seen the act of mounting, which in his mind implied going up a hill or a mountain. Their mother frowned and did her matter-of-fact voice. 'A man-dog became very friendly with Anna, and now there are puppies inside her tummy,' she explained.

Henry was still puzzled, because adults' explanations rarely told you what you needed to know. He was friendly with all sorts of people, but they didn't swell up and give birth to puppies. He wasn't sure how you could get babies in your tummy either, because that was a place for food. Women must have a different kind of stomach, he guessed, but he wasn't sure. 'How can you tell if it's a man or a woman dog?' he asked, one Sunday lunchtime, because it had been preying on his mind. All dogs looked the same to him, except that some were big, or lame, or patched, or smelly, or frightening, or pathetic.

They were eating roast beef and Yorkshire pudding. There was a silence of chewing. His father stared at his roast potatoes and began cutting them into very small pieces.

His mother frowned and took a breath. 'Well, if you look at a dog carefully, Henry, you'll notice that a male dog has similar... parts... to what little boys have. Private parts,' she added.

Henry didn't know which parts she meant. Many of his own parts were private — his mind, for example, because he liked to go there and daydream; and his hands, of which he was sometimes ashamed, because they had dirt under the nails, and because they were short-fingered like his father's, not long and tapering, like his mother's. For this reason, he tended to keep them in his pockets.

'Which ones?' he asked, and saw Alice rolling her eyes.

'Your winkle,' his mother said. Sometimes Henry called it his winkle and sometimes it was his ninkle. A ninkle was the thing that did a tinkle, because rude words sometimes rhymed.

'Oh.' Henry considered this, cutting up a bit of the grey meat that sat in a puddle of brown gravy. He wasn't satisfied. 'But when two dogs are *friendly*, why does that make them have babies?'

His mother looked at their father again. He was hacking through the crust of Yorkshire pudding into which she had put onion. The pudding was creamy on the inside, but tough and burnt on the outside. Henry's dad put some food in his mouth and began chewing, as if that were his only comment on the situation of dogs and babies.

'Well,' his mother went on, setting down her knife and fork, 'the man dog jumps on the back of the lady dog, and...'

Henry's mind drifted. He was unsure why jumping on someone's back made babies. Chloe sometimes jumped on his own when he piggy-backed her up the lawn and nothing happened. He became aware that a peculiar atmosphere had descended, and that it was his fault. On the radio, *Family Favourites* warbled away. There was a song playing, something about a mouse wearing clogs, right there on the stair, going clip-clippety-clop in a house in old Amsterdam. The song was funny and annoying, and everything had become stiff and strange in their house because of Henry's questions. Henry looked at his plate. 'And when a *woman* has a baby,' he went on, for he must know, however much Alice's eyebrows were trying to silence him, 'what happens then?' Grandma Ivy had said that a lady grew a baby in her tummy and kept it there for a while, and then the lady had an operation in hospital, because birth was a kind of illness. The doctors lifted the baby out, all clean and perfect, and then the woman was well again, and this was a miracle, Grandma said, and the miracle was birth. Henry ventured this theory now and wanted to know if it was correct, because sometimes Grandma Ivy said things which, his mother said, stretched the truth.

'Oh, no, it doesn't come out of her tummy,' she said. 'Or, at least, not usually.'

Alice groaned and shook her head.

'What's wrong?' he asked.

Alice looked away. 'Can't we just eat lunch without you asking these stupid questions?'

'Why are they stupid?'

'Because they are.'

That was the kind of non-answer his sister always gave.

There was more scraping of knives. On the radio, Frank Sinatra was singing about someone who had got under his skin, which was what happened when you had a baby, only a man couldn't do that, give birth, that is. Henry was confused. He had been told that it was good to have an enquiring mind. Only those who asked questions learned the facts, and facts were important, his dad said. They had a magazine in the house called *Tell Me Why* that was full of intriguing facts, like how tall the Empire State Building was. Henry looked at his mother to supply the facts he needed, because his father kept filling his mouth with food. She sighed. And then, finally, to the accompaniment of their scraping knives and The Beatles' *Yellow Submarine*, she told him the truth.

Later, when it was time, Anna gave birth, and the children were allowed to watch. Anna, who had swollen into a strange, waddling sausage of a dog, lay on her side, panting. Their mother had laid newspaper in her bed, the way his dad did under shoes when he cleaned them. Anna kept on panting and, after a while, made a shivery, straining motion with her sides. 'They're coming,' their mother said quietly, as if something delicate might be broken if she raised her voice. The children drew closer, although it seemed a very private thing to be watching, and not quite decent. As they looked, squatting with their hands on their knees, a shining thing like a bubble slowly blew out from Anna's rear end. It wobbled in a funny and disgusting way, then flopped onto the paper. They peered down. Inside the bubble was a crumpled shape, and that was a puppy. It had a squashed-up face and folded legs. Through the blue-grey gummy stuff, it looked strange and alien. Chloe began to cry because it was dead.

'It isn't dead,' their mother reassured them. 'Anna will wake it up. You'll see.'

Anna began to lick away the bubble. It broke into raggedy bits, and they saw the folded shape of a tiny fawn-coloured puppy, its eyes tight shut. Anna patiently worked at it with her long tongue, swallowing the cobwebby stuff so they could see the soggy-looking thing more clearly. Finally, it moved its muzzle blindly to and fro, as if trying to work out where it was. Anna continued washing it until it began making faint whimpering noises. Then, Henry's mother picked it up and set it against Anna's swollen teats. It began drinking, making contented grunts and tiny movements with its clawless paws. Its eyes were tight slits. Chloe complained that the puppy couldn't see, but their mother said it was normal, and that its eyes would open after four or five days. And this was birth, this straining and helplessness and mess, but it would be all right, she said, because the puppy would live.

Anna had nine puppies in all, and the children were the audience, watching the bluish bubbles blowing one by one from Anna's behind, the babies emerging as clay-like things that slowly awoke and became toy-dogs that stumbled about. Their legs would give way suddenly so that the puppies sat down, surprised; and this made the children laugh. Some puppies were black and white, others suede or piebald, and from this they deduced that the daddy dog had been brown. Henry wondered if all male dogs ran away, not wishing to see what they'd created after doing the mounting thing that Mummy had explained over Sunday lunch.

When they were a few weeks old, the puppies were allowed in the garden, although you had to watch them carefully. Once, one of them went down the gap beside the shed, and Henry had to grab it by its squirmy tail and drag it back, because there was broken glass and old bricks and sharp brambles down there, and when he did so, the puppy turned its head and tried to bite him with its white, needle-sharp teeth. Baby dogs could be as annoying as people, and they didn't know when you were trying to help them. But, generally, Henry liked the puppies, although Mummy explained they wouldn't be able to keep them all, because nine was too much of a good thing.

One evening, Chloe was crouching down and playing with the pups. She was leaning forward so she could touch them and tickle them under the chin, stroking their soft, vulnerable bellies and fondling their velvety ears. As she reached out her hand, she overbalanced and fell, and then she was lying in the bed with the dogs, and everyone was crowding round and talking at once. Something squeaked and yip-yipped, and when Chloe got up, they saw what she'd done. Alice lifted out one of the puppies, the one Chloe had fallen on. Something was wrong with it now, because its head hung at a funny angle. It was the fawn-coloured pup with white on its nose and tail, and it was their favourite. Mummy said it wasn't dead, only hurt. 'I expect it'll be all right,' she said. She took the pup and inspected its crumpled shape. 'We can nurse it back to health, poor little thing.'

Henry knew then it wouldn't be all right, because of the way his mother had said 'expect' and 'thing.' He left the kitchen and went down the far end of the garden and hid among the fruit trees. As he went, he kicked at a fallen pear, and it rolled away. He remembered all the windfall apples he had smashed that summer, the hard skin yielding under the sole of his shoe, so that the apples squeaked as they opened, then lay where he left them, then browned and died in the sun, remaining there until the wasps came and buzzed in the ruins he had made.

After a while, he heard a voice calling. At first, he ignored it, letting his name drift into the branches of the trees and disperse like smoke. Only when he grew cold and shivery, and the evening went blue and smelled of damp and bonfires, did he go back in, taking the bonfire smell with him. His mother asked why he'd run away like that, and why he hadn't come when she'd called. He didn't say anything. He couldn't explain what he'd half-believed, which was that if he stayed away long enough, when he came back everything would be different, and the puppy wouldn't still be crushed; time would have done something else in the space he'd left. But it hadn't.

His mother wrapped the puppy in a blanket, because broken things must be kept warm. Henry had once seen a woman lying in the street next to a smashed-up car. A man had draped his coat over the woman, and the woman's feet were poking out of the end, and that was an accident. The victim had to be kept warm, because breaking a body let all the heat out.

That night, they sat with the fawn puppy and stroked it and watched TV. The puppy wasn't grateful, however, and didn't want to be stroked. It wouldn't drink when they offered it warm milk from a little medicine dropper, letting the liquid dribble out of its mouth onto the blanket and wasting it. It made small, whimpering sounds and restless movements with its paws, as if it couldn't get comfortable. In the end, the children went to bed, leaving it downstairs to sleep in its own cardboard box where the other puppies couldn't disturb it. Sleep, like warmth, could also heal you, their mother said. And in the morning, when they woke up, they discovered their mother was wrong, because the puppy was dead.

They buried the puppy at the end of the garden and put up a stone to mark its grave. Henry wanted to bind two sticks together to make a cross, the way he had seen someone do it in a cowboy film when his buddy died, but his mother said no, because animals didn't have crosses, and when Henry asked why, she said because Jesus hadn't died for dogs, but for human beings.

In the end, they gave most of the puppies, which Anna had pushed so laboriously into the world in their shiny blue-grey bubbles, away. They kept only one — the black and white pup who'd tried to run off and had bitten Henry with needle-sharp teeth when he tried to rescue it. Their mother named him Peppy, short for peppermint, explaining that peppermints were black and white in the olden days. And although they grew to like the little black and white pup, Henry never forgot the one his sister had killed, and that they had buried at the end of the garden under the fruit trees, with no cross over the turned plot of dirt, because Jesus had died for people, not dogs.

Chapter 4

An Inspector Calls

People died as well as puppies, and one day it happened at school. Then Henry knew that death wasn't only for old people and dogs, and flies on window-ledges, and the birds he found in gutters with their eyes glassy and unseeing.

Colin Platt was always in trouble. Afterwards, everyone said that if anyone was going to die, it was bound to be him. He was the one who had thrown a wheel-shaped toy with suckers on each arm at a school window, and the glass had cracked into a crazy cobweb-pattern. The other children were scared of what Colin had done, and no-one wanted to be there when a teacher saw what had happened. They would be guilty by association, and then they would have to face the wrath of Mrs Wheeler. Then a teacher came and found Colin trying to unstick his toy from the cracked glass. She led him away, and the children were glad, because Colin should have known better. No-one had ever broken a window before.

Mrs Wheeler was the headmistress. Her name fitted her, because she was a short, round woman who rolled and wobbled and trundled along corridors. She had swollen ankles, and legs like sausages crammed into the thin sausage-skin of her stockings. She was terrifying and never smiled. She wore a hairy suit of bracken-coloured tweed, and her perfume was sweetish and unpleasant. This perfume hung in the air, and it sometimes appeared in a ghostly way without her. And this was even more frightening, because it meant you didn't know if she had just been past, or was about to roll around a corner to catch you. Even when you weren't doing anything wrong, she would manage to accuse you of something.

Once, in assembly, Henry was sharing his hymn book with Alistair Cairns, and Alistair sang the hymn in a high, silly voice and with different words from the ones in the book. Henry tried not to laugh but couldn't help himself, and Mrs Wheeler spotted them. 'You two will remain behind when everyone has gone,' she said. All the children went quiet, and turned and looked at them because they had done a very bad thing. A space opened up around Henry and Alistair the way it had around Colin Platt when he broke the window, only this time Henry was standing beside the bad boy and had been caught red-handed.

Mrs Wheeler took them to her office, which smelled so strongly of her perfume you could hardly breathe. Your eyes watered so that you were crying even before she had scolded you. 'Why were you two disrupting my assembly in that disgraceful way?' she asked. She said '*my assembly*' as if she owned it and they had stolen it from her. Her voice was cold and green and hairy like her suit.

Henry and Alistair stood side by side as if they were friends and collaborators, which they weren't. They were silent and hung their heads, because that was what you were supposed to do when accused of something and were showing contrition. Henry hated Alistair now, although he had quite liked him before the assembly. Alistair had snot that came out his nose in two slow trickles which he sniffed back up, only for it to come leaking out again. His hair was dirty and stood in stiff spikes, even though you were supposed to keep it clean because of nits. He had smudges on his face like a drawing gone wrong. But now Henry and Alistair were the same in the eyes of Mrs Wheeler. They kept looking at their shoes and didn't answer her question about why they had interrupted her assembly, because there was no answer. And then Henry spoke, because someone must, and because he found that there was an answer after all, and because he knew he must distance himself from the dirty boy beside him. 'Alistair sang the song all wrong,' he said, 'and it made me laugh.' He heard his words fall into the quiet room.

Alistair looked sideways at him. 'No, I *never*!' he hissed.

Henry shook his head, but said nothing more in the voice that wasn't his. He would let Alistair condemn himself out of his own mouth. Henry would never have made a grammatical mistake like that. 'No, I never' was a double negative, and his mother said that was an ugly and incorrect way of speaking. Only common people spoke like that, and Henry wasn't common. He was a nice, polite child, and now he was playing the role of a boy he'd seen in a film. That boy had been accused of something he hadn't done, and he had stood straight and spoken clearly, and in the end, he had been proven innocent. He'd been forgiven and praised for his honesty and pluck, and that would happen to Henry.

Mrs Wheeler seemed to agree, because she reached out and slapped Alistair on the back of the legs. It made a loud, wet sound and Alistair said 'Ow!', opening his mouth wide like a cartoon boy in a comic.

'Don't you *dare* speak to me like that, you nasty little child!' Mrs Wheeler said. This was strange, because Alistair had been talking to Henry, not Mrs Wheeler, but Alistair didn't say anything more because now he was crying. Mrs Wheeler spoke very quietly. Quiet could be worse than loud. Her voice was a slow, whispery sort of voice. It reminded Henry of one of those caterpillars covered in hairs that crept over the pavement; if you touched it, the hairs would break off under your skin, and you would be poisoned, and die.

Alistair kept snivelling and saying he had done nothing wrong, but he'd done two things wrong. One was laughing in assembly. The other was having the wrong kind of voice, and that was why Mrs Wheeler had hit him. The wrong voice meant you were nasty and conniving and a common-little-guttersnipe. You could be slapped on the legs for that. Henry looked down and saw Mrs Wheeler's red handprint on Alistair's thigh. It marked him out as a boy who would come to no good. Henry had not been hit, however. The skin on his legs was pale and unmarked, and even though his knees were wobbling with fear, they were innocent knees and innocent legs, because he was a good boy. And then Mrs Wheeler said they could go and let that be a lesson to them.

So, if that day Henry had had to make a prediction, he would have said that Alistair Cairns would be the one to die at school, because he sang the wrong words to hymns, which was blasphemy, then dragged others down into the trouble he was in. Not only that. In the playground he'd called another boy a wog, which Henry knew was an ugly word, even though he didn't understand it. Another time, Alistair had asked all the boys in the playground to lie on top of him in a great pile, in order to show that he could withstand any weight, but after a while he had told them to get off, because they were hurting him. He said it like they were the ones who'd had the idea, and he was the victim of their cruelty. That was the kind of stunt he pulled. He was also cheeky to teachers but got away with it. He did dangerous things for no reason and had come in once with a cut on his arm where he'd hurt himself juggling with his mum's kitchen knives. No-one else did stuff like that.

But it wasn't Alistair who died.

On the day it happened, Colin Platt didn't come back to the classroom after lunch. When Miss Pringle asked where he was, no-one knew. In the end, someone said they had seen him going into the toilet, and she went looking for him, even though she wasn't supposed to leave them in the classroom unattended. There was a long wait. Then they heard a scream, and some of them ran out into the corridor because there was no-one to tell them not to.

Miss Pringle was a small figure at the far end of the corridor. She was carrying Colin's limp body in her arms and saying *Oh My God* over and over. Miss Pringle was calling on God to make Colin come alive again, but Colin's feet just dangled and swung loosely like a puppet's. And then the children couldn't see any more because Mr Jackson appeared in the corridor, blocking the view, and he told them to go back into the classroom and stay there until he said otherwise.

It was only later that they found out what had happened. Colin had hanged himself from the drum of the wall-fitted towel, the one you tugged to get the dry bit that came rolling out like a blue tongue. He'd been playing parachutes, which was where you climbed on the sink and slid inside the loop of towel and hung there, limbs dangling, like a commando falling over occupied France on a night-raid during the war. Only Colin played that game. Colin was very small and light and no-one else dared do it, because they knew they might pull the towel-dispenser off the wall, and a teacher might come in and find you, and there would be hell to pay. But Colin didn't care about teachers or hell, because he was a soldier in the war and full of derring-do.

A policeman came into their classroom and stood there, tall and blue in his uniform like the man in *Dixon of Dock Green*, only without the helmet strapped under his chin. In a gruff, blue voice, he asked if anyone had gone to the toilet at lunchtime and seen Colin playing with the towel. He asked it in an accusing tone, the way adults asked if you had been playing with a ball in the house when a vase had been found broken to pieces on the living room floor. No, sir, they said, chanting the words together. He frowned and repeated the question, as if he had wanted a different answer. 'Other people must have been involved,' he said. He held his pen poised over his notebook. 'Are you sure no-one went in there?' He paused. 'That's a long time without anyone needing the toilet.' He was giving them a last chance, and they looked at him in his stiff uniform with his silver buckles and buttons that shone in the classroom's electric light. Yes, sir, they said, we're sure. The policeman shook his head as if he were disappointed in them. His bristly eyebrows said that there was a murderer in their midst whom they should identify.

'Colin was absent a long time,' he said again, putting the pen to his lips. 'Are you *absolutely* sure no-one saw anything?' He tapped the rhythm of the words on his mouth, angling the word '*absolutely*' as he levelled his gaze at them. They looked at him, and then they looked at their hands and picked at scabs and hangnails and finger-dirt, because they didn't know what he wanted them to say. There was a new smell in the room, and that was probably Sarah Judey, because she sometimes pooed herself when she was nervous. Once, though, when they had accused her of doing it, they found that Duncan Steele, who was the brightest boy in the class, had brown stuff on his seat when it came to stacking the chairs at the end of the day, and he had rushed from the room with brown liquid running from the hem of his shorts down the back of his leg. And that showed that the answer to a puzzle was sometimes where you least expected it.

The policeman was still waiting, pen poised, because he needed his answer, too. Henry wanted to stand up and admit it was him, but he didn't because it wasn't true. In the end, the policeman wrote something on his pad in an angry way, stabbing in a full stop. Then he marched from the room.

Miss Pringle didn't come back that day, because Colin's accident had hurt her in some way. You couldn't touch a dead body and not get sick, because corpses were contagious. Another teacher came and told them to open their books. 'It's quiet reading time,' she said, speaking solemnly like someone in church, 'and a time for silent reflection. If you need to speak, please use your whisper voice.' Henry couldn't concentrate. He didn't want to be quiet. He wanted to shout and scream and dance and smash things and turn cartwheels and whoop like an Indian brave. Then he noticed the empty seat where Colin had sat that morning. It was a blue chair with metal legs and pulled out at the angle Colin had left it at. Now Colin was dead and would never sit on it again, and the chair seemed to know this, and be sorry.

At the end of school, Henry was full of a kind of wild joy. He ran out and asked John if he'd heard the news. John, who was in Mr Plunkett's class, said he had, but he wanted to know if it was true. 'Of course it's true, you idiot,' Henry said. And then they smiled, because deaths never happened at boring old school, and it was exciting and not quite real, like something in a story or film. Everything had gone electric. Henry needed to tell someone else, because everyone at school knew now and they were swarming and tumbling and whispering and chattering with the thrill of it. He ran down the long, concrete, tree-lined drive and out of the gate to the car. His sisters were already there, because Henry had been a long time chattering and racing and asking and telling.

He closed the door with a thunking sound which was louder than the sound the door usually made. It was quiet in the car, and then he knew that Alice hadn't said anything. Chloe was singing to herself, too young to understand. Alice looked at him with her face all serious and disapproving. She was waiting for him to do something, and so he did, because he was bursting to tell. He explained exactly what had happened, but his mum didn't act excited. She covered her face with her hands and leaned against the steering wheel. They sat in silence and watched her, hearing her breath catch in her chest. It took a while to realise that this was crying, because adults did it differently from children, and it was embarrassing, and strange to cry for someone you had never known. Chloe wanted to know what had happened and why Mummy was sad, but their mother didn't explain. She wiped her eyes and said they were going home now. But she didn't start the car; she just sat there. Then Alice said the thing she'd been waiting to say, which was that Henry had come charging out, asking everyone if they'd heard 'the news'. And then his mother turned and looked at him and said, 'Oh no, Henry, you didn't say that, did you?' He didn't answer. Instead, he waited for an explanation to enter his head, or for his mother to start the car, but neither happened. He didn't understand why you couldn't call a death news, when it was. It was the most exciting thing that had happened in his life. And anyway, Colin Platt was a bad boy, and baddies always died at the end of things, because they deserved it. You couldn't cry for someone like that. And yet his mother had cried.

In assembly on Monday, there was a table covered with flowers and a big wreath, and Mr Loveday said Colin Platt would never be forgotten. Then some of the female teachers began to cry as Henry's mother had done. Then assembly ended and they went back to their classrooms and never spoke of Colin again.

Chapter 5

Mothering Sunday

Sunday was unlike other days. It was a day that had nowhere to go. In the distance, you could hear bells. You knew men were pulling the ropes, and the bells jangled in and out of sequence, losing their rhythm and finding it again, and that was Sunday: things falling in and out of rhythm, and making a kind of clanging music that descended the scale, like God coming down the belltower to bring his message of love to the Earth, but finding everyone asleep or otherwise occupied.

Henry had sometimes gone to church with the Cubs. Once, he had had to carry a flag and march up the aisle in his uniform, but when he left Cubs he didn't go to church anymore, because his parents weren't religious, although his mother talked about God and heaven and whether animals had a place in it. Henry thought this was odd, because she hadn't let him make a cross for the dead puppy's grave, but now she said she thought animals deserved a place in heaven more than most people, because animals were innocent and incapable of malice. So, as Henry sat on his bed, he heard the bells in the distance calling to him, and he tried to ignore them, although something inside him yearned to go somewhere, he didn't know where.

The day yawned. The garden stretched and seemed bigger than on a weekday. If it was warm, Henry explored the far end, where the neat lawns became jungle. There were plum trees and pear trees and a tree that bore tiny red apples, like the ones his grandmother had seen when she'd gone to heaven. There were black ants which were safe, and red ants that bit, and yellow ones he wasn't sure about. There were white raspberries which were strange, because raspberries were supposed to be pink. Things in the garden were often weird like that. Sometimes, there were newts or a dead bird or the skeleton of a mouse, because the garden contained death: rotten fruit, or bones, or the feathers of a pigeon a fox had eaten. Once he saw the fox that had done it. It loped with an odd, guilty, sideways movement up the garden, then disappeared through the hedge, a flash of red and white, then gone. At other times, a hedgehog came out of a bush and curled up into a spiky ball when he prodded it with a stick.

There was only one thing he was sure of, and that was that you were never alone in a garden. The tall shapes of the trees surrounded you, and the flowers looked out of the rockery, and the fish slid gold and sleek and speckled under the surface of the pond. In summer, the dragonflies whizzed electric blue through the air like tiny biplanes on four whirring wings. Sometimes, Anna and Peppy ran around and woofed at squirrels but they were too slow and fat to catch them.

Henry climbed trees. He liked, especially, to climb a tall tree that produced large Golden Russet apples. They had a different, faint, faraway taste, like a musty perfume. Henry liked to sit at the top of the tree and eat the Russets and look out over a world where everything was very small and distant. He could see but not be seen in his nest of leaves, staying there until Mum called him in for tea. If she'd known, she would have told him not to climb so high, because a neighbour had once fallen out of a tree and broken his back, and he was in a wheelchair now.

Sometimes the reason he wasn't alone in the garden was because Chloe attached herself to him. This was boring. He couldn't play war with her, because she didn't see the point of holding a stick and saying 'ratatatatat' while he died spectacularly near the rockery. Girls didn't understand the importance of death, or the need to act it out. Chloe thought playing at death was silly, but Henry knew it was heroic to die, and noble to be caught by enemy gunfire, like in the war films when John Mills was hit, and said his last words with a streak of blood on his head or dribbling from the corner of his mouth, and violin music played and everyone cried, but in a reserved British way, which meant sniffing but not weeping. It was always the Germans who killed the British. These were the same Germans who appeared in cartoon-form in his copy of *The Victor*. They wore strange helmets that were stepped at the side, and they threw stick grenades, not pineapple-shaped ones. Their planes were different too, and more stylish than the British ones, but you couldn't admit that, just as you couldn't admit that a Luger was more stylish than an Enfield service revolver. Sometimes, evil things looked better than good ones.

'Take that, Fritz!' the Tommies in the comics said, blasting the Germans with their guns, which were called Tommy guns. The Germans said '*Mein Gott*!' and threw up their arms and died. But it was far better to be killed than to kill, in Henry's opinion, because nothing was more noble than dying for a cause. So, Henry practised dying. He practised it again and again on the lawn, because practice made perfect. 'You shoot me, and I'll fall,' he said, when Chloe wanted to play with him.

'Don't want to,' she said. 'Why should I?'

'Because that's the game,' he said.

'It's a silly game, then.'

'We'll climb a tree afterwards. I'll show you how.'

She weighed this. 'Okay, then.'

She held the stick awkwardly and didn't even point it at him properly. Her 'ratatatatat' was half-hearted and Henry could tell she didn't believe in it. Nor did she think Henry heroic when he spun, clutching his chest and toppling backwards, although this took a great deal of courage, for he'd just given his life to save others, defending this end of the garden against enemy invasion.

'Let's climb a tree now,' Chloe said, after two blasts from her gun, flinging it into the undergrowth as if that's all it was, really, a stick. Henry regarded her coldly. He knew she wouldn't be able to climb a tree. 'No,' he said. 'I'm going in now. I've had enough. And you don't play properly. Girls never do.' He got up and sloped off, hearing her wail, 'But Henry, you *said*!' He strode on. Part of him wanted to go back and keep his promise, but something else made him steel himself, like a soldier in a war film. 'Play your own stupid games!' he yelled.

'You mustn't torment your sister,' his mother said, when he went into the kitchen. She'd left the door open because it was warm, and she must've heard what had happened.

'I wasn't tormenting her. She didn't want to play the game I wanted to, that's all.'

His mother was cooking lunch, the chicken sizzling in the oven and releasing its savoury smell. Henry began to think about food, because he was hungry, and he could imagine how it would be. There would be bread sauce and forcemeat balls and little sausages, and a sherry trifle for dessert. His mother had done a course in *Cordon Bleu* cookery. At dinner parties, she served food to guests in large scallop shells. There were napkins folded into special shapes and placed inside wine glasses, or secured with a wooden toggle. Sunday lunch was different, however. It wasn't food to impress people, but it took a lot of effort anyway, and his mother wanted them to notice this, because normally they didn't. His eyes wandered. Saucepans clattered their lids, releasing exhalations of steam. He saw that his mum was steamy too, and there was a dangerous, over-heated look about her, as if she were a saucepan whose lid might fall off and the water flood, hissing, onto the gas jet, putting it out.

'She said you promised to show her how to climb a tree,' his mother said. The radio was playing *Two-Way Family Favourites* as usual. Soldiers stationed overseas were missing home and wishing they could be back for a lunch such as this. The last song had been *How Much is that Doggie in the Window?*, which Henry hated, because it reminded him of the puppy that had died.

'But you won't allow her to climb trees,' he pointed out.

His mother stirred the gravy. Sometimes she lifted a whole joint in its tin from the oven and tipped the juices into a saucepan, so the gravy would have the flavour of the meat. The juices spat and popped, and if the fat landed on your arm, it hurt. His mother had small cuts on her fingers and burns on her arms, and that was part of being a housewife, she said. When she cut her finger, she bound it with a bit of white rag, and the blood showed through, brilliantly red.

'Well, you could have *pretended* to show her, Henry.'

Henry looked at his right sandal, which had scuff marks on the toes. If he'd been a real soldier he would've worn boots. He had a pair of shoes with a compass in the heel. To find the compass you had to lift a hidden flap. They would have been better than sandals.

'I don't know how you *pretend* to teach someone to climb a tree,' he said, because his mum was looking at him.

She knocked the wooden spoon against the saucepan. 'You know what I mean, Henry. You could have shown her how to climb a *little* way and then helped her down again. Don't be difficult, please.'

He stood there sullenly, being difficult. His mum often asked him to do impossible things. Teach your sister to climb a tree, but don't do it really. Play fighting games with her, but don't be rough.

'Go and wash your hands,' she said. 'Dinner's nearly ready. And tell Dad it's time to come in.'

'Where is he?' he asked, although he knew.

His mother was prodding the carrots with a knife, her head enveloped in steam. Cooking food involved cooking yourself, he saw. 'Up the garden, digging, or mowing.' She paused, lowering her voice. 'You know, Henry, your father's a strange man. If I ask him to do something in the garden, he goes and attacks some obscure corner that no-one will ever see. Now, who would do that?'

Henry considered this. He thought 'attack' a strange word to use about the garden, especially as she was attacking his father by saying so. But it was true in a way. He had seen his father driving the three-pronged fork into the earth like a Tommy driving a bayonet into the guts of the enemy, and knew people had a way of directing anger at things that had done them no harm. Sometimes his mother was an angry cook, peeling vegetables with a flashing hand, chips of carrot or parsnip spitting across the wooden board and landing at his feet. Or she crashed joints into the oven, slamming the door as if forcing someone she didn't like inside. It was the same when she cleaned the house, thumping the hoover against Henry's bedroom door when he was reading. Noises were a way to express the things you couldn't say. The banging of the hoover meant, 'Why do I have to do this endless housework? Because *you* won't, that's why!' It wasn't fair, because Henry sometimes helped with the drying up, and on Sundays washed insects off the fins of their Singer Vogue, slooshing them into oblivion with the hosepipe.

Henry waited for her to say more about his dad's unfathomable behaviour, but she didn't. Her rages were short-lived, because anger in their house simmered and spat like a joint of meat. You ate it and swallowed it down and it went away.

His mother stuck a sharp knife through the crackly, golden skin of the chicken, prising up the flesh to see if the juices had run clear. If it was red, you couldn't eat it, because swallowing chicken that wasn't cooked properly could make you ill. Food could kill as well as sustain you, she said. He knew then that food was a thing made from anger and resentment and love, but it was also a poison. He wasn't sure which emotion his mother would serve up today along with the potatoes and greens. You never knew until the meal was over, and then it was too late.

Henry watched his mother carefully, because if you watched, you could read someone's mind. His mother had a book upstairs called *Body Language*. She also had *Lady Chatterley's Lover* and *The Life that Lives on Man*. The last one had pictures of skin mites viewed under an electron microscope and expanded to the size of monsters. It wasn't nice to think of tiny things living invisibly in your armpits, or up your nose. But they did, and those photos were the proof. His mother had shown him the pictures and sometimes told him things he'd rather not have known.

He watched her now. Today, she was wearing tight brown slacks with seams running down the back like a pair of stockings. They made her bottom look bigger than normal. She was a tall, elegant woman with long legs, and people always called her slim, but his mother told him she wasn't slim at all, not really. 'I have rolls of fat around my middle and a big fat bottom,' she said.

Her bottom was why she went on diets. Diets were when she would only eat soup and crispbreads. Her bottom was the source of all her unhappiness.

'What are you looking at?' she said, pausing, because he was still staring at her, daydreaming. 'Come on, chop-chop! Lunch is served!'

She smiled then, and Henry realised she wasn't angry anymore. Her anger hadn't been about her bottom, or him. It had something to do with the patch of ground his dad kept digging at, uselessly.

'Go and fetch him,' she said. 'I'm serving up.'

He walked down the garden. It was a slightly different garden from the one it had been two hours ago, because the grass had been cut in stripes, pale green, dark green, the same colours as the outside and inside of a cucumber. The lawn felt cooler when you looked at it, whereas before, when the grass had been long and full of buzzy things, it had felt hot. There was the sweet smell of cut grass and the faint tang of petrol, and these were exciting smells, and they told you summer was here.

The noise of the lawnmower had stopped. On the top lawn he saw the machine where his father had left it. It was standing idle with its handles in the air as if it had surrendered to the enemy. It had a throttle for power and a hopper for the grass. There was a tank you filled with petrol from a can and wires that ran like veins to the motor. It had sharp blades at the front that revolved on a little drum.

His father was lying on the ground next to the mower. He had taken his shirt off. His chest was going up and down, his soft white belly quivering and wobbling with the counter-rhythm of his heart. Henry had never considered that his dad might die, but the way he was lying now, with an arm across his eyes and his stomach shaking, looked mortal, for his father was not a young man. He was bald and tubby. Then Henry noticed there was black hair on his father's chest, and long damp hair under his arms. His father didn't usually take his shirt off and there was something faintly repulsive about that soft, pale body. Henry watched his father breathing and matched his breaths to his: in, out, in, out. Then his father cleared his throat and moved his arm very slightly. 'Dad?' Henry said softly. 'Dinner's ready.' They called it dinner sometimes, and sometimes lunch.

His father gave a sigh, acting as if he'd known Henry had been there all along.

'All right,' he said in a tired voice. 'I'll come in a minute.'

Henry timed a minute on his new Sekonda watch, a watch they'd bought from Mr Shroeder's shop because he would give them a discount. It had a background that looked like bumpy wallpaper, but when Henry looked up after sixty seconds nothing had happened. He knew then that his father didn't mean a minute, because adults seldom meant what they said. Henry looked away and waited. Beyond where his father was lying was where the jungle began. That was where they'd buried the dead puppy, although its burial mound was now lost under a little pile of twigs and leaves and grass clippings and vegetable peel. He saw a new mound of turned earth and his father's garden fork stuck in it. It was in this part of the garden that the tortoise lived, sometimes emerging to lumber across the lawn, scowling and angry under the weight of its shell.

The tortoise had no name, and no-one knew where it had come from. It had migrated from somewhere and begun living in their bonfire, as if this were a perfectly sensible place for a tortoise to live. When it woke up and grew warm in the sun, it came down the garden on a mission, rowing itself along on four jerky legs. It was hungry after its long sleep, and would accept pieces of cucumber from Henry's hand, snapping at them with a bony mouth, then hissing air through its slitted nostrils. It ducked its head under its domed shell if Henry raised his hand and his shadow fell across it. Usually it trusted him, however, blinking sad, ancient, rheumy eyes, as if it understood him and forgave him for being human.

Henry walked back to the house, for he had done what his mother had asked him, and his father would come in his own time. In some of the grass lanes his father had cut in the lawn lay the remains of cooking apples that had fallen off the tree. The mower had smashed them open, and wasps blundered and throbbed in the mushy, brown sweetness that lay inside.

Chapter 6

The Hunger Artist

There were five of them around the table. *Family Favourites* still burbled in the background. First it was voices and then it was music: *All You Need is Love* by The Beatles, which was a song that began with the French national anthem, a tune that was called *La Marseillaise.* His mother said French things were more sophisticated than English things, which is why she'd studied *Cordon Bleu.*

Henry's mother had set the table and there were dishes of vegetables: sprouts and carrots and swede and sweet little peas. Their plates were steaming with thready white chicken that had golden skin around the edges, and there was crumbly yellow stuffing with herbs in. The sausages wore bacon cummerbunds and bent to the side as if bowing to the meat, because the chicken was what his mother called *la piéce de resistance.* The gravy lay oily and rich in a jug they called the gravy boat. The bread sauce was in a bowl, white and thick. It smelled of cloves. Cloves were bitter things like tiny wooden versions of the stick grenades the Germans threw in the war. If he got one in his mouth, he took it out and set it on the side of his plate, which his mother said was all right, even though it was bad manners.

Henry couldn't start eating because not everyone had been served. This was etiquette. His mother had a book about etiquette. It had a picture on the cover of a tall lady in Edwardian dress, because they had more etiquette in the past. It was full of important things that were still true today, his mother said.

They passed the dishes. Steam rose from them, a little cloud of vapour that hovered and dispersed. Alice sat prim and straight, her hair hanging down her back. Now that she had gone to High School, she was growing out of plaits. Hairstyles were things you could grow out of, like clothes. Henry didn't have a hairstyle yet. He would have one when he was older. His mother cut his hair. His hair had no shape, but that was all right, she said, because boys weren't supposed to care about how they looked. Neat and tidy was what mattered. When he had a haircut, he sat on the high stool while his mother steadied his head, her scissors snipping and clumps of his fair hair falling. She cut his hair carefully, because his head was still flat at the back and domed at the front, and some people would tease him for its shape if she cut it too short. When she cut his hair she pressed against him, and she was soft and warm, and he could smell her breath, which had the faint bergamot perfume of Earl Grey tea.

His father did not like Earl Grey. He drank another kind of tea and let it sit in the pot until it was very strong and dark. His mother took her tea weak and pale, 'like mother's milk'. Mother's milk made Henry think of Grandma Ivy, who was his mother's mother. His mother was tall and slim, and Grandma Ivy was neither, so you didn't have to look like your parents if you didn't want to. He couldn't imagine his own mother drinking milk from his grandma's breast, but she had. Many things you couldn't imagine had actually happened. His parents must have liked each other once, but it was hard to believe it now.

When Chloe was very small, Henry had watched his mother breast-feeding her. Chloe was just a baby and hadn't really become Chloe yet. One day, half-way through feeding, his mother had pulled her breast away and her sticking-out nipple had squirted a jet of milk on the floor. She'd laughed and said, 'Oh, dear!' Henry, who was three, wasn't sure if he should laugh or not, because his father had tutted, and said it wasn't the sort of thing you should do in front of a child.

Alice sat opposite Henry. Her face was solemn and pious. She ate carefully, dividing her food down the centre with her knife and fork the way she parted her hair at the front. She took small, dainty mouthfuls and chewed them discreetly. This was being ladylike. Alice knew about etiquette too, which was a thing more for girls than boys.

Alice didn't play with Henry now; instead, she sat in her room and listened to music. Henry heard her singing along to a record when he was trying to read his comics. Alice was 'almost a teenager', and Henry's mother said he must make allowances, because girls went through changes. These changes included new hairstyles, and singing the words of love songs in a bedroom with the door closed, and spending too long in the bathroom, and looking at your brother as if you hated him.

Chloe was still a baby and made eating into a game. She was too small to appreciate the formal appearance of food and wouldn't eat it unless she had subjected it to her own design. She made mashed potato into a landscape, channelling chasms and canyons with her spoon, then flooding them with gravy. The sausages were boats, and she made splashing noises. Then she took a spoonful of peas and poured them on top in a green shower. 'It's raining peas,' she said, and laughed. Her hand shook and some of the peas bounced off her plate onto the floor.

'Eat sensibly,' his mother said. Chloe smiled, but carried on with her game.

His mother sighed. Like Alice, she sat in a straight and formal way. There were rules for eating. This was also in his mother's book, the one he had found hidden.

His father hid things too, but they were not like the book of etiquette. Behind the sliding mirror in his father's wardrobe, Henry had found a magazine. It had a woman in a bikini on the front and strange stories inside.

On his father's dressing table was a bullet made of brass that tapered to a rounded point. It was a live bullet. When Henry turned it upside down, he saw the dot where the hammer would strike. The bullet scared Henry, because if he dropped it and the end struck the floor, it might go off. But he liked it too. When he held it in his hand, it felt cool and warm at the same time. His father never talked about it and Henry never asked. It wasn't a secret, because his father made no attempt to hide it the way he hid the book with rude stories in.

His mother's things were different. She had a dressing table with mirrors and a pink, quilted seat where you could sit and look at yourself. On the glass top of the dressing table there were powder-puffs and creams and cosmetics. She had a pirate's treasure of jewellery in a wooden box: ropes of beads, and earrings with a thin spike to go through the tiny holes in her earlobes. There was a Japanese fan, and lipsticks that were bullet-shaped but waxy and fragrant when you twisted them up. Sometimes, on the floor of the bedroom, he found crumpled tissues with the shape of his mother's lips on them. She kissed the paper with an open mouth, so her lipstick didn't leave red marks on the cigarettes she sometimes smoked, elegantly, like an actress in a film, blowing the smoke with a theatrical puff, or making rings that floated up and away.

It was in her wardrobe that he'd found the book on etiquette. The lady on the cover looked like his mother, except old-fashioned and in the past. The word *Etiquette* was written in a script that looked like the lady did: long, thin letters with little leaves on them, as if they were tendrils growing into the shape of words.

Etiquette meant manners, and manners were important to

Henry's mother, especially at the table. There were words and formulae to use with eating. Please may I have the salt? Please may I leave the table? Henry only used the word 'may' at meals. Chloe was too young to know the rules, which is why she played with her food. She never asked permission and never apologised. She just giggled.

His mum was 'Mother' today, and he thought of it with a capital letter. Lunch could be dinner, and Mother could be Mummy or Mum, but at the dinner table she was Mother, because things had different names for different occasions. Some occasions were formal, and some weren't. Eating at the table was formal, especially on Sunday.

Part of correct etiquette was to eat slowly and to set your knife and fork down between bites. You should never invert your fork and shovel in food as if it were coal going into a boiler. Holding your fork that way was only acceptable if you moved it to your right hand and were eating spaghetti Bolognese, which you sprinkled with a thin dusty cheese called Parmesan, that smelled faintly of vomit. The smell made it sophisticated and more Italian, his mother said. Sophisticated meant eating food that was slightly disgusting. This food was what was called an acquired taste.

Even if you were ravenous, you should pretend that you weren't. You should eat with elegance and a kind of indifference, relishing the food but pretending not to. This was like having to teach Chloe to climb a tree, but not. Two opposite and impossible things at once. This was elegance. This was etiquette.

His father didn't follow these confusing rules. He ate coarsely and brutally. He piled his plate high, pushing food into his mouth while there was still food inside, so you could see what he'd partially eaten. He chewed as if he was angry with the food, not looking up, just staring at his plate and working through it in a methodical way, disposing of it as quickly as possible. When he spoke, it was to give a command. His mouth was invariably full. 'Get your elbows off the table, Henry,' he said, spitting a little bit of potato onto the white tablecloth.

Henry hated his father then. How could a man who ate like that scold him for bad manners? But he did as he was told, because he had no choice. He moved his offending elbows off the tablecloth, and a feeling welled in his chest and behind his eyes. He couldn't eat. The food cooled on his plate and no longer seemed delicious. It looked like the mush his father had chewed in his cement-mixer mouth. His father had shown him what food really was: bits of liquidised animal and vegetable matter; fuel to be shovelled in any old how.

'Would you like another potato?' his mother asked. She was using her consoling voice.

'No, thank you,' Henry said. He hadn't touched the ones on his plate.

'Eat up,' she said, encouragingly. Then, changing tack, 'Isn't this nice?' she said, addressing the room.

'Yes,' said Alice, delicately cutting her chicken.

'Yummy,' said Chloe, her cheeks full. Her mashed potato was now a log flume for sausages. The peas were balanced on the sausages and those were the 'pea-ple' riding the logs. She laughed as if this was the funniest joke.

His father grunted, piling more on his plate. Then he noticed Henry sitting silently. 'What's wrong with him?' his father said. 'Is he ill?'

'He's all right,' his mother said, quietly. 'Come on, Henry.' She touched his arm.

Henry tried to eat, but it was very hard. He found that if he didn't look at his father or listen to the sound of his father's chewing, he could manage a little. He got through a few more mouthfuls, but his father had spoiled it.

When it was time for dessert, he waited until his father had finished before he started his own. His mother did the same, because she liked to 'rest' between courses. Then the two of them ate the trifle she had put sherry in — trifle that was very cold and delicious — eating it in tiny spoonfuls to make it last, while the others looked on enviously because they had finished theirs. In the end, Henry set his spoon down in the fluted glass dish the way his mother had done, with elegance and decorum. She smiled at him. And that was when he made up his mind: he would try to eat like her from now on. He would never eat like his father, because his father was a pig shovelling swill into its mouth. You could never teach etiquette to a pig.

Chapter 7

The Boy Who Couldn't Feel Fear

His father came home late every night. He sat in the kitchen and ate alone, working his way through the fried potatoes and slightly burned vegetables Henry's mother had warmed up for him. They never ate together, because the children must eat early, and she must keep them company. She left his father to it, retreating to the other room to watch the television with the rest of the family. The dogs were his dad's only company. They lay in their beds, waiting for what would come later. Then Henry's mother would call them through to the lounge, and they would get up stiffly and run across the linoleum with a clatter of nails. Not even the dogs wanted to stay in the same room as his dad any longer than they had to.

Then his father would be alone with the clock, and the small TV he hadn't turned on yet, and his cigarettes, and the airer near the ceiling heavy with the weight of the day's washing. His father would remain there until Henry went to bed, and afterwards Henry would hear the old man shouting at the television as if it had angered him in some way.

Sometimes his father left the smoke-filled kitchen and climbed the stairs that had a banister and newel post with a sphere on top like a wooden cannonball. He would come into Henry's room and read to him. He sat stiffly on the bed-end and intoned, in his clipped, reading-a-book voice. He still had his suit on, a pinstripe that smelled of onions and sausages and fried potatoes and cigarettes and train carriages and airless offices. It made Henry's mother angry that his father never changed out of his suit. She said he carried the reek of his work around the house with him. Her own father had always changed out of his office clothes when he came home, because her father was a gentleman. To keep your work clothes on when you had the option of changing was lazy and uncivilised, she said, and yet his father continued to do it.

Henry thought he would rather have a father who wore a suit that smelled of food and offices than no father at all.

His mother's and father's bedtime stories were different. His mother read him *Alice in Wonderland* and *Through the Looking Glass,* and these were books that sounded like a dream, because when Alice fell down the rabbit-hole she fell slowly, which was impossible. She could change size in a few moments, which was also impossible, and speak to animals that could reply to her in perfect English. In the book's coloured-plates that Henry pored over, Alice looked like his sister, and it was odd that they shared a name and were similar in appearance. Despite this, Henry felt that *he* was more like the book-Alice in temperament than his sister was, which was why he became the girl in those stories, arguing with the queen, or nibbling the food and drinking the potions, and finding everyone and everything oddly arbitrary and exasperating. He liked the Tenniel illustrations almost more than the writing, especially the ones showing the flat playing-card-men, and Alice with a long, telescoped neck, and the red-faced queen, and the terrifying beast called the Jabberwocky that the small boy fought with using his vorpal sword, killing it when his blade went snicker-snack through the creature's long, snaky neck. He loved, especially, the part where the boy came galumphing back to show his father what he had done, for the son was a hero now, and a 'beamish boy'. *Galumphing* was the best word Henry knew, and *beamish* second best. But he loved the other ones too, the words that were English but not exactly, because they were looking-glass words, really: *slithy, mimsy, brillig, outgrabe.* His mother told him once that her parents had called her Mim when she was a child, and that was because *Jabberwocky* was her favourite poem and mimsy her favourite word. Grandma Ivy still called her that sometimes. 'Shall I make some tea, Mim?' Grandma would say, and it was strange, because his mother had another name and identity Henry knew nothing about, and a name that had come out of a book.

His father's stories weren't like that. They weren't dreams with funny words in, and didn't have pictures you could look at, or words that had become his father's name as a child. They were nightmares, and there were no heroes who galumphed anywhere.

His dad read from *Tales of the Brothers Grimm.* This book had a hard black cover with embossed gothic lettering on it. The authors' name suited the stories perfectly, the double 'm' like a pair of pursed lips. His father's voice was tobacco-dark like the tale, which that day was about a boy who couldn't feel fear. The boy in the story had to face various hair-raising challenges, and if he survived them without showing any terror, he would win the hand of the princess.

One challenge was sleeping under a gallows where men had recently been hanged. Their corpses swung above him, their legs dangling and moving in the wind, and looking as if they were still alive. The boy wasn't scared, however. He pitied the corpses, unhooking them from the gallows and sitting them around his fire, because they must have been cold up there, alone in the sky. None of this or any of the other challenges scared the boy, and he was annoyed, because he wanted to be afraid, so he would know what fear was like. He didn't care about the hand of the princess. It was fear he wanted.

In the end, because nothing could be found to scare him, the boy won his prize and married the king's daughter. But they didn't live happily ever after, like in normal stories. Eventually, his new wife played a trick on him, because it was boring having a husband with no feelings. When he was asleep, she filled a bucket with icy water and live fish and poured it over him. The young man woke up shivering and his wife laughed, because she'd succeeded where everyone else had failed.

His father closed the book. 'There,' he said, tapping the cover, as if the story had proved a point that he wished Henry to grasp, a point about women, and marriage, and fear. Henry was confused, 'because shivering isn't the same as being afraid, and the princess cheated,' he said.

His father smiled. 'You're right,' he said. 'She did cheat. Women do, sometimes.' He looked at Henry as if that was the moral, and Henry nodded as if he understood.

'Good night, then.' His father got up and raised his hand in a gesture of farewell, as if he were going away on a long trip, although he was only descending to the smoky kitchen. 'Sleep well,' he added, as he walked out with the book under his arm.

Henry lay awake and watched the light fading behind the curtains. The wind rose, making them to billow and flap. When they moved, the faces in the fabric came alive. They were sly, goblin faces with mouths that yawned and eyes that winked.

Henry wriggled deeper under his blankets. His wardrobe loomed like a coffin standing on one end. He knew there was a dead body in the wardrobe that would come to life as soon as he closed his eyes. Sometimes, drifting off to sleep, he felt the gentle bump as someone or something sat on the end of his bed, then all his muscles would jerk him awake. But if he opened his eyes and stared, no-one was there.

Chapter 8

La Télévision

Within a year, Peppy was bigger than Anna and much naughtier. He liked to chase other dogs and attack them, and Mother said he would have to be castrated, because being too much of a boy could be a problem. In the evenings, the children would sit in the lounge with her, watching the television in front of the gas fire, which purred and creaked and complained. The dogs lay on the rug and slept, their paws twitching. In the dogs' dreams they were always whimpering and running and chasing things. It seemed to Henry that they were never at peace, even in sleep. He wondered if dogs had nightmares like he did.

In his nightmares, something terrible chased him down the garden. He would run towards the apple trees, but the lawn was too soft to support him, or his legs too heavy. Then the thing, whatever it was, would gain on him until its hand touched his shoulder, and he would wake to find he had pressed himself against the headboard, and his shoulder was sore where the monster had rested its claws on him. When he looked under his pyjama-top, the marks were there. Or he lay in bed and saw grey wolves slink like smoke through his doorway, and knew that if he remained there, they would climb in his bed and devour him. In the end, he could bear it no longer. He got up and went into his parents' bedroom. He saw their humped and sleeping shapes and turned his head back the way he'd come. The door was open, and he knew the wolves would come flowing around it if he waited any longer, so he went forward and crawled under his father's bed. He lay amongst the balls of dust on the cold, bare floorboards, because he knew the wolves could not get him there. A draught came up through the gaps and made his teeth chatter, so he got out from under the bed and crept in beside his father. His father didn't wake, but in the morning he asked what on earth Henry was doing there. Henry explained and his father frowned. 'There are no wolves in the house,' he said, 'or anywhere in England. Don't be daft.' But Henry knew his father was wrong, because there *were* wolves, and he'd seen them. Anyway, his father was stupid, because it wasn't England in your dreams; it was another place where anything could happen. He couldn't tell his father this because he wouldn't understand.

Henry often had nightmares. In another, he was running across the park which was empty except for him. This dream was in colour, which dreams normally weren't. A green-faced witch in a spaceship pursued him, cackling and gleeful. She pointed down with her long, thin finger. There were no trees to hide behind and she was all-seeing in the glass cockpit. Henry knew she was the Wicked Witch of the East from *The Wizard of Oz*. In the film, the witch had been killed when a house fell on her, and all you saw were her red-shoed feet sticking out from the rubble. But this witch was in a spaceship and nothing could harm her.

When he awoke, he knew he couldn't go into his father's bed again, so he crept down the landing to Alice's room. He opened her door and crept inside. Then, lifting the blankets, he slid in beside her long, bony shape. He was surprised to find that her back was warm, like Chloe's had been through the material of her dress when he'd pushed her on the swing. He knew then that Alice wasn't as cold a person as he'd thought. It was nice to lie behind her and feel the warmth radiating from her back. In the end, the sound of his sister's breathing was soothing, and it rocked back and forth like the movement of the swing under the conker tree, and soon he was asleep, cradled on the rhythm of her breathing and the movement of the swing that took him up into the leaves of the conker tree and down again.

Their father seldom joined them in the lounge where the dogs slept and jerked and dreamed. When he did, he lay stiffly in an armchair and smoked, ticking his cigarette into an ashtray he had placed on the armrest, and tutting because he couldn't hear what was being said on the screen. He thought it impolite to talk over the television. In his opinion, TV was an extension of the classroom or lecture theatre; you should be silent and attentive, and, in that way, you might learn something.

Their mother made a face and winked at the children. TV wasn't a person or a classroom, and anyway, this was a programme with singers and dancers so there wasn't anything to learn. It was entertainment, which their father didn't believe in, and this was because he was what their mother called 'a stuffed shirt.'

'They're just having fun, Arthur,' she said, when their chattering and giggles had started up again. The children tried to hide their laughter behind their hands, but it came out anyway, squeezing and bubbling through their fingers, because the dancers were wriggling and writhing in a funny way to the beat of the song. After a while, their father said a bad word, picked up his ashtray and walked out, slamming the door behind him. The children and their mother looked at each other. Their father was frightening when he was angry, but at least they could enjoy the programme now he was gone.

Some people had colour sets, and they knew this because neighbours and friends at school talked about it. Having a colour TV was better than black and white because it was like having a cinema in your own living room. Their mother said you could hire colour TVs from Radio Rentals, and it wasn't expensive. 'But your father says no,' she said, 'so that's that.' Their father always had the final say, and he always said no to things that were fun.

It was *Top of the Pops* again, and Pan's People were gyrating to *In the Summertime* by Mungo Jerry, which Mum said had rude words in it. Mungo Jerry sang that you could 'make it good in a layby,' and this was funny, although the children weren't quite sure why. Alice said she knew but wouldn't explain, and they were stupid not to know. Their mother said, 'Now, Alice,' which was a sentence where 'now' had a meaning only Alice and their mother understood.

Then Peppy broke wind and sat up, looking behind him in surprise as if something unconnected with him had happened. It was mostly Peppy who did this, farting and denying it, although sometimes their grandma did and said it was just her slipper squeaking. Mother called it flatulence or wind, because fart was a rude word. Peppy's wind was terrible, on account of the rubbish he gobbled up in the garden: windfalls, and mouldy bread that had been thrown out for the birds, and vegetable peelings. It made them laugh, the way a dog could be frightened of its own farts. Their mother picked up the *Radio Times* and flapped it up and down because of the smell. She made an amused but exasperated face. If a dog had flatulence, it was funny, because a dog knew no better, and etiquette couldn't be expected of them, but if Henry did, it was disgusting.

Their mother usually defended the children, but she made an exception for Henry, because he went too far. Sometimes, Henry did something stupid, like swinging a conker on a string, spinning it like a propeller so it went all blurry and flew out of his hand, shattering the glass-front of a cabinet. Once, he bounced a tiny rubber ball inside the house, and it jumped off a wall in a way he couldn't have predicted and broke a vase. Then his mother summoned their father, who'd just come through the front door in his rain-spattered mackintosh, and told him to punish Henry, because she was at her wits' end, she really was. Henry had tormented his sisters all afternoon, and now this. His father ran his hand over his wet, bald head. 'I've just come in,' he said. 'Can't I even take my coat off?'

A row began then, because it wasn't a matter of taking bloody coats off. His father said it was. He'd just walked up the hill and was soaked, and anyway, he didn't know what had happened, and he couldn't punish someone for something he hadn't seen. This wasn't Nazi bloody Germany. Their mother said his analogy was stupid, and he never took her side when it really mattered. Then there was a fight, and the children ran away to their rooms.

After a few weeks, their father relented, and they got a colour TV. It showed a world that was better than the one they lived in. There were American programmes on TV sometimes, and they were the best of all. Americans lived in huge houses and called their gardens yards. They had bigger, happier, brighter lives than English people. In *The Brady Bunch,* arguments were only disagreements, the parents never fought, and there was always a moral about sticking together and being kind. Everyone smiled at the end of that show, because a family was a 'bunch,' not a group of people who didn't understand each other. And that just went to prove that TV was better than real life. If Henry could have been American and lived his life inside a TV, he would have done, as long as he could take his mother with him.

Chapter 9

The Swimming Pool Season

Henry liked swimming. They went to a big, modern swimming pool in a place called Morden, which was an anagram of the word modern, so the place and the pool matched in a way names normally didn't. Henry had never felt that he was his name, although that was what everyone called him, and it was the name on his school exercise book, and the name his mother had sewn into the back of his school sweaters: Henry Truffle. Sometimes, when he said his name aloud or looked at the combination of letters, he wondered at the arbitrariness of a name, and how it was like a sweater: something you wore sometimes, but took off when you weren't at school or were alone in your own head. In your own head, you had no name.

Other names didn't fit, either. His mother had called Anna's black and white puppy Peppy, but that dog had never been anything like a peppermint. You bit into a peppermint, but Peppy bit into you, because he was a struggling, snapping devil. When they let him off the lead in the park, he would sprint away and head like an arrow for the nearest dog, knocking it over, snarling and biting and nipping, and then they were apologising and chaining him again because he couldn't control the rage inside him. Sometimes, when Henry let him out the back door, Peppy would run round and round the lawn like a demented greyhound on a track. Henry's mother said Peppy needed a good walk every day, but she didn't always have time, which was why he ran like that, circling the flowerbeds and going nowhere. And that was why she'd had him castrated, she said, because he had too much pep. Boy dogs, his mother said, could have too much maleness for their own good, and it made them mad. It made Peppy mount his own mother, Anna, when she was in season, and then everyone had to look away, because a glint had come into Peppy's eye, and an odd, clockwork mechanism was working his hindquarters. And that, Henry's mother said, was being a boy.

And now Henry was being a boy, but a different kind. He was at the swimming pool, the one where there were three boards at graduated heights from which people — mostly men — dived.

The last time he'd come, Henry had gone off the lowest board. Even from that height the water glittered very far away, and the echoing voices made him dizzy. He'd tried jumping from the second board, but the slap as he struck the surface had stung his arms and tummy, and he'd gone very deep, descending into a bubble-filled silence. Then he'd felt the pressure in his nose, and there was a little click of adjustment in his head. Streams of tiny bubbles came out of his mouth, and, as they'd cleared, he'd seen the lower halves of the swimmers, their legs kicking in silent spurts of energy. It had been strange to watch the half-people floating in space, and odd to see the pale legs and buttocks and bellies when the owners of those body-parts didn't know he was there. And then there was a whoosh as he was drawn upwards, the silence breaking into a roaring clamour as he re-entered the world above.

Jumping from the board had felt brave, but it was cheating, because you weren't supposed to do that. You were supposed to dive, your vulnerable head going towards the bottom of the pool. You had to have courage, and he didn't have much of that. For that reason, he had no intention of diving, or even jumping, off the boards today.

He undressed in the hot cubicle, put on his swimming trunks

and went outside. The floor was grooved under his feet and the air smelled of chemicals. He found an empty locker and stuffed his clothes inside, forcing in his heavy shoes. He closed the metal door, which bulged in one place and caved in in another, as if someone had kicked it in a fit of anger. He took out the key attached to a thick yellow armband and slid the band onto his wrist. It looked like a bracelet. His wrist was too thin, and the rubber flopped over his hand. He tested it by shaking it, but it didn't fall off, so it would be all right. He knew that he must on no account lose his band, or key, because if he did, the lifeguards would be angry and have to dive to the bottom for it. If they couldn't find it, he wouldn't be able to open his locker, and then he would have to go home in his wet swimming trunks and leave his clothes behind, and that would be humiliating.

He inspected his band. Yellow was the colour of cowards, and cowardice was something to be ashamed of. 'He's yella,' they said in cowboy films, when a man ran away from an Apache attack. Henry didn't want to be yellow, so he would do something brave today. Perhaps he would dive off the middle board after all. Robert, his friend, could do a swallow-dive and cut the surface without a splash. Maybe Henry would do that.

He left the changing room and walked past the showers. Men were soaping their bodies into a white lather, while boys stared up into the water falling from the showerheads with pinched-up eyes that were reddened from the chlorine. There were six showers. Behind the fifth shower was an orange stain of rust that ran down the wall. No-one used that one.

It felt odd to be staring at people he didn't know, and some returned his gaze with a sullen or enquiring expression, so he walked on, passing a drain where a sticking plaster, a sweet wrapper and a clot of dark hair lay in the plughole. The hole was blocked, and the water welled up in a swirling eddy. The hair moved as if it were alive, and the sweet wrapper and plaster bobbed like little boats. He felt sick, because he knew he would be swimming in water polluted by other people's bodies and dirt. That was why they had chlorine, and someone told him the stronger the smell of chlorine, the more people had peed in the water.

He moved away, splashing through the trough of green stuff you had to go through to stop verrucas spreading. He'd had a verruca once, and it was a lump on your foot that had a hard black dot in the centre like a little eye, and it hurt when you walked on it.

He went along the chilled corridor. On the wall was a metal sign explaining what *patrons must kindly refrain* from doing. The sign was written in red and the THANK YOU! at the end looked irritated, as if people shouldn't need reminding. There were pictures showing the forbidden activities: *no running, no pushing, no acrobatics, no shouting, no ducking, no petting, no bombing, no smoking.* Henry wasn't sure what petting was, but next to that word was a picture of a man and woman with their arms round each other and a background of showering love-hearts.

'Robert's doing underwater swimming,' said Robert's mum, when he found her. She was called Mrs Harris, and she was a large woman who wore her makeup into the pool. Her rubber swimming-cap had flowers on it, and her nipples made two hard bumps like buttons on the front of her costume. Her name suited her, because she had hair under her arms and on her upper lip, and bits of it curled out of her swimsuit at the top of her thighs. She had a husband who was short and fat and drove a green Jag. He honked his horn if Henry left his bike on his drive and didn't get out of his car to move it. Henry didn't like Mr Harris. He got drunk in the afternoon and asked funny questions that weren't funny at all. But he wasn't here now, only Mrs Harris. She was strange too. She swam a very slow breaststroke and did widths, then stood up and talked to other women in the shallow end. These women stood with their arms folded over their breasts, and they did more chatting than actual swimming, because for them swimming was socialising and not exercising.

'He's over there somewhere.' Mrs Harris waved her arm vaguely. 'Underwater swimming,' she repeated, as if that would make it easier to find him.

Finally, Henry found Robert, and he wasn't underwater at all. Robert was with his sister, Julia, and Henry's sisters, and they were standing in a line along the edge of the pool. They were playing a game, and they hadn't waited for him. 'You took too long getting changed,' Alice said, with a bored expression. 'You're always so slow. Never mind, you can join in now.' She was the leader on account of her age, and she had placed the other children in order of height, all facing the water. She made Henry stand at the far end. 'Ready?' she said, when she'd arranged them to her satisfaction. 'Yes,' they replied, knowing something good was coming. Then she walked behind them and pushed them one by one into the pool. There were splashes and shrieks. Then they climbed out did it all over again, because that was the game.

Alice did it out of sequence, so you never knew when she was coming, and that made it even better. Sometimes, to add variety, she pushed them hard. She did this even though one of the instructions as you entered the pool had said: NO PUSHING. Either she hadn't read the sign or didn't think the rules applied to her. The children began to improvise. The next time he was shoved, Robert did a somersault and slid into the water without making any ripples. Henry stood, not knowing when his turn would come. And then, when he wasn't expecting it, she pushed him. His legs went forward and up in the air, and his head flew back and hit the side of the pool. There was a dull crack and everything in his head went red.

He floated for a while and the sound of voices went far away.

Then someone grabbed his arm and pulled him up. They dragged him towards the side, and his body made a little wave of resistance. People were pointing and drawing back, because there was blood in the water. He found himself in front of the ladder-thing and tried to climb out, but his legs were wobbly, and it took a long time. Then he was out and standing on the side, holding one hand to the back of his head to stop the brains coming out. Then Mrs Harris was bending over him, her face looming close. Her breath smelt of coffee, and the pores of her skin were too large. He saw that sticky mascara had run from her eyelashes. She was asking him what on earth he'd done, when he hadn't done anything at all.

Then a man in a tracksuit appeared. He took Henry by the arm and led him to an office. When they arrived, he asked what had happened. Henry said he'd slipped and banged his head, and this was a lie, but you couldn't tell tales on people.

'You need to get dressed,' the man said. 'Then we'll get you to a hospital. Where's your armband?'

Henry stared at his wrist and saw that the armband had gone. 'I don't know,' he said.

The man muttered something and shook his head. 'Well, I'm not going snorkelling to find it. What's the number?'

Henry knew this. It was two numbers which, added together, made his age. 'Sixty-three,' he said at last.

'Christ,' the man said. 'They only go up to fifty.'

'Thirty-six,' he said. A pain was beating in the back of his skull. 'Or twenty-seven. I can't remember. I'm sorry.'

The man whistled. 'Luckily for you, we've got spare keys for all the lockers because people keep losing them,' he said. 'But we need the number.'

'Thirty-six,' Henry said, more firmly. He felt dizzy and sick. Blood was leaking in a warm trickle down the back of his neck.

The man looked at the ceiling light for a while, then he picked up a clipboard with a chewed biro tied to it by a piece of string. He wrote the word 'Incident' and underlined it. 'Wait here,' he said, and went away.

The man didn't tell Henry to sit down, so Henry didn't. He looked at the floor, where there was a crushed cigarette-end, and wondered if he could lie there and go to sleep. After a while, his teeth began to chatter. Then the man came back with a plastic bag full of clothes. "These yours?' he asked.

Henry looked at the socks and shirt and the heavy shoes with muddy treads. The clothes didn't look like his because of the way they were all squashed together.

'No,' he said. 'I mean, yes.'

'What?'

'I think so,' he said.

'You *think* so?'

He looked again. 'Yes. They're mine. I'm sure.'

The man breathed out slowly. 'It *was* thirty-six,' he said. 'Your number. A right song and dance we've had, I can tell you. You'd better get dressed quickly. The ambulance is here.'

Henry took the bag of squashed clothes, and his shoes fell to the floor because he couldn't hold it all. Then he tried to get dressed, pulling on the clothes without drying himself. He kept his damp trunks on because he didn't want the man to see him naked, and his trousers got stuck on his legs and a sock wouldn't go on.

'You done?'

'Yes.' His wet hair dripped onto his shirt-collar.

'Come on, then,' the man said, jingling his keys. 'Follow me.'

Henry was lying on a hospital bed, and a nurse was about to give him an injection. Mrs Harris and Robert were there, Robert looking bored and Mrs Harris restless because she'd left the girls in the waiting room. 'Pull a face to make Henry laugh, Robert,' she said. Robert put his fingers in his mouth and tugged sideways while going boss-eyed, then stuck his tongue out. The nurse pushed the needle in Henry's arm, and Robert's stupid face was no help at all.

'He was so brave,' the doctor said, when his mother picked him up. 'He didn't make a sound.'

His mother smiled. Henry's head was wrapped in a bandage and there were six new stitches in the back of his head. He had lain face-down on the table while the doctor repaired the skin on his skull. He had clawed his nails into his palms to stop himself from crying. He knew he mustn't make any noise, and he hadn't.

'So, what happened again?' his mother asked. They were in the car, and she was driving him home.

Henry was silent for a while. 'I went to dive in the water and my feet sort of slipped,' he said at last.

His mother sighed. 'I expect you were running, weren't you, or playing some silly game?'

He nodded, but said nothing.

'You really must be more careful, Henry. Were you running?'

'Yes.'

'Well, then. You know who to blame, don't you?'

When he went back to school, all the kids wanted to know why his head was wrapped in a bandage. John said he looked like the creature in the poster for *The Curse of the Mummy's Tomb*. 'What happened?' they asked. 'Were you in a car crash?' Suddenly, he was the most popular boy in school.

'I slipped on the side of the swimming pool,' he said. 'I cut my head open, and the doctors gave me twelve stitches.'

They stared at his head. It was the same head they had once laughed at and called triangular. Now they were in awe, because he must have done something brave to earn a bandage as big as that. Even Alistair Cairns was impressed. 'Did it hurt?' he asked, wanting to know despite himself.

'Yes,' Henry said, 'but I didn't cry.'

'Was there blood in the pool and everything?'

'Of course. Everyone had to get out so they could clean the water. '

'Oh, wow!' said Alistair Cairns. He sucked his lips, because even he had to admire a lie as big as that.

At lunchtime, Henry walked around the playground like a king, acknowledging the nods, and answering the questions that were humble requests from mere menials. With each re-telling, his tale became grander. He'd got concussion, he said, and the doctors had worried he might have brain damage. Then he said he hadn't slipped at all; he'd dived off the top board and bumped his head on the bottom. He told it so convincingly he believed it. He remembered the bodies he had seen under the water, their silent kicking motion, the click of adjustment he'd felt in his head, due to a change of pressure. 'Go on,' his audience murmured, rapt now. 'Then what happened?

Smiling, he told them the lies they wanted to hear.

Alice never referred to what had happened. It was as if she hadn't been involved at all, as if the lie he was telling to protect her, about slipping on the side of the pool, was the established fact. When Henry caught her eye, which he tried to do, she stared back blankly, or glanced away with a sort of tired shrug. She couldn't care less what he said or did, or didn't say or didn't do; that shrug meant he certainly shouldn't martyr himself on her account. But Henry knew what the noblest course of action was, and how a brave Tommy in the war would have behaved. So, he kept silent. Or, as his mother would have said, kept mum.

Chapter 10

The Reinvention of Grandma Ivy

Their grandmother came to the house most days. If you were playing on the front lawn, or taking a letter to the post-box, you sometimes spotted the blue waterproof macintosh she always wore as she walked uphill from the bus stop. She had short, curly, blue-white hair and the stout forearms of a prize-fighter. Once, she had lifted Henry's bike clean above her head, turning it upside down, then setting it on the ground so Henry could fix the chain. Even Henry's father couldn't have done that. His father said they didn't make women like Ivy anymore, and he didn't mean it as a compliment.

If their mother was at work, their grandma would be there, and she was always in her pinny and the slippers with flapping soles. She was never still, because idleness was next to sinfulness. Flap-flap, her slippers said, as she moved up and down the kitchen doing her chores. She was suspicious of any activity that involved sitting down. Henry's mother told him that, when she was a child, his grandma would snatch books out of her hand if she caught her reading in the daytime. 'We'd all like the luxury of putting our noses in a book, Miss,' his gran would say, 'but some of us must work. Floors don't sweep themselves, you know. And there are no servants kept. So, chop-chop!'

Henry remembered then that he had never seen his mother reading a book unless she was in bed and there were no chores left to be done. This was because reading was a pleasure to be performed in the privacy of your room; it was enjoyable, but a form of indolence and therefore slightly suspect.

Despite her strict laws about daytime reading, Henry loved his grandma. She cooked huge meals, which were most often great bubbling stews full of scrag end. Scrag end was fatty bits of lamb that became, when boiled in a pot, a sort of greasy soup topped with a rainbow-hued scum. Into this, Grandma added coarsely chopped vegetables and huge floury dumplings that floated on the surface in an ominous cluster. The dumplings were heavy and sat in their stomachs all afternoon. This was war-time food, Grandma said. It was good, but you felt exhausted after eating it, as if you had to fight another war digesting it.

Sometimes, their grandma tired of scrag end and brought sausages in a greasy paper parcel that she carried in a pocket of her macintosh. In the pan, the sausages sputtered and crackled and spat hot fat across the room. Grandma Ivy laughed when this happened, and said 'no harm done', turning the sausages with a spatula. Grandma had lived through doodlebugs and the Blitz, so she could take spitting bangers in her stride and expected others to do the same. She also had standards that were different from those of Henry's mother. For, although she wore white gloves when she went out and hated anything 'common', she sometimes said things she shouldn't. One day, she was cooking as usual, and Henry was watching. He noticed how the sausages had transformed into charred lumps that burst in pink oozings from their ruptured skins, and it was then that his grandma said something rude. She said the bangers looked like 'men's doodahs'. Doodah was a grandma-word from before the war, and it meant a winkle. Henry agreed with her, but he knew she shouldn't have said it, because winkles were not a subject for polite conversation, especially for an old lady.

Grandma Ivy always did things differently. She made food that wasn't healthy, but her bad food was nicer than healthy food. This food was called traditional fare. She fried eggs into a frizzy, lacy lump, and then balanced them on a tower of crinkly, home-made chips. She boiled puddings in a cloth. Sometimes they were suet puddings with a nest of steak and kidney hiding at the bottom in a mess of rich brown gravy; sometimes they were ginger or treacle puddings, with the dark sweetness in the middle when you dug there with your spoon. She made sponge cakes that were dry and hard with a crisply baked shell and a generous filling of cream, jam or chocolate: fillings that squished out over the side when you bit into a slice, as if the cake were salivating over its own gorgeousness. Mother said these cakes were 'technical failures', but the children thought they were delicious anyway. Grandma often got things wrong, but she got them wrong in a way that seemed right.

Grandma did things the old way, the way things were before the world discovered calories and dieting. If a woman got fat in Grandma's day, she put on a corset and cinched herself in. She wore her fat with pride and donned a girdle and oozed out the side of it, the way cream oozed out of Grandma's cakes. Fat was curves and curves were seductive and that was all right back then. This was why grandma hated slimming. She cut bread into doorsteps and slathered it with butter an inch thick; she made enormous tins of Toad-in-the-Hole where the blunt heads of sausages sat up and looked up at you as if asking to be eaten.

Grandma Ivy was different in other ways, too. When Henry was ill, his grandma changed from someone strong and frightening into someone gentle and kind. She called him 'dear' and dripped lavender from a small glass bottle onto his pillow, so that the fresh scent might remove the sourness of his sickness. And she did other nice things. She removed the plastic bucket, cleaned it, and put a splash of Dettol in the bottom; and that helped, too. Then, when he was a little better, she brought him a plate of dry toast and a bottle of Lucozade that he sipped through a straw, the liquid flowing, cold and fizzy and orange, into his tormented stomach. 'Never mind, dear,' his grandma said soothingly when he brought it all up again, before removing and cleaning the bucket once more. 'It's rotten being ill, isn't it?'

'Rotten' was a grandma-word. Rotten was like a windfall apple. When you were ill you were rotten, and that was what it felt like inside. You were full of wasps that circled and buzzed and stung.

Grandma was musical, too. Sometimes she played the piano in the living room, improvising a song and finding the melody in mid-air, her hands rippling over the keys and her heavy rings clattering on the ivory. 'How does it go, dear?' she would say, and when they sang it, her fingers would find the notes. While she played, Chloe capered and Henry did a lunatic hop. Alice, who only danced in the privacy of her own room, watched quietly, because she was growing out of Grandma now. Grandma was behind the times and didn't understand what it meant to be a teenager.

Henry liked the fact his grandma had come from a different age. Her stories were different, and she didn't read them from a book. She made things up out of her head the way she found music in the air and not on a sheet of paper, so the children were never quite sure if what she told them was true. Nonetheless, Henry liked the tales of how people were punished in the past; her stories were even gorier than the *Tales of the Brothers Grimm*. For example, Grandma Ivy said that, in the past, a man who sold rotten fish would be placed in the stocks and pelted with his own stinking wares. 'In those days, they knew how to treat a criminal,' she said, meaningfully, as if the past was both better and worse than the present.

Henry began to realise how old-fashioned his grandma was. She wore white gloves on a hot day and said things like 'meelk' instead of milk, daintily sounding the 'l' in that word like a cat licking milk from a saucer.

Grandma couldn't cope with new inventions. They all laughed when she called the new fifty pence pieces 'fifty-pent pieces'. It had all been silver sixpences, sovereigns and guineas back in her day. Henry had a cardboard chart where all the new coins fitted into shaped slots. His grandma peered over his shoulder, frowning as he prised out the 50p to show her. He read her the information because it was interesting. The 50p was '...the world's first seven-sided coin made of light cupronickel,' he read. It was 'an equilateral-curve heptagon, replacing the old ten-shilling note.' Grandma sniffed. She didn't trust things that were seven-sided and made of cupronickel. 'There was nothing wrong with the old money,' she said. 'Why did they have to change it?'

Words like decimalisation and up-to-date and European did not satisfy her. Europe was a dark and distant place and not entirely to be trusted. She liked counting in twelves and missed the threepenny bit, which she called a 'thruppence', saying that word affectionately as if it had been a friend who had died. As far as she was concerned, decimalisation was the end of something great, and the beginning of something worse, something not quite English.

Chapter 11

End Game

When Grandma Ivy was well, she made teddy bears and dolls, moulding their bendable limbs from wire, then padding and clothing them. She had completed a doll-making course and must put it to some use, Henry's mother said. She gave a doll to each child as a gift, even though Alice was too old for one. She made stripy socks and football boots for Henry's doll, and a flouncy, pink ballet dress for Chloe's. She had found some plastic faces and set one into each doll so that it had a personality or character. Henry's doll had a lion-like mane of hair and looked mischievous. She made one for Alice in the style of a teenager. It was a cloth and fabric model of a girl in a short skirt with ankle socks and a little handbag. Alice didn't want it because Grandma had given the doll breasts and a coy, simpering face, and it was embarrassing. When Grandma went home, Alice put it in a plastic bag and buried it beneath the underwear in her chest of drawers.

Grandma had other hobbies, and one was cards. Because he liked playing cards too, Henry sometimes accompanied her to whist drives, putting on his best clothes and boarding a coach to distant places like Eastbourne. The whist drives had nothing to do with driving, although the journeys were part of the experience, his grandma said.

Henry was sitting in his seat in the coach and listening to the old lady behind him. She was explaining how Eastbourne was a favourite spot for suicide. She said the cliff path at Beachy Head was full of wreaths and floral shrines dedicated to those who had jumped to their deaths. The suicides had chosen this place because it was where England and people's hope ran out together. The old lady spoke in a loud voice and had no-one sitting next to her, so Henry thought she was speaking to him. He turned and gave her his full attention. She was a white-haired lady with a thin face and lipstick that had missed her mouth in the corners. 'But I'm sure we'll all have a lovely time,' this lady said, unwrapping a bonbon and putting it in her mouth. 'It's a beautiful spot. I suppose that's why people go there to die.' Her eyes twinkled at Henry. She offered him a sweet, which he accepted, and Grandma gave him a look, and he didn't know why.

The other old ladies didn't speak about death. They made a fuss of Henry and fed him Old Jamaica chocolate that had rum in it, saying, 'Be careful my boy, don't get drunk!' and pinching his arm in a friendly way. They told his grandma she was lucky to have such a fine grandson, which made Henry sit straighter in his seat. He was acting that role today, his hair neatly combed to disguise his triangular head, a new Timex watch on his wrist, and his shorts held up by a belt that had an s-shaped clasp.

When they finally reached Beachy Head, the old ladies didn't go and look at the suicide cliffs but shuffled into a low building, where tables had been set out for cards. Grandma gripped the flesh at the top of Henry's arm, leaning on him as if the two-hour journey had exhausted her. The wind blew her dress against her bandy legs and Henry thought she might fall, but she said she was stronger than she looked.

The old ladies sat at the round tables and ate more food and drank more tea, even though most had sipped from thermos flasks all the way down, something that had forced the coach driver to stop at service stations several times for what he called 'comfort breaks.' After a while, little groups of old ladies went off to the toilets to 'powder their noses'. Henry had noticed their commitment to powdering before and had often wondered at it, because it was something men never did. Younger women did it too, and his mother said it was it was important to stop her nose from looking shiny. His mother powdered her nose using the compact with the broken mirror. She didn't have to go to the toilet to do it; she sat at her dressing table and let Henry watch. 'I'm putting on my face,' she would say, dabbing away with the little puff, then touching up her 'lippy' with the bullet-shaped tube that she turned to allow the tip of the lipstick to screw out. 'I'm putting on my physog.' Physog was one of his mother's words just as 'impertinent' was one of his dad's. It was strange the way a woman put on her face, but a man just had the one he was born with.

Henry liked watching his mother putting on her face. She applied mascara with a sooty little brush, angling the compact because her face was divided along the crack. Henry didn't understand why his mother kept her broken old compact when she could have bought a new one. She explained that it had sentimental value, and that not everything old could be thrown away, and one day he would understand that. Henry said that was silly, because a broken mirror would bring her seven years bad luck. His mother shrugged and said that she'd had the compact much longer than seven years. Whatever bad luck was in it would have done its mischief by now.

When the old ladies came back from the toilet, they began playing cards. They talked loudly as they played and made jokes, then laughed until the tears ran down their faces. They blew their large, powdered noses into tiny lace squares that were wet after one blow. They ate biscuits and shortbreads and large wedges of Dundee cake and swigged more of the hot, sweet tea until the room grew steamy and sour with the smell of it.

A seat was found for Henry near his grandma. He let his eyes roam the room as he nibbled at the food they pressed on him. They were of the opinion that feeding a boy was the one thing you must do keep him happy. They didn't let him join in their games, however, because card playing was a serious matter and for adults only. He watched, and saw how they kept a tally of their wins on little score-cards that they filled in with the stub of a pencil. A win was a trick but there was nothing especially magical about it.

When he grew bored, he wandered across the noisy hall to look out of a window. It was greasy with breath. He ran his finger down it, and made a dripping trail through which he could see the coach and green grass and the road that led to the suicide cliffs. He caught an acrid waft of smoke and realised he wasn't alone. Their coach driver was beside him, looking out at the same view. He was a thin, sallow man.

'Raining,' the coach-driver said, nodding at the window.

Henry was forced to agree.

'Typical,' the man said, as if it were raining to spite him. 'Always rains at Beachy Head.'

Henry was unsure if this was true or a joke. He looked up at the driver, but the driver's eyes had pinched shut as he blew out smoke, and Henry couldn't read his expression. The driver had a big Adam's apple, and when he sucked on his cigarette, he drew the smoke into his thin cheeks so that they collapsed like a paper bag. Then he blew the smoke out in a long stream and said 'Ah!', as if letting out something angry from inside him. He looked down at Henry and contemplated him for a while. 'What's a young shaver like you doing here with all them old biddies?' he said at last.

Henry considered his reply. He didn't want to have a conversation with this man, and he didn't think it polite to call old ladies biddies. Nor did Henry like being called a young shaver, as if he were a man and not a boy. He noticed then that the driver smoked his cigarette upside down and with his hand bent over the top of it, as if he were hiding it. It was a roll-up cigarette with bits of hairy tobacco poking from the end. He didn't hold it between two fingers as Henry's parents did, and when he finished it, he dropped it on the floor, grinding it out with his foot until it was just a dark stain on the linoleum. He didn't crush it out in an ashtray, which was what polite people did. Then Henry noticed that the man was staring at him. He was waiting for an answer to his question about the old biddies.

'I don't know,' Henry said at last. He was there, he supposed, because his grandma had asked him.

The man nodded. 'No, I bet you don't.' He rolled his eyes, as if he could think of a million things young shavers might get up to, and none of them involved sitting in a room and watching old biddies drink tea and play cards. '*You* don't play cards, then?'

'Yes, I do, but they won't let me, because I'm too young.'

'Typical,' the driver said, blowing out a jet of smoke. 'So, you just come all this way for the ride?'

'Yes,' he said. 'My grandma's here.'

'Oh, your *grandma*, is it?' He turned and scanned the hall, as if he might be able to guess which of the double-chinned, tea-swigging old biddies belonged to Henry.

'Yes.'

'And you don't gamble, like?'

'Pardon?'

'You don't play cards for money? Some of them biddies is playing for cash, y'know. I seen 'em.'

'No. I'm too young.'

'Shame,' he said. 'You might've won a few bob.' He paused. 'Half of 'em's senile.' He tapped his head.

Henry didn't know what this meant.

‘Doolally,’ the man explained, making his eyes wiggle in a deranged sort of way.

Henry didn’t like this man’s way of speaking, or the way he treated Henry as if they shared a similarly low view of old ladies and their activities.

‘I have to go now,’ Henry said.

The man blew out another jet of smoke. ‘All right, then. You toddle off.’

Henry ‘toddled off’, and went to join the old ladies who were senile old biddies now.

Cards were best when you played them at home. Grandma had taught them canasta, rummy and pontoon, sharing out spent matchsticks to gamble with when she had no change, which she called ‘coppers’, in her purse. Sometimes, she removed all her chunky gold jewellery and let them bet with that, and if Henry won, he had a hand weighed down with rings, which he waved around like an emperor, or king. He loved these rings, the smooth gold inset with gemstones and with the hallmarks on the inner side of the band in a square lozenge. He wished he didn’t have to give them back when the game was over, because they almost fitted him now. His grandma laughed, and said she would leave him some of her rings when she died.

He loved his grandma, but it was a different love from the love he felt for his mother. His grandma had strange ways and phrases, and Henry’s mother said it was because his grandma lived in the past. In Grandma’s life the war was still going on, his mum said. It was true. He had been to his grandma’s flat, and it was dark and cold and smelled of gas. She kept some windows open, and his mother said it was because of her asthma. Grandma felt she couldn’t breathe if all the windows were shut. But the real problem was with her lungs, not the windows.

His grandma's flat was strange in other ways. Instead of a garden, it had a jungle out the back full of thick blackberry bushes. The thorns tore and snagged at your clothes if you went outside to pick the fruit. Grandma said she was too old to cut them back. Grandma's flat also had sinks where a gas burner sat on the wall above the basin with a blue pilot light always on. The flame popped and roared when you washed your hands, and Henry was scared the whole thing would blow up and kill them one day, but it never did.

Grandma often spoke of the war, and air raid shelters, and of hearing the sirens and the droning of planes overhead. It was strange to think she had ended up living in a kind of unexploded bomb.

Henry and his grandma watched wrestling on Saturday afternoons if he went to her flat for a visit. In wrestling, fat men in leopard-skin leotards grappled with each other, while an audience of old women screamed and shook their fists. This showed Henry that not all old women went to whist drives and ate mint humbugs and made dolls with football boots or ballerina costumes. Some old ladies wanted men to tear each other apart while they cheered them on. Once, when they were watching one of these wrestling matches, Henry stole a glance at his grandma. She had just brought in a plate of biscuits. As he ate one, he wondered whether his grandma also wanted to see men hurt each other. She certainly liked to tell stories in which people were tortured in the cruel punishments of the past. Then he remembered the old lady on the coach who'd laughed at the suicides at Beachy Head. You could never be too sure of people, because even nice old ladies sometimes enjoyed other people's suffering and ate bonbons and biscuits while they watched it happening.

Chapter 12

There Was A Crooked House

Henry's father wasn't practical, but sometimes he put up shelves, albeit at an odd angle. He also tiled the kitchen but ran out of energy, so that tiles meandered across the wall and ended abruptly in a patch of grey plaster. 'Your father doesn't finish things,' Henry's mother said, shaking her head. 'He isn't thorough.'

Henry stared at his father's failed attempts at DIY and made a decision. He would take part in these practical activities, if on a smaller scale, because in that way he might win his mother's approval. Unlike his father, he would be thorough. He wouldn't abandon projects in the middle and exasperate people.

Henry had his own little workmate with a clamp to which he attached small pieces of wood. These he could saw at or hammer nails into. He also had a stub of pencil and a small spirit level in which a mysterious bubble lived. The bubble appeared from nowhere, wobbled across a green gauge, and settled between two markers, but only when the wood was level.

Henry could never quite understand this obsession with things being level. Nothing in their house was. Doors hung drooping on hinges. Cabinets that his father had fitted were slightly 'out of true,' attributing this to an obscure thing called 'subsidence,' which was where a house sank into its foundations. His father also blamed the general asymmetry of things on other factors that were not strictly his fault, such as the shaking of the property caused by the main road that lay just beyond the hedge. It had been a country lane between farms when they'd bought the house, he said, but now it was a trunk road on which lorries and cars thundered, day and night. Henry found it hard to imagine their road as a trunk, which he pictured as a pink-ended elephant's snout, sniffing and wavering this way and that. He tried to think of their house on a country lane with just an occasional cart or tractor going by, but he couldn't do that either, because the traffic, with its swish of tyres and bang of lorries and roar of music from open windows, had always been there, ruining the peace that should by rights have been theirs.

Everything in the house was skew-whiff. Henry's mother spent much of her time adjusting the angles of things, especially the framed pictures. These were mostly prints of horses by George Stubbs, or landscapes in which country maids stood at gates with a view of fields behind them. They were pictures that showed an older, quieter England. These pictures also told the viewer that his mother had taste and was familiar with the works in The National Gallery. Taste, Henry gathered, meant favouring rural compositions — hunting scenes with dogs, misty views of country estates where simple folk did their labour — over images of cities. The only picture of a city on their walls was a Canaletto print of London, and it didn't resemble any version of London Henry knew. It showed an image of St Paul's and the Thames, and there were pavements where ladies in ballooning dresses strolled with little dogs, and black-robed priests paced about, and on the water, men punted ferryboats over the silver waves. In the background, the dome of the Cathedral floated like a bubble, while dozens of church spires held up the tent of the sky.

Henry found that he always looked at these pictures from the perspective of the artist or member of the gentry, but when he suggested to his mum that he was descended from a line of painters, landowners and gentlefolk, she told him that, on the contrary, his ancestors had been a riff-raff assortment of 'gardeners, coachmen and labourers'. Henry was dismayed. This was almost as bad as being told his head was triangular. His mother said that this was why it was important Henry made something of himself in life, because otherwise he would become another peasant like the stunted and sunburned men in the paintings.

When she said this, Henry looked down at his dirty, short-fingered hands, the ones that he'd always imagined were those of an artist. They were a peasant's hands, he saw now, not an aristocrat's. He was descended from the exhausted workers and coarsely clad boatmen in those pictures, not the elegant folk on horseback or in ecclesiastical finery. And that was also skew-whiff — Henry's sense of himself as a king in disguise — when the truth was that he was from a long line of undistinguished nobodies.

He liked his mother's pictures anyway, even though they were cheap imitations and not actual paintings, and even though they hung at odd angles on the wall.

The misalignment of the artworks was mainly Henry's fault. He bumped against them when he answered the phone, which was a big white plastic thing with the curly cord and the cup over the speaking part that smelled of lipstick and tobacco and other people's breath. Henry hit the pictures with the tennis balls and shuttlecocks he wasn't supposed to play with in the house. He knocked against them when climbing on chairs to retrieve the paper darts that dived and swooped and looped the loop due to the ailerons he put on the wings. His mother told him that she spent all day putting the house straight only for him to come along and in five minutes knock it sideways. 'Why can't you be more like your sisters?' she said, waving her duster, a technicolour nylon thing on a stick, as if she would dust him out of existence, or at least, into femininity. This was an unfair comparison to make, because his sisters were lazy creatures who thought lying on a bed and dully turning the pages of a magazine while feigning to have a 'tummy-ache' was a productive use of time.

Despite his mother's unjust accusations, Henry determined to put things at the correct angle, even though time always seemed to unbalance things again. He could, at least, help with the chores. In a spirit of self-sacrifice, he sometimes did the drying up after dinner, while Chloe lay in front of the TV watching cartoons, and Alice sat in her room listening to music. Alice believed drying-up was beneath her dignity now that she was thirteen, and had spots, and liked boys, and listened to Motown records. She got away with this behaviour because she had moods and rhythms that were something to do with the phases of the moon. This wasn't fair. There was no excuse for Henry's moods that he could attribute to the movement of the sun or any other astral body. So, when another load of drying up had to be done, it fell to him to do it, because his sisters couldn't be persuaded to help. They were girls; they had strange fits of weakness where all that would console them was cake and music and cartoons on TV. Henry knew then that girls would always get away with things that he couldn't, and that, all things considered, he would have been better off born female.

As becoming female was beyond him, Henry occasionally made half-hearted attempts to be more like his father. He kicked at an old football and played passing with his dad on the soggy lawn; he sat with him and watched football matches on TV. His father smoked as he watched these games and did so until the room was blue and the screen appeared to get further away. His father grew irritated with players who didn't play as well as he would have played in their stead. He lay sprawled in the armchair. He looked like a tubby version of Nobby Stiles, one of the players who'd helped England win the World Cup in 1966. Despite this, he considered himself an authority on tactics, and thought most players were 'bloody idiots'.

In a cardboard box upstairs were old photos of Henry's dad when he'd had more hair. They were team photos, and his dad was sitting on a chair and surrounded by footballers in long shorts. The pictures were black and white. The men had different hairstyles, and the kind of moustaches men didn't have any more. The captain held the leather ball delicately on his lap as if it were a giant egg that might hatch at any moment. His father's face in the photos was very young. He was thin, and smiling, and not quite the father Henry knew, because his father never smiled now.

They watched in silence. Whenever his father grew angry, he lit another cigarette, because anger and smoking were connected. You lit up the cigarette and the end burned brightly. When your rage was done, you crushed it out in the ashtray. Henry's father got angry about forty times a day, which meant there were forty butts to throw out each night. When Henry's eyes grew sore and his chest thick (his father had been angry ten times in this match already) he asked his father not to smoke any more. His father kept his eyes on the screen and told him to bloody well shut up and go away if he didn't bloody like it, and Henry did, getting up and walking out and closing the bloody door and missing the end of the bloody game, but hearing the roar of the crowd through the walls, because his father had the bloody volume turned too high. His father was a little deaf, but that was no excuse for telling Henry to bloody well shut up.

Despite this, Henry tried to be the kind of boy a father might be proud of. He cut up pieces of wood; he played conkers and made paper planes. He played football on his own, up and down the lawn, kicking it too hard and destroying his mother's roses, then knocking over the pot plants on the terrace and spilling earth everywhere. When he tired of this, he turned to his Action Man, because he was a more reliable companion than his dad.

Action Man suited outdoors better than indoors. In the garden,

Henry posed him in fighting stances, kitting him up in his accessories of fur-lined parka or wetsuit or desert fatigues, each suited to the various kinds of terrain afforded by different parts of the garden. The rockery was a mountainous escarpment, the uncut lawn a jungle, the pond where the carp swam, a lake or an inland sea. Henry put Action Man in dinghies and fitted guns into his moulded plastic hand. He tried to build heroic adventures around him. But it grew boring after a while, because Action Man always had the same expressionless face with the scarred cheek and sightless blue eyes. You had to face the truth in the end, which was that Action Man was just a stiff and rigid doll with ugly joints and plastic seams. If you stepped away and left him alone, he just lay there in the dirt, inert and fixed in the rigor mortis of his crawl-posture. They should have called him Inaction Man. In due course, Henry came to hate him, too.

One day, Henry's mum came home to find he'd hung Action Man along with Teddy and Looby Loo from the banisters. They dangled and swung by their necks on the end of long lengths of string. His mother asked him to take them down, please, because executing old toys wasn't nice. It would upset Chloe, she said, and it had upset her, because hanging wasn't something you joked about, even if it was in a game. Then Henry remembered how his mum had wept when Colin Platt had died by hanging himself. Women were different, he saw, because one thing reminded them of something else, and that was why they cried at songs or in films, and boys didn't. They saw the wider symbolism of things, whereas for a boy, it was just a song or a teddy-bear hanging from a bit of string. So, understanding this, Henry took Action Man and Teddy and Looby Loo down from the gallows and untied the string from their necks. Then his mother said thank you, and peace resumed.

Henry tried Airfix models next, because he didn't need his father for those, and because there you could deal with death and war in a more straightforward way than just hanging toys. He bought models of Hawker Hurricanes and Wellington bombers and Spitfires, but also German planes like the Messerschmitt 109E. The German designs were more stylish, he thought, although he knew he couldn't say that, and his father wouldn't approve. Sometimes, he bought the model of an old biplane such as the Sopwith Pup, getting the correct tins of Humbrol paint so he could decorate it and make it authentic. He'd heard from friends that it was best to paint the planes' interiors before assembling the model, so he did so with a fine brush, delicately filling in the instrument panels, then painting the wings and fuselage while they were still held in the plastic frame. Next, he put on the slippery transfers — the target shapes and numbers and swastikas — sliding them carefully in place. Then he had to assemble the whole thing, following his little illustrated map of instructions, dabbing the glue that made his head spin and fused to his skin and left long trailing spiders' webs that hung from his fingertips.

Sometimes, things went wrong. Once, when Henry came to put the two halves of the fuselage together, they didn't fit properly, sliding out of alignment when his fingers applied pressure; and then glue got onto the carefully painted bodywork and spoiled it. After an hour of wrestling with the plane and failing to get it right, Henry took the whole lot, including the little pilot sitting stiffly on his moulded plastic seat, down to the jungle at the far end of the garden. He put the model on a flat stone that looked like a blacksmith's anvil. Then he picked up the biggest rock he could find and smashed the plane and the pilot to bits. Afterwards, his chest heaving, he buried the pieces under the earth where no-one would ever find them.

A week later, his dad came in from the garden and wanted to know why there were bits of an Airfix model in his vegetable patch, and Henry said he didn't know, they must have been there from the time of the previous owner.

Chapter 13

The House on the Borderland

Their house had many rooms, and some were outside. Henry's favourite was the garage. Great cobwebby lengths of wood rested on shelves above the car and were supported by rusty metal brackets. It was always dark, despite the naked lightbulb that hung on a length of frayed flex. The switch to the light sat in a cracked plastic dome and bulged off the wall. Everything in the garage was old and unsafe, but Henry liked it, just as he liked the attic, because it was mysterious — part of the house but not really the house at all: part of the present but also part of the past.

The attic was a place where you had to be careful to walk on the planked area, or you would tumble through the ceiling into one of the bedrooms. You heard the skittering of birds on the tiles outside and the road's distant rumble, and you saw bits of blue sky caught between tiny gaps in the joists. In the attic, there were ancient suitcases and rusty trainsets and boxes bursting with old clothes you could use for dressing up. The beams were draped in more grey cobwebs that were full of dead woodlice and moths. The attic was a whole floor that no-one thought about, a room you never remembered until you were in it. It reminded you that a house was a tall thing that lay under the sky and wasn't quite sheltered from it.

The garage was different, but it also had gaps that let in the outside. Water crept in and puddled on the floor. Spiders came in, and mice. Despite this, his father used it to store things. It was a place full of drawers of screws, nails and hinges. There were old jam jars crammed with rusty fittings, and a metal box that opened to reveal mysterious tools like gimlets, chisels, files and claw-hammers. Saws hung on wooden pegs: the thin-bladed hacksaw, the long-fanged, rainbow-hued one Henry liked to shake because it made a wobbly noise. In a corner, and attached to a tap, lay the long black snake of a hose that had coiled around itself and turned into a stiff fossil because it had lain there so long.

'You mustn't lose your temper,' his father said. Henry had just lost it again, because when he tried to hammer nails into a plank of wood, they went in sideways. He looked at his father, remembering the way his dad swore at inanimate objects. If a screw wouldn't go into a wall, it was a '*bloody thing*'. If a piece of wood barked him on the shin, it was a '*silly sod*'. His father was a hypocrite, Henry knew then. Hypocrite was a word Henry's mother used.

His father was lopsided, like most of the things in the house. When he was angry, he clamped his tongue between his teeth, so the end sat in the corner of his mouth like an indicator turning left. It was the same with his glasses. There was a twist in the frame that meant one side sat higher than the other, making his father's face look like he'd had a stroke. Henry's uncle had had a stroke, and one half of his face was frozen now, his mouth hanging down with a droopy lip.

His mother was lopsided in a different way. She'd been born with scoliosis and had had an operation when she was a child to correct it. Henry had seen the long scar on her shoulder, and it looked like a splash of white paint. The operation hadn't worked, however, because one shoulder was higher than the other, giving her back a snake-like twist. To look normal, she built up one side of her body with wads of tissue-paper, balancing them in the scoop of flesh behind her collar bone. Sometimes when Henry went into her room, he found the bits of balled paper that had fallen off her collarbones and lay on the floor. These were the parts of his mother she had shed, leaving them around the house for him to pick up.

Nothing in their house was straight. Being straight also meant being truthful, a thing Henry found difficult. Once, when he was playing football in a park with some boys, he told them his name was Harry, and they accepted it, and carried on as normal. He'd chosen Harry because it seemed a stronger, more confident name. He played football better as Harry and enjoyed being someone else for an afternoon. He decided lying had its place in the world.

The problem was he couldn't stop. One day, at school, he said he had a rich uncle who owned a Rolls Royce with a TV inside and a cocktail cabinet and electric windows that wound down at the press of a button. This uncle lived in a mansion and took Henry for car rides in the country. The boys at school were impressed, just as they'd been when he'd told them he'd had twelve stitches in his head after his sister pushed him in the pool, when in fact he'd only had six.

He lied about his house, too. Once, when his friend's father was bringing him home from a party, Henry told the man to stop two doors down from where he lived. He got out and walked up the wrong drive, going past the sign that said *Lumberland*, waiting there until his friend's car had gone away. He had chosen this drive because the house was bigger than his own, and grand enough to have a name that suggested it was an actual land and not just a house. His friend would respect a boy who came from a house like that; a house that was also a principality, and where the prince was Henry himself.

The worst lies you could tell were the ones you told about other people. It was usually his dad he lied about. He was ashamed to have a father who looked like a monk and drove a clapped-out car, while his friends had young dads who were tall and straight and had hair and drove new cars like Lotus Elans and Jensen Interceptors and

Citroëns, a car that had air suspension and rose into the air when you turned the ignition. One Saturday, after a football match, when a boy asked if the bald man in the car was his dad, he said no, that's just an old uncle come to pick me up. The boy nodded and said okay. All the way home, Henry loved his dad a little bit more than before, because he'd lied about him, and was sorry.

Chapter 14

Of Mice and Men

They had few visitors at their house. The milkman came for his money now and then, and it was always a shock. It was his mother who opened the door, and the knock was a thing of dread. 'Who on earth is *that*?' she would say. His mother was usually in her dressing gown, because the milkman came so early. She looked like an actress caught unawares: she hadn't put her face on yet and her hair was what she called a 'frizz-bush.' She stood at the open door, pulling her collar together while the milkman showed her his calculations in the book he kept chained to his belt. His mother relaxed and flirted as she paid the money, even though he called her Mrs Troofel not Mrs Truffle, and a freezing wind blew through the house, because the milkman always brought a bit of the coldness of the winter and his icy milk with him.

But it wasn't always the milkman who knocked on their door and it wasn't always winter. Sometimes it was summer and later in the day, and then it was the rag and bone man wanting any old iron and not rags or bones at all. When you looked outside, you could see his cart at the bottom of their drive and the horse nodding its head and jingling its bridle. Their mother didn't have any old iron, thank you very much, and when Henry mentioned the old mangle with chapped lips that stood rusting in the yard, she told him to be quiet. Or it was the man who offered to sharpen their knives; or a gypsy woman selling sprigs of lucky heather which she pushed into his mother's hand before she could say no, and once his mum had touched it, she had to pay, or the woman would turn nasty. Whoever it was, their mother was on her guard, because people weren't to be trusted. They either wanted to sell you something or take something from you. Your children, your property; your dignity.

People calling round unexpectedly, or the phone shattering the afternoon calm, were causes for alarm. You never knew who it might be. A person who rang and then hung up when you answered was a burglar checking to see if anyone was home. His mother never explained how the burglar had got their telephone number, and Henry never asked because he knew she was right. They had been robbed twice, and his mother had been on tenterhooks ever since. Tenterhooks were hooks on a beam where you hung cloth to dry, and his mother said she felt like that now: up in the air, like a piece of cloth hanging in the wind.

Henry remembered the police coming round, and a woman in uniform standing awkwardly in the hall, while his mother sat crying on the bottom stair. The front door was open, and it was cold. Upstairs, there were clothes on the floor and drawers turned out, their contents sifted through. All his mother's antique jewellery had been stolen. Downstairs, the front door had been forced with a jemmy and the wood was all splintery and pale under the varnish. Their father wasn't there. He was never at home when they needed him, his mother said, and always there when they didn't.

It was strange having policemen and women in the house. Henry had only met a policeman once before, and that was when the officer had come into their school after Colin Platt had hanged himself.

And then, one day, the police came for a different reason.

He and Alice had been on their way to see Robert and Julia, their friends who lived around the corner. It was a sunny day and only a twenty-minute walk. They would come to no harm, their mother said, as long as they didn't talk to any strangers. So, they set off and turned down the quiet side road where the richer people lived. They passed the post-box and the house with a stained-glass window showing a sunrise and its spreading beams. Soon they would reach the witch's house, which was a dark building with a pointed roof that looked like a witch's hat. It was surrounded by fir trees which were a deep, dark green, and you always felt cold walking past that house even in hot weather, as if there was evil inside it. That day, a car was parked near the witch's house and a man was at the wheel. He saw them coming and wound down the window and beckoned them over. 'What do you think of that?' he asked, when they approached his car. At first, they didn't know what he meant. *'That,'* he said. They followed the direction of his eyes and the tilt of his head and saw what he meant. His thing was out of his trousers. It was very interesting, but at first Henry didn't know what it was.

'Do you like it?' the man asked. He stroked it, and was keen to have their approval.

'Is it real?' Henry asked, because it didn't look it.

'Of course it's real,' the man said. He was a normal man, apart from the thing that had come out of his trousers. 'You can touch it if you want,' he added.

Henry looked at Alice. They knew that what the man was asking them to do was wrong, although Henry wasn't quite sure why. When his mother had said don't talk to strangers, he didn't think she'd meant men in cars with strange, skinless things that sat up and looked at them. 'No, thank you,' they replied, speaking as politely as they could, because they mustn't anger him or the thing he was showing them. And then Alice gave Henry a look, and they ran away before the man could do anything else.

When they got home, they told their mother what had

happened. She didn't think it was an exciting and funny adventure like Henry did. Instead, she made a phone-call, and then a policeman and woman came to their house. The officers were very serious. They asked them lots of questions about the 'gentleman in the car'. All Henry could remember was the man's thing, which he described in great detail, especially the bit about it twitching and looking a bit like a skinned mouse. The policewoman covered her mouth when he said that, but the policeman frowned at her, and she stopped smiling. Then the policeman cleared his throat and asked about the make of the car, its colour and the registration number, none of which they could remember, because these weren't interesting details. He asked what the man had looked like, but neither of them could remember his face, which was anyone's face, really. Henry repeated his description of the man's thing, and added that it had twitched sideways at one point, as if the man had it on an invisible string and was jerking it. The policeman and woman looked at each other again but didn't write this down. Then they left, and nothing more was ever said about the man who had a skinned mouse living in his trousers.

Chapter 15

The Go-Between

They were sitting at their desks in the wooden hut on stilts and Miss Clarke was reading to them from *The Hobbit.* As she did so, the walls of the classroom fell away, and Henry found himself carried deep underground. It was stiflingly hot, and he was lost in caverns under a mountain where goblins lived. It was cold and damp, and he was in a cave where Gollum came paddling across a lake, his pale eyes gleaming like lamps. On other days, he stood with Ged in a frail boat in the middle of an unnamed sea, a magician's staff held aloft to ward off dragons. Or he was Piggy on a desert island where there were no parents, and Piggy's shorts, which were his own shorts now, were chafing his thighs, his body soft and white and quivery. Then he was Ralph, tall and strong and laughing at Piggy for being so fat and clumsy and wheezy and asthmatic. In books, you could be all the characters at once, and none of them.

Miss Clarke was a progressive teacher, and they loved her. She thought eleven 'an appropriate age to encounter difficult ideas', and the children agreed. They enjoyed *Lord of The Flies*, the book in which schoolboys became savages and fought each other, because it seemed real to them. In the playground, there were fat kids who got picked on, and a ginger boy who flashed his willy in the toilet entrance and was laughed at, and two kids from Malta who spoke English with an accent. There were fights where two boys tangled in a dusty heap until a dinner lady came and separated them, and there was a girl who dragged a boy around by his hair when he made a joke she didn't like.

So, they believed in *Lord of the Flies*. If you were on an island with no grown-ups that was what would happen. Fighting and killing and madness.

One lunchtime, Alistair Cairns picked up Miss Clarke's copy of *Lord of Flies* when she wasn't there. He flipped through the pages and turned to the end to find out what happened. He read the violent bits aloud in a confident voice, the other children standing in a huddle and leaning in, because he was the teacher now. They shuddered when they heard how the fat boy's head got crushed by a rock, and pink stuff came out, and the sea breathed in and washed the pink stuff away.

They didn't tell the truth when Miss Clarke came back and found her bookmark on the floor. 'Has anyone touched this?' she asked, picking it up. They sat solemnly, hands on the desk, eyes on her. 'No, miss,' they chanted. It wasn't a lie because Alistair Cairns had touched it and they'd only listened, so in that way they'd all done it, and no-one had.

Miss Clarke was the prettiest teacher in the school. She wore low-cut tee shirts and short skirts, and some of the boys were in love with her. She was twenty-four years old and very friendly. She told them lots of things about her private life. She had a cat called Mr Tibbles. She did yoga and took French evening classes. She never mentioned a man, and told them she was single. When Alistair Cairns asked if she wanted a boyfriend, she said no, she was quite happy with Mr Tibbles; he was the only man in her life. They all laughed at this. Henry imagined Mr Tibbles as a human-sized cat in a dinner jacket and bow tie, having candlelit meals with Miss Clarke in their cosy little flat.

Miss Rogers, who was Miss Clarke's friend, was small and plump and wore kaftans like the singer in The Mamas and the Papas. Miss Rogers ran the art club, and her room always smelled of paint. Miss Rogers didn't have a cat, but she did have a boyfriend. Henry knew this because he'd heard Miss Rogers and Miss Clarke talking about him in Miss Rogers' hut.

It was breaktime and their voices came floating through the window when Henry was standing outside. Henry didn't want to eavesdrop, but he had no choice, and he didn't move away because what he heard was interesting. Miss Rogers was talking about her boyfriend. His name was Paul, and sometimes he was nice and sometimes he wasn't. Henry remained there, listening to this conversation because the window kept being open, and he kept being curious. It was like a story in a book that you had to follow to the end.

Once, Miss Clarke asked Henry to carry a message to Miss Rogers, and he agreed. It was good to be trusted. After a while, the one note became many notes, and soon he was running back and forth several times a day. The messages were written on graph-paper folded into tight squares. Miss Clarke and Miss Rogers knew that Henry would never read these notes because he was an honest boy who wouldn't let them down. He always ran as fast as he could, then stood with the eyes of Miss Rogers' class on him as she wrote her reply. When he'd been given the answer, he ran straight back again. He knew this was how marathon running had begun, with an ancient Greek carrying a message announcing victory over the Persians to distant Athens. It made Henry feel heroic to be carrying messages of war or victory or whatever it was the letters contained.

Then, one day, he became curious about the notes he was carrying. He wasn't Greek and there wasn't a war on. It was hot and dusty, and he was sweating, and he was just a schoolboy carrying stupid bits of paper, so he stopped running and stood there and thought about what he should do. He found a place where he couldn't be seen. He unfolded and read the note, which turned out to be two notes in one.

Hi L,

Paul's been horrible again. He expects me to stay with him but shows NO commitment! He disappears at weekends and doesn't tell me where the fuck he's going. He could be seeing another girl for all I know!

Men = bastards, eh?!

Are you free after school? I need to talk!!

Jane x

Under this note was a reply.

Yes, sure. Kevin isn't much better! 4pm, my room?

Liz x

Henry re-read the notes with his heart bumping in his chest. He had to decipher the information quickly and absorb its meaning. The teachers had adopted a strange writing style, especially Miss Rogers. He had never seen an equals sign used like that before and was unsure what a bastard was, but he knew it wasn't good. Miss Clarke was *Liz* and *Jane* was Miss Rogers; that was easy to work out. Their Christian names looked odd, and he understood that he wasn't supposed to know about teachers' private lives, but it was their fault for speaking loudly with the window open and then giving him these bits of paper with rude words in. Then he noticed that Miss Rogers had overdone the exclamation marks, and hadn't always written in proper sentences. She had also used the f-word, which he had only heard his dad use when he got lost on a motorway and his mum was navigating, and they had missed their exit, and then they were stuck on that road for the next twenty miles and were going, as his dad kept reminding them, in the wrong bloody direction.

There was something else he noticed, and it was the worst part. Miss Clarke's reply suggested that she *did* have a boyfriend after all, because who else could Kevin be? Henry's image of Mr Tibbles, in a dinner jacket and bow tie, fell to pieces. Miss Clarke had lied to them.

Then Henry realised he'd been reading the notes for too long and might get caught; and if that happened, he would be in big trouble, and no-one would ever trust him again. He was standing under a tree that dropped sticky buds like date shells on the ground. He re-folded the paper carefully and ran to deliver it to Miss Rogers, the buds sticking to the soles of his shoes. He worried that Miss Rogers would see them and know he had gone off the path to read the notes, but when he passed her the piece of paper, she said nothing except thank you, and then wrote her reply.

Chapter 16

The Dutch House

A new boy called Mark joined the school. He was tall and thin and wore glasses and had buck teeth, and he was one of the cleverest boys in the class, even though he wasn't English.

Mark's family had come from Holland. They had two cars, a Mini and a Volvo, and both cars were bright orange, because orange was the official colour of the Netherlands. It was a colour few English people liked because it was gaudy and vulgar, but when the Van de Schoerrs drove around in their cars, no-one felt that way; they thought orange was distinctive and bold. Mrs Van de Schoerr was slim and blonde and had black edges to her teeth because she smoked, but all the mums said she was beautiful, and so stylish in that bright orange Mini.

Things were different at the Van de Schoerrs' house, too, as Henry discovered when he spent the night. Mark's family didn't eat cereal or egg on toast in the morning. They had single, buttered slices of bread with chocolate sprinkles on top, and these were called open sandwiches. Other things were open about them, too. Mark had an older sister who was sixteen and had breasts almost as big as Miss Clarke's, and instead of being shy about them, she wore a medallion with 'The Magnificent Two' written on it, and arrows pointing left and right. Alice would never have worn a medallion like that. When Henry whispered to Mark about his sister's badge, she overheard him and said, 'Well, Henry, I'm glad you think they're magnificent,' and Henry blushed. He didn't know how to reply, because he hadn't written the words on her badge and the perception of their magnificence wasn't originally his idea, although he did agree.

When they played football in the garden, Mark was always Holland, because Holland had Johan Cruyff, and he was the best footballer in the world. Mark had an interesting stamp collection, too. His stamps were all Dutch, with modern designs in bright colours. They were not like the British ones that showed Polar explorers and old buildings and members of the royal family in profile. Mark also had a book of war photographs, and one was a picture of a man who had been hanged from a beam by a length of piano wire. His face was swollen and his tongue poked out of his mouth, and it made you sick to look at it. A sign in German said 'No Photographs', but there was a grinning Nazi in the picture, and someone had taken a photo anyway because they were looking at it.

Henry wasn't allowed pictures like this in his house. If *The World at War* came on the TV and it was about the holocaust, Henry's dad came in and turned it off, because, he said, Henry was too young for such things. In Mark's house, they didn't think you were too young. There were no secrets, no hidden magazines and mysterious bullets on dressing tables, no garages full of lumber and spiders. Mark's garage was clean and organised and empty except for a Volvo estate in bright orange.

Henry knew that in the war the Dutch had been on the side of the British, and he decided he liked Dutch things better than English things. He couldn't support the Dutch football team more than England, but he wanted Holland to beat Germany whenever they played each other. And in this way Mark had become Henry's best friend, and not John, the weedy boy whose mum sometimes gave him a lift to school. It was more fun to be friends with a boy from a different country, one whose sister wore a medallion saying, 'The

Magnificent Two', and whose parents let him look at gory pictures, and whose country had been Britain's ally during the war.

Chapter 17

A Clockwork Orange

They were learning about the body at school, and Henry had brought in his mother's book of human biology. It was called *The Wonderful Story of You.* It had fascinating illustrations, one of which showed a woman with her skin peeled back. In her belly, little men were toiling away, shovelling food into a furnace, and this gave you an idea of how the digestive system worked.

Miss Clarke stood beside Henry and looked at the picture he loved and that the other children had admired. She said it wasn't very realistic, because digestion depended on stomach acid and bile and the pyloric sphincter and other things that sounded complicated and disgusting. She said it took several hours for food to pass through the gut; it wasn't just a case of throwing fuel onto a fire. And in any case, why were there little *men* doing this in that picture, when the body was supposed to be a woman's? 'Women don't have little men living in their bodies,' she said. The children laughed.

Alistair Cairns shouted, 'What about if the woman's *pregnant*, miss?'

Miss Clarke said that was enough. The children knew pregnant was a rude word. Alistair was being cheeky, but her comment shut him up.

Henry closed his book on the picture of the digestive system and the little men with shovels and the stomach that looked like a furnace. Miss Clarke had said his book was silly. He wondered why his mum had sent him in with such a babyish, old-fashioned, unscientific thing.

Later, they were doing reproduction and Miss Clarke drew a man and a woman in sideview on the board. The man's parts were plain to see and everyone giggled. Miss Clarke told them to be sensible or the lesson wouldn't continue, so the children concentrated, because it was interesting. Miss Clarke's drawings didn't help, however. It was hard to understand the picture of a woman in profile because it looked as if she had a twisting passageway somewhere inside her hip. Then Miss Clarke sketched a front view in chalk and said this is a womb and eggs, and this throat-shaped thing with animal horns like a ram's head, well, that's the fallopian tubes. Henry looked at the side-view sketch again. He couldn't understand how a baby could come out of the sealed skin on a woman's hip, or out of a ram's head. Miss Clarke didn't explain, because today it was conception and not birth, and before he could ask a question the bell rang, and the lesson was over.

One day, Alistair Cairns brought a magazine into school. The boys all gathered round in the toilets. There were pictures in it of strange, orange-coloured women with no clothes on. The boys looked at the pictures but didn't speak. They studied the images carefully, to learn the things they hadn't been told. They breathed a bit too hard as Alistair turned the coloured pages where the women posed and showed themselves. There were things in these pictures people didn't want you to know about.

Henry learned the truth about the female body in other ways, too. Once, Amanda May invited some of the boys into the book cupboard during wet-break, and when she lifted her skirt she had no knickers on. She had taken them off without telling anyone, and that was part of the game. 'Come in and see my show,' she said, and one by one the boys went in and one by one they came out again, looking shocked or delighted or slightly crazed. Then it was Henry's turn to go into the stuffy book cupboard. He went in and closed the door. Amanda was up in the air because she was standing on a chair, and this was because it was a performance, and he was the audience. She smiled and showed him what she had, and then she put the end of a daffodil in the crack and said, look, isn't it cute? His heart began beating very fast and he felt dizzy and sick. He said yes and thank you and opened the door and ran outside to get away from her and from it, the thing into which she had placed a flower.

And now, in the boys' toilet with the magazine, Henry had the same excited, vomity feeling, because the bodies of the naked women were mixed up with the smell of urine and toilet-cubes and the jets of water fizzing in the stained ceramic stalls, and the guilty feeling that they would be caught at any moment. Then someone shouted *'Teacher!'* and Alistair stuffed the magazine up his jumper, and they ran away.

Chapter 18

Babes in the Wood

Henry and John still saw each other outside school, even though John was often sick and couldn't play very often. John had a weak chest and wasn't allowed to go out if it was cold or damp. He was pale and tall and had thin ankles he kept twisting and spraining. They were permanently wrapped in yellow bandages that reminded Henry of strips of cloth dipped in urine. John was only a half-friend, because he was weedy and other people made fun of him. It was hard to like someone other people didn't. Other boys used John as a target if they had a pump gun that shot tiny potato pellets with blasts of compressed air; or they pushed him off a wall to see what would happen, because John was dreamy, and his skin was translucent, and he never retaliated.

John was only second or third best at things. He flinched and stuttered and twitched, and he was only reserve goalie for the school team. He was never higher than tenth on the popular girls' lists of their favourite boys. Nonetheless, although there were better people to hang around with at school, when Henry had nothing to do, John was always there, the boy around the corner with a bike and a cloud of dusty hair and lots of empty time in which he did little but sit around and read.

When John was well, he and Henry went adventuring in the scrubby bits of woods that lined the roads. These places were not actual parks, but dense patches of scrub and nettles and small trees that backed on to the rear of people's gardens or golf courses. It was in these non-places that they found litter and car-parts such as rusty exhaust pipes and hubcaps. Sometimes they came upon rain-damp magazines, their pages swollen and mouldy, not like the one Alistair Cairns had shown them in the toilets, which had been clean and new. The boys looked at the images of naked men and women, studying them and trying to grasp what they meant. It was hard to see, because often the rain had stuck the pages together or the sun had baked them and made them brittle, so that the pages tore or crumbled to pieces when the boys tried to turn them.

It was never whole magazines. Often it was a single page or fragment of a page. Sometimes the technicolour body parts of a woman were snagged on twigs and brambles, or thrust deep inside a spiky hedge where the boys couldn't get at them. They harvested what they could, then tried to assemble them in a way that made sense, because each was part of a jigsaw or mosaic of things they imperfectly understood.

Every now and then, they would hear something rustling and look over their shoulders, but there was no-one there, just a bird hopping or a squirrel running up the bark of a tree. Then they'd search the wood again, because the more they found, the more they needed.

One day, Alistair gave Henry a dirty magazine and said he could keep it. It contained whole pictures and pages you could turn, not soiled and grubby fragments; and even though Henry didn't want the magazine, he took it home. He smuggled it in his satchel and then hid it in his cupboard under the crumpled tissue-paper in a shoe box where no-one would ever find it.

But his mother did find it, because she found everything.

She sat him down one afternoon and said she wanted a conversation. Her expression was very serious. She had never asked for a conversation before, because conversations just happened. She told him she'd found some horrible pictures and wanted to know what Henry knew about it. He looked at the shoebox and pretended to be surprised by what she had found there. Then, when he saw she didn't believe him, he explained that he was hiding the magazine for a friend who didn't want to get into trouble. His mother nodded, then said maybe he should choose his friends with more care from now on. She said she was disappointed to find such a magazine in their house, because the pictures were disgusting, and she thought Henry was better than that. Henry hung his head and didn't know what to say. He'd only looked at the pictures once before hiding them away. He wasn't sure they were horrible and wasn't sure his mother thought so either, but he didn't argue.

In that box were images of women whose sly eyes watched him when he looked at them. It was both looking and being looked at. They were women whose honey or red or coal-coloured hair lay smooth over their shoulders. Some of them had their legs open, and some were teasing their pubic hair with a hairbrush. The women's private parts were not private now. They weren't slits or keyholes like the ones he had seen before, or forests like those in the magazine Alistair had shown them in the toilets. They were glistening and succulent, like the hothouse plants he'd seen in the greenhouse at Kew Gardens, a place that was steamy and humid, and where the air smelled of rankness and raw earth.

Chapter 19

Station 11

They didn't really tell him what the 11+ was all about. During the exam, he mainly looked out of the window, because there was a beautiful Cedar of Lebanon in the distance, a tree whose branches made peaceful sideways lines like pacifying hands, and the hands meant that everything would be all right. Around him the others scribbled furiously, but he didn't understand the questions, and couldn't bring himself to resolve the problems that involved magical boxes whose rows and diagonals must add up to 30. He didn't care how much Yvonne spent over six months, when she spent x pounds on school lunches and y pounds on a bus pass, because he didn't know Yvonne. If she were a rich girl, the cost would be irrelevant, whereas if she were poor, she might have to go without her lunch.

There were pages filled with spiky numbers and angles that made his skin crawl. He mistrusted anything where a letter like x masqueraded as a number, because it seemed to him a category error, like having a cat represent a dog in a story, or a man, a sheep. There were missing numbers in sequences of grimly marching digits like lines of parading soldiers, some of whom had been killed in action and weren't there, so that he must guess their ages, as if that mattered when they were dead anyway. There was a Venn diagram about chocolate and vanilla ice cream, where some children liked one, and some the other, when he knew that all children loved both, so the question was pointless. Finally, he was asked how many faces there were in an octagonal prism. At first, he misread the question and pictured the face of a man in an octagonal prison, and that man was somehow him, and he had no idea where the door was. When they said 'Two minutes left', he wrote 'eight', knowing it was wrong.

He flicked back through his answer book. He saw that he had left many blanks, but he had drawn a little sketch of the Cedar of Lebanon with its outstretched arms and its offer of peace. Maybe they would give him credit for that.

Chapter 20

The Sound and the Fury

The news came that Henry had failed his 11+ and would be going to the comprehensive school, the one that adjoined his primary. It had large grounds, and after school he stood at the fence and watched the girls playing hockey, their sticks moving and the ball flying away, and, a few seconds later, the clack of the ball and the reverberation of the clashing sticks reaching his ear. It was like watching a film that hadn't been properly synchronised. It was odd watching those girls, because there was a dreaminess attached to their actions, and it made it seem that what he was watching was already in the past, and these were the ghosts of girls who had died a long time ago and weren't really there.

The day he learned he'd failed, the new headmaster, Mr Brouton, took him out of class and walked him around the grassy area between the buildings. Mr Brouton placed his hand on his shoulder, the two of them tracing the path that Henry had covered in his role as a note-carrying go-between. Now he was being delivered to a different future from the one that others had planned for him. He felt sad, but only because Mr Brouton did. The sadness was in Mr Brouton's gravelly tone, and in the weight of the arm he'd now put round Henry's shoulder as if he needed consolation, and the way Mr Brouton said words like 'disappointment' and 'adjustment'. Henry nodded, but he didn't really care. For, despite Mr Brouton's arm, he felt lighter. If grammar school taught the things those exam papers had been full of — spiky calculations and theoretical propositions, unreal people making fictitious journeys on phantom buses to pointless and unspecified destinations — he didn't want to go. He was pleased he'd failed.

At the comprehensive school, there was a sports hall for indoor football, a beginners' Latin class, and a teacher called Mr Morris who exuded evil when he came into the room at wet-break. Mr Morris decided that Henry was causing mayhem, even though Henry was only looking at a noticeboard and talking quietly to another boy. Mr Morris was a tall, thin man with a dry, wheezy whisper that made something in your spine go cold. He had a metallic gleam at the back of his eye that suggested he would love to hurt you, but couldn't, because the rules didn't allow it. And because he couldn't hurt you physically, he took it out on you in other ways. He punished you for looking at a noticeboard, and for reading out to your new friend Tim some of the funny things you found there. And that was how Henry got his first detention.

Even though Henry had Tim, he remained on speaking terms with John, who was at the grammar school now. John had succeeded when Henry hadn't, and Henry's parents were disappointed. Henry's father lied when relatives asked about how Henry had done in his test, for he said they hadn't heard yet, when everyone knew the results had come out ages ago. Henry was a failure his father had to hush up.

Even though Henry didn't care about not going to the grammar school, it seemed wrong that John, with his stutter and asthma and unpopularity with girls, should have passed when he'd failed. He hated John a little bit because of it. Nonetheless, John came round on Boxing Day like before, and he was just the same — perhaps a bit taller and louder with his new grammar-school voice that showed no sign of the old speech impediment. After lunch, they sat around the TV watching *Chitty Chitty Bang Bang* with Henry's mum and sisters. John had seen it already, and he began to tell them what was going to happen next, and who the Child Catcher was, on and on. He took no notice when Henry's mother said, 'Let's just see what happens, John, shall we?' because he already knew what would happen. He knew the future and they didn't, and so he told them about it, and in that way, he ruined the film.

Afterwards, Henry and John sat on the hall stairs. Henry was on the step above, looking down at the boy who had once been his friend, the boy who now had floppy hair and a fake laugh and yellow teeth. Henry was full of the restless feeling that always came on Boxing Day when you had eaten too much and there were no more presents to open.

They sat in a yawning boredom of not liking each other and of having nothing in common. Henry was going one way in life and John the other, and John thought he was better when he wasn't, because he was down there on the step below Henry, his blandly simpering face grinning up at him and within easy reach. And that was when Henry leaned down and slapped him with all his strength. John's face quivered, and then he was standing, shaking with rage, his fists balled up. For once, Henry was a little afraid of him. John asked why the hell Henry had done it, when he was a guest who'd come round for dinner, and it was Christmas and everything. All he'd done was talk about *Chitty Chitty Bang Bang*, for God's sake. And Henry said he didn't know why he'd done it, he just had.

Chapter 21

Chronicle of a Death Foretold

Grandma was often ill. Her asthma was getting worse, the older she got. When she had an 'attack,' she had to sit down and concentrate on her wheezing. She sucked on her inhaler, which made a wheezing noise of its own, and then there was another noise in Grandma's chest, which was a kind of metallic whining. It made Henry feel that the inhaler was giving his grandma the wheeze, not taking it away.

If they were out together and they were running for a bus, his grandma would suddenly stop and say, 'I can't.' Then she would sit on a wall while Henry waited, watching as his grandma's chest rose and fell in stiff gasps, up, down. 'Oh dear,' she said when the attack didn't go away. Henry stood patiently, but it was hard to know what to do. You could only watch and wait until she could breathe again.

Worst of all was when Grandma was taken ill and stayed the night. Then her terrible coughs filled the house and Henry couldn't sleep. It was like a piece of paper being torn from end to end, again and again. After a while, he became angry with his grandma for being ill, and for bringing her illness into their house. He wished she would go away and have her asthma somewhere else. He put the pillow over his ear, so he didn't have to listen.

Then, as if the modern world had suddenly grown too much for her, Grandma was taken ill. 'Bowel cancer,' his mother said in a quiet voice, as if the words were contagious. Grandma disappeared to hospital, and they didn't see her for a while. They must pray for her to get well, his mother added, although Henry knew his mother never prayed.

His mother believed in luck and superstition. She touched wood to make good things happen, and to avert bad things. She believed in extra sensory perception and sometimes exclaimed when she turned on the radio, because the song she'd been humming in her head was playing right now, and that just showed you, didn't it? The brain was a mysterious thing, and sometimes sensitive people like her picked up radio frequences without knowing it. Henry wondered why his mother didn't pick up the play that was happening on another radio station, or the sport that was on the TV, but these were questions he kept to himself.

His mother read her star sign in the *Daily Express* every day. 'That could apply to anyone,' she'd say, putting down the paper. 'It's so general. I could make up rubbish like that myself.' However, it was clear she half-believed it, because she insisted on reading out all their destinies for the coming week. Even so, studying their horoscopes didn't help her predict that Grandma would fall ill.

Henry went to the hospital with his mother. At first, he hardly recognised his grandma. She was small and frail in the bed, her head propped up on the pillows and her white-yellow hair spread out around her. A tube came from her side and hung outside the sheets. Henry, leaning forward to ask a question, caught his leg in the tube and his grandma winced. 'Never mind,' she said, when he apologised. 'You weren't to know it was attached to me, were you, dear?' But he should have known, and his clumsiness had nearly killed his grandma.

After two weeks, Grandma came home again, and she was like a new person — thin and pale and holy. It was as if her recent victory over death had purified her, and she waved away offers of food because she had moved beyond the world of human need. When his mother insisted, his grandma said that 'a glass of water and a slice of dry toast' would suffice. Then she smiled at Henry, as if he alone understood the monastic necessities of illness.

From that time on, his grandma no longer made Toad in the Hole, or fried bangers in a pan, or bustled around in her pinny. She no longer lifted bikes over her head so Henry could repair a puncture. Instead, she sat and looked at things. She played cards, the gold rings loose on her fingers now and coming off more easily. She stroked the dogs as if she loved their uncomplicated animal lives. 'Yes, I know *all* about you,' she said, in a strange croon, rubbing the pale belly and dried-up teats of the black Labrador who'd grown grey around the muzzle. It was two old ladies appreciating each other in their dotage. And Henry knew with a sudden clarity that both his grandma and the old dog would die soon, and there was nothing he could do about it.

Chapter 22

The Jesus of Suburbia

The place where Henry lived was changing fast, and his father didn't approve of it. The town at the bottom of the road had spread sideways and lengthways, generating a concrete wave of tower-blocks that was flowing uphill towards where Henry and his family lived in their lopsided, mock-Tudor house. This was a threat, his father felt.

'There are too many people,' he said, looking at the new buildings that had sprung up around them. 'We'll soon be part of south London. A somewhere will become a nowhere, like everywhere else.'

Henry understood what his father meant. There was nothing to make their hometown special, nothing of any interest to rest your eye on. Nothing beautiful. Only one thing stood out as different from all the other suburban places around them, and that was Jesus, who sometimes walked up their road with an enormous cross on his back.

Jesus, his mother told him, was clinically insane. He was 'delusional and couldn't distinguish reality from fantasy'. Henry's mother had begun to speak like this lately. She had a new job as a secretary at a psychiatric hospital, so she knew about mental disabilities and was an instant authority on them. She had started to pepper her speech with words connected to her job, and now spoke of the unconscious and repression and psychosis and deviance, in the way she had once spoken about clairvoyance and astral travel and ESP. She felt Henry's father had mental issues of his own and should be in therapy. She thought she herself was the model of sanity.

Henry saw Jesus quite often. He was usually walking up the hill towards Henry's house. 'Poor man,' his mother said one day, as they drove past him again. It was raining and Jesus was wet. He was a tall man with long matted hair and a loping stride. He was barefoot and dressed in white robes, and he had the wooden cross slung over one shoulder, his body sagging under the weight of it.

'He's probably one of our patients,' his mother said airily. 'They sometimes let the non-violent ones out to interact with the normal world.'

Henry considered this. He didn't think walking up a hill while people beeped their horns or yelled things out of their car windows was interacting, but he didn't say so. His mother paused, watching Jesus in the rear-view mirror. 'Mad people often think they're saviours. It's a common delusion.'

Henry nodded, turning to watch Jesus disappear from view. He noticed that the man's lips were moving. 'Perhaps he's preaching,' he suggested, 'to the people in the cars?'

'No,' his mother said firmly, 'he's just nuts. He should be inside.'

It was strange, because they only saw Jesus on this stretch of road. You never saw him in town, and he never seemed to reach Henry's house. You couldn't imagine him at the shops, doing normal things like buying a loaf of bread or sitting in a café. You couldn't even imagine him in an asylum. He was just a figure perpetually walking the same path up and down their road and not getting anywhere.

Chapter 23

The Crow Road

Henry settled into his new school, the one where he'd once seen ghost-girls playing hockey on a field, their movements oddly detached from the clacking sound of ball on stick. He was twelve now. He knew that light moved at 186,000 miles a second and sound at 767 miles an hour. Sound was slower, because it required a medium like air or water to travel through, whereas light didn't. That was why the girls' movements had seemed disconnected from the sounds of their hockey game. The girls hadn't been ghosts at all; that was just the silly, ignorant way he used to think.

When you went to another school you made new acquaintances and forgot the old ones. His new best friend, Tim, was different from the Dutch boy, Mark and his old friend, John, who were tall and skinny. Tim was small and had freckles and curly hair. He had tiny white teeth that looked as though someone had whittled them down to the stumps.

Tim's mother was very short because she hadn't had enough to eat in the war, and it had stunted her growth. This just showed that the war had affected everything. Henry's father watched *Dad's Army* and *Colditz* on TV because he was still fighting the war in his head, while his mother told stories of how she'd been evacuated to Yorkshire as a child. She had gone with a friend when they were ten years old. On their first night, their host-father had sat on the end of their bed and told them stories to help them get to sleep. As he talked, he stroked the girls' folded underclothes, and the stories had become peculiar, and after a while he went away, taking one of the girl's socks with him. The girls had crept out of the house and run down the street to find the warden, knocking on her door and waking her up. The warden wasn't angry. Instead, she found them somewhere else to stay, somewhere a man didn't touch their knickers or steal their socks or tell them funny stories about people with no clothes on when they were trying to get to sleep.

His mother's nerves came from the war. It was the feeling that a bomb might drop on your head at any moment. His father's nerves came from there not being a war. That was why he kept an old gas mask in the attic and a box with his service medals in a drawer and that bullet on the dressing table. That was why he had a battered old suitcase with Flight Sergeant A.C. Truffle painted on the side. It was a reminder, and a reproach to the present for its slackness and lack of grit.

Henry found that there were different kinds of wars to be fought at the new school. Sometimes it was wars with people and sometimes it was wars with things. Once, he'd gone to a water-fountain to get a drink, and an older boy had come over and pushed him away, saying he could wait. When Henry objected, the boy turned and slapped him round the face.

Another time, he was running on the field, and a wasp had flown towards him and stung his finger. That afternoon, he couldn't pay attention to the lesson about the Dead Sea Scrolls and papyrus, because his finger had swollen to twice its normal size. He asked the teacher if he could go out to the water fountain to bathe it, and she said yes. It was as he washed the hot skin of his finger under the stream of cold water that he remembered how he had once summoned the devil in his bedroom, and the devil had appeared in the form of a wasp. So now he knew that bad things in your past could turn up in the present and hurt you.

You were 'in the wars' when you got hurt, his father said; but battles with insects and bigger boys were ones you couldn't win, because wasps and bullies didn't follow rules. When he watched *Colditz* on TV with his dad, there was something called the Geneva Convention that protected the men in the camp, and even the German officer seemed scared of contravening it. But in normal life there was no Geneva Convention.

He'd hated Belinda Evans at first sight. Belinda was what his mother would call *common*. She said 'meself' instead of myself and chewed pink bubble-gum with her mouth open, juggling the juicy gumball from one side of her tongue to the other. She was tall, with greasy, waist-length hair and thin legs, and her knees were wider than her thighs. She wore clumpy shoes and went around with a girl called Monica, who was short and had a twisted face like a gargoyle. Monica and Belinda had a witch-like way of dressing and talking and conspiring. They also had the knack of appearing from nowhere when you least expected it.

When the boys were playing football, the girls would follow them. Sometimes they materialised in the place the boys were heading to, arriving there before the boys did. The girls would be sitting and waiting on a felled tree, chewing gum and speaking to each other, their mouths half-hidden behind cupped hands. The boys didn't like the girls being there but started their game anyway. They ran and yelled, kicking the leather ball towards the blue school jumpers that were their goalposts.

Although the boys tried to ignore them, they played differently when the girls were watching. They showed off and were more argumentative. They kicked the ball harder, tripping and shoving each other when there was a corner kick and a chance of a goal. They spat and swore and flicked vee-signs, turning their voices into coarse footballer-voices.

One day, they were playing as usual, the midday sun burning on their backs, their pale-blue shirts sticking to their skin. When the ball came to Henry, he dribbled past a defender and kicked it. The ball traced a high arc and sailed over Mark's head. Mark did an acrobatic leap and fell in a hot tangle of limbs. To his surprise, Henry found that he'd scored.

'Goal!' cried his team, which was Tim Pryor and David Taggart and the giant, Quentin Newbolt.

'Over the bar,' said Alistair, spitting.

'There is no bar,' said Henry. 'That was in.'

They argued about what constituted 'too high,' and whether it should be calculated according to the relative sizes of the goalies. After a while, Alistair's hands became fists, and a light came into his eyes. Then he looked over to the girls and shrugged, unclenching his fists and making them hands again. 'All right,' he said. 'One-nil. But if I kick a high one like that, you'll have to allow it.'

Henry agreed, and the game went on. The girls remained, perched on their log. They were watching the boys but pretending they weren't.

'What are they doing here?' Henry asked Tim, as they went to fetch the ball which Alistair had booted towards the hedge.

'Dunno.' Tim was chewing a stalk of grass. He could split a blade and blow through the hole so that it made a sound like a seagull.

Henry kicked a stone. 'Why don't they just go away?'

Tim shrugged. 'Can't force them, I suppose.' He pulled the ball from the hedge where it had wedged itself. 'Here,' he said, passing it.

They went back to their game, but something had gone out of it now; a listlessness was rising from the ground and making their legs heavy. Then Henry's team went behind when Quentin Newbolt fumbled a save, and the ball trickled into the goal. The bell rang and it was too late to play on. The game broke up.

'We won,' said Alistair Cairns, coming over to talk to the losing team. 'Bad luck.' Then he walked across the pitch and kicked Henry's blue jumper, which had served as a goalpost, into the air. 'Oops,' he said, and sauntered away.

Henry did nothing. The other kids went in for afternoon school, shirts untucked, top buttons undone, hair plastered to their brows. He walked too, carrying his jumper. It had bits of grass on it now, and he picked them off, one by one. Whenever he thought he'd finished, he found more of them, spiky and straw-like.

A shape appeared in front of him. 'Bad luck.' He looked up and saw it was Belinda.

'What do you want?' he asked. He noticed her ugly accomplice, Monica, hovering in the background, grinning.

'I just wanted to say that your team was better,' she said. She said the word 'better' without any t's in it. 'Alistair shouldn't have kicked your jumper like that. It was mean.'

'Yeah, well,' Henry said. 'It doesn't matter anyway, because we lost.'

He turned and walked into school. Belinda tried to say something else, but he ignored it. He didn't need the sympathy of a girl as ugly and common as that.

Chapter 24

Mouth Stories

Henry had to have four teeth out because his mouth was overcrowded. If they didn't take them out, he would grow up with crooked teeth, and then no woman would like him, his mother said.

He was sitting in the leather chair, his head tilted back and resting on a leather pad. He gripped the armrests. Then the man injected his gum, sliding the needle in. First the sharp jab, then the hot flow of the numbing agent, then the paralysing ache. The dentist bent over him. He had a masked face with wide, hairy nostrils and whistling nose-breath. Sweat came out of the pores in his nose as he moved his plier-things inside Henry's mouth. After a while, the dentist grew annoyed and began to wrestle with something that resisted him. Then there was a crunch as each tooth came out, and the dentist breathed more noisily, dropping each one into a metal dish. Even though he was supposed to keep still, Henry moved his head to see. The teeth the dentist had removed were long, rooted objects that dripped blood. They were nothing like the small white things he brushed each night before bed.

Afterwards, Henry's tongue explored the hollow pits in his gum. They told him to sluice his mouth with the pink stuff in the cup and spit into the metal drain that would suck it away. Then they said he could go.

His mother was in the waiting room, leafing through a magazine. Gilbert O'Sullivan was singing on a loop. The music got muddled up with the sick feeling in Henry's tummy and he decided he didn't like Gilbert O'Sullivan anymore.

'All right, dear?' his mother asked.

He nodded.

'Come on, then.' She took his arm. 'I've got you a cake.'

'Okay,' he said. It was hard to form the word because his mouth had a new shape. His tongue felt clumsy, like a piece of leather.

In the car, Henry looked at the paper bag his mother had put on his lap. She told him he couldn't eat his cake yet because his mouth would be numb for a while. He would bite his tongue and injure it, she said. He wondered why she'd bought him a cake he wasn't allowed to eat. 'Wait until the medication wears off,' she said. 'It's a doughnut, by the way.'

He looked at the greasy bag. The paper had gone translucent on one side and there was a splotch of red from the jam.

'Did it hurt?'

'Not much.'

'That's good. You've gone very pale. It's probably the shock.'

He nodded. He couldn't tell her about the long bleeding roots of his teeth — those alien things that lived in his head.

He went back to the dentist a week later to have the brace fitted. This man was an orthodontist, and he told him that wearing a brace would affect his speech for a while. Henry looked at this new thing that was to become part of his face. The brace was a dome of ridged pink plastic that matched the roof of his mouth. There was a retaining wire that fitted over his incisor, the one that stuck out. 'No public speaking for you,' the man said, as he fitted the brace. 'Not until you've got used to it, at any rate.' Henry nodded. He didn't say that he never did any public speaking.

Henry had given a speech in his last year at primary school, and it had gone horribly wrong. He had captained the football team because the regular captain was away, and when the game finished, the coach, who was his form teacher in a purple tracksuit, told him to write a report. He would have to read it out in assembly, he said.

Over the weekend, Henry scribbled down some words. He wasn't sure why he was being made to do what his teacher could have done perfectly well. But it was too late to get out of it now.

'I feel a bit sick,' he said, looking out of the window as his mother drove him to school on Monday morning. He had his speech in his satchel, which his mum said was really a briefcase. Sometimes he made people at school laugh by saying, 'It's a sad case,' holding his hanky to the case's silver latch, then making a sound as if the case were crying and blowing its nose. A sad case was how his mother described a person with mental disabilities at the psychiatric hospital where she worked.

'Butterflies,' his mother said, 'Just think, in an hour's time it'll all be over.'

'I know,' he said. Outside, the houses flashed past. They were getting closer to his school. The sunshine lit the front of the houses and suddenly Henry wished he could stay outside in the sun and not go into assembly.

'You've written it, remember,' his mother went on. 'It's not as if you'll have to make it up as you go along.' She looked at him in the rear-view mirror. 'Reading aloud's easy. You're a good reader, aren't you?'

'Yes,' he said. She should have known reading to a parent wasn't the same as reading to a room full of people. When you read things to other people, they judged you if you made a mistake. They waited to pounce.

At school, Henry showed the report to the teacher who coached the team. He ran his eye over it, then made changes with lightning flourishes of his pen. 'This will improve the flow,' he said. Henry nodded, trying to decipher the new words. 'There you go,' the teacher said, handing it back. 'It'll be fine now.'

In assembly, Henry was given a chair near the front. The headmaster read the announcements, and they sang *Morning has Broken*, accompanied by Cat Stevens on the Grundig tape player. Henry gripped the paper on which his script was written, in case he lost it.

'And now,' said the headmaster, 'Henry will tell us about the first eleven's performance this Saturday.'

It was funny hearing his name said aloud, and his heart jumped. He stood up. He was confused by the word performance, because playing football wasn't performing. Performing was acting or dancing or singing. His team hadn't performed, anyway. Their goalie had dived the wrong way when a boy took a shot, which was why they had lost. Henry's dad was watching from the touchline, and Henry had been embarrassed by the small, bald man who didn't look like other people's dads. Afterwards, his dad had praised Henry's teammates but not Henry, whose boots pinched and who could only do defending. Some people might have performed on the pitch, but Henry hadn't.

He stared at his speech and cleared his throat. Some of the words leaned forward as if into a headwind while others lolled backwards. He had never noticed that about his handwriting before, that it went in two directions at once. Over the top of his script lay the teacher's corrections. He saw that the page was shaking, the words sliding about. Then someone coughed and he knew that he had delayed too long.

He began, and heard a monotonous croaking sound that he realised after a while was his own voice. He carried on but it was hard to breathe. The room had begun to spin, the children's faces melting into one another. Nonetheless, he kept reading until he reached the place where his script was covered in the teacher's scrawl. He stopped then. There was silence and children shifted in their seats. Then the teacher was beside him, whispering the words he should say, because it was all perfectly legible, couldn't he see? He only had to read it.

'Yes,' Henry said. 'All right.'

But it wasn't all right. When the teacher sat down and Henry tried to go on, he couldn't make the words into sentences. They marched towards the gate of his teeth and got stuck there. *Breathe*, his teacher mimed from the front row, spreading his arms. So, he breathed, and then all the words came out in a jumble. 'We played really well for most of the game then made careless mistakes one of their attackers took a shot near the end and our goalie couldn't reach it so we lost 3-2 thank you for listening.'

He ended breathlessly and sat down with a bump.

The headmaster waited a while, then stood up. He smiled and thanked Henry for his report, which had been most informative. He made some concluding comments that Henry didn't hear on account of the blood roaring in his head. Finally, the headmaster asked the children to leave, one row at a time, and return to their classrooms, quietly now, please, and no talking.

In the car on the way home after school, Henry's mother asked how his speech had gone. 'It was fine,' he said, looking out of the window. 'There,' his mother said, smiling. 'I told you it would be, didn't I?'

Chapter 25

Do Androids Dream of Electric Sheep?

In his dreams, things he didn't want to happen happened. Sometimes women appeared naked, and he couldn't help but look. They were never the kind of women he'd seen in magazines. They were teachers and librarians and lollipop ladies, and they had lumpy bodies with floppy breasts and quivering buttocks. He didn't know why they were in his dreams, or why they were naked. Sometimes they chased him and he couldn't escape, because his legs were made of water; sometimes he found that he was running after them, and one of them turned and fell, sprawling in front of him as he tumbled on top. 'Henry Truffle, what are *you* doing here?' they said, sitting him on their laps and letting him touch their breasts, so that he grew flushed and confused. Because he didn't know what he was doing there, either.

Then there were other dreams. In one of them, he was in his classroom, but the children were different from his normal classmates, and the proportions of everything had changed. It was summer and very hot; despite this, all the radiators were on. One of these radiators was behind his chair and when he touched it, it burned his hand. He sucked his fingers to cool them, and the skin came off in strings like the scum you picked off hot milk. No-one noticed. Meanwhile, the teacher droned on about Neolithic man, the Beaker People and the Bronze Age. 'The discovery that fire could transform not only raw food through cooking but also metals into alloys was a great leap forward,' the teacher said. Henry yawned, his eyes roving the room. There was only one student he recognised, and she returned his glance. It was Belinda Evans, the girl he hated. But he found it hard to look away now, because she looked pretty, and was smiling.

Then he was outside and the sky high above him, the field stretching to the horizon. He saw the goalposts made by the dropped blue jerseys, then a series of discarded items — a pair of shoes, a shirt, a pair of trousers — and, near his feet, the sheath of an ice-pop wrapper with red liquid pooled at the end. He didn't know where everyone was. Perhaps there had been a fire-drill and he hadn't heard the alarm. An empty crisp packet blew past, and he tried to catch it, but missed.

Belinda Evans was sitting on her log and watching him. The wind blew in gusts and as the crisp bag was passing her she caught it with her fingers, like a creature taking an insect from the air. Then she rubbed it between her palms, and it crumbled to pieces. 'Crisp bags are made of dried leaves,' she said. 'Didn't you know?' He didn't know but saw that it was true. He noticed that she was different now but still pretty. She wore jeans and a tee-shirt, and her hair wasn't schoolgirl hair, but styled and elegant. She had little earrings, and make-up, and her chin was dimpled. 'Are you okay?' she said, brushing fragments of leaf-crumbled crisp bag from her hand.

'Of course.' He looked around to see where the others had gone. 'Why wouldn't I be?'

'No reason,' she smiled, shrugging. 'Only I was just wondering, because you're naked.'

He looked down and saw she was right, just as she'd been right about crisp bags being made of dried leaves. He tried to shield himself with his hands, but couldn't.

'You shouldn't have taken your clothes off,' she said. 'Not unless you're showing off or something.'

'But I didn't take them off,' he said, trying to turn his back on her.

She smiled again. 'What do you think that is over there?' She pointed to the lines of cut grass on the school field, and then Henry saw that the clothes littered across the grass were his own.

'It's okay,' said Belinda. She got up from her log and walked towards him. 'Come here. It's all right.' He walked towards her obediently, but she turned her head suddenly and frowned. Then she disintegrated like the leaves she'd rubbed to powder in her hands, because Henry's mother was calling and calling; she was telling Henry to get up, because breakfast was on the table, and he'd be late for school. And when he awoke, his pyjama bottoms were sticky and smelled of pollen, and he had to go and wash himself before he went downstairs.

Chapter 26

Biographia Literaria

Because Henry had done well at his new school, he was to have an interview at the one John had gone to after passing his 11+. If he impressed them favourably, he would start there. He would be joining them a year and a term late, but better late than never, his father said. He would be at the school they'd always planned he would attend, and all would be well.

The Grammar School was a redbrick building that faced a busy road. It looked like a man who'd drunk too much wine and had waddled over to a seat and then sat down heavily in a frowning heap to look out at the world. The school seemed to disapprove of the view. What it saw was the London Road with its ceaseless roar of traffic, a row of modern apartments and a trail of scruffy shops.

Henry and his mum got out of their car and walked across the forecourt. To the left, there was a large, soggy-looking rugby pitch, framed by a pair of H-shaped rugby posts. Henry remembered that they didn't play football at this school, and the rugby pitch announced that everything would be different from now on. There were only boys here, and they played a sport that used a curious, egg-shaped ball, one which you carried over a line or kicked over and through the gallows-like posts. That was a conversion, which Henry had previously thought was a religious word. There was nothing religious about the rugby pitch, which looked rather frightening, and oddly like a place of execution.

They went inside and Henry had his interview, wearing his old school blazer and with his hair combed and his face scrubbed. His mother sat beside him, holding her handbag in her lap. The headmaster was a tall, thin man who sat under painted portraits of other tall, thin men with similar names, all beginning with the letter H: Hitchens, Hutchings, Hastings, Huntley. It was as if the rugby posts had come into the school and attached themselves to the front of each headmaster's name.

After the introductions, the headmaster looked at the typed page on his desk. 'So, Mr Truffle, what is your favourite subject?'

Henry had never been called Mr Truffle before, and it was as if he had suddenly become his own father. 'English,' he said, as if announcing his nationality to an interrogator. He sat very straight, as his father would have done. 'And history and Latin.'

The headmaster nodded, as if expecting more. Another man, white-haired, and seated to one side, smiled encouragement.

'Your Latin will be very useful here,' the headmaster said. 'The boys in the A-form do Latin. And your hobbies, Mr Truffle?'

'Reading,' said Henry, unsure if reading was a hobby.

'Ah, yes. But reading *what,* I wonder?' The headmaster's big-nosed face wished to know this most particularly.

Henry tried to think of all the books he'd finished and enjoyed, but he couldn't remember any of the titles. Mainly he'd read the same book again and again, because if he liked something he never wanted it to end. '*The Lord of the Rings*,' he said, looking down at his hands, which were strange today, and a mottled purple and white. He was wearing a ring he had made in metalwork at his comprehensive school, shaping the iron around a mandrel, hammering it flat and soldering it, then sinking it, hissing, into the trough of cold water. Afterwards, he had dinted the surface with a little round-ended hammer to give it a faceted patina like that on the pewter tankard they had a home. He turned the ring on his finger. If it were Bilbo's or Frodo's ring, he would disappear. He would become invisible.

'Ah, *The Lord of the Rings*,' Mr Hitchens nodded. He looked at Henry, whom he could still see, evidently. 'That's Tolkien, I believe?' Mr Hitchens' nose wrinkled, as if he didn't wholly approve of the fantasy genre, but would make allowances for the young. 'I think that's more in Mr Evans' line than mine.' The white-haired man beside him nodded and wrote something down.

'Well, Mr Truffle,' the headmaster went on, 'in a moment, Mr Evans will take you away and introduce you to some of the masters who will teach you if you come here. In the meantime, I'll have a chat with your mother. I must say we were impressed with your recent report.' He tapped some other papers on his desk. He smiled at Henry's mother, and she blushed. Then Mr Hitchens turned. 'Mr Evans? If you don't mind? They should be ready now.'

Mr Evans arose and led Henry away.

Henry sat in a different room while the masters, who were like ordinary teachers but different, came in and out. They were brisk men in black, bat-like gowns, and they quizzed him on books and tenses and dates and conjugations and declensions. A man in glasses wanted to know why, if a woman was wearing stilettos, she would leave marks upon a wooden floor, but the same woman in flat shoes would leave no such marks. Henry gave his reply, and the man nodded, wrote something down and went out. After him came the Latin master. He was a wide-shouldered, military-looking man with a side-parting that looked as though it had been made with a ruler and pencil. He asked about the first and second conjugations. How familiar was he with those? Very familiar, Henry said, although he wasn't sure what they were. Jolly good, the man said, I think we're speaking the same language. '*Puella, puella, puellam*?' the man said, tilting his head on one side, and Henry nodded. '*Amo, amas, amat*?'

Henry nodded again. The man said this was all splendid and tickety-boo and first class, which were words Henry's father used. 'Oh, and one other thing,' the Latin master added, tapping his teeth with his pen. 'It's best to stand up when a member of staff comes into the room. Boys do that in this school. Matter of courtesy and all that.'

Henry understood that the man was telling him he had been rude; that what passed muster at his old school would not do here. 'Yes, sir. I'm sorry, sir.'

'No need to apologise, old chap. I expect they do things differently at, um...?'

Henry provided the name of the school the Latin master had forgotten.

'Jolly good. Never mind. All paths lead to Rome, eh?'

Henry didn't know what that meant. 'Yes, sir.'

'I'll see you anon, then.' After this, the square-shouldered man marched from the room.

Mr Evans came back. He asked Henry about English, inviting him to say more about *The Lord of the Rings*. Henry relaxed then. He forgot that he needed the toilet and that his collar pinched. He spoke normally, without that weight on his chest. When Mr Evans asked how Frodo had succeeded in his quest, Henry explained how he almost hadn't, because he'd faltered at the last moment. It was only when Gollum had bitten Frodo's finger off and had fallen into the Crack of Doom with the ring of power in his grasp, that Sauron had been defeated. And this was strange, because it suggested goodness needed evil to succeed, and that power would drive a good person mad. Henry touched his own ring, for now he was talking about Tolkien he felt invisible at last.

'And what's your favourite part?' asked Mr Evans, whose face was red and enthusiastic and boy-like, despite his mad white hair.

Henry said it was the descriptions of the moon waxing and waning, because he had never heard these terms before, and it made him imagine a moon smeared in the sky like a smudgy bit of candle wax, or waning away like a spent firework. It was the only thing he could think of, and he wondered if perhaps it was a stupid answer.

Mr Evans smiled, however, and seemed satisfied.

'Did you know,' Mr Evans went on, speaking as if they were friends sitting around a fireside in The Shire, 'that the name Frodo comes from a very old word — a word in Anglo Saxon?'

'No, sir.'

'Well, it does. It's from Fróda, and it means wise. And that's what you'll become if you join us in this school, Henry.'

Then Mr Evans arose and smiled and shook Henry's damp hand. He led Henry back to headmaster's office, where his mother was still sitting stiffly in her chair as if she hadn't moved in the previous hour. The headmaster looked up. 'Ah,' he said. 'Here is the man himself.'

Henry was unsure if this meant Mr Evans or him.

'Take a seat, Mr Truffle.'

Henry did so. Then, when he was sitting beside his mother again, Mr Hitchens spoke to Henry's mother as if Henry wasn't there. He repeated that they were very impressed with Henry, who was not only grammar school material 'but very good grammar school material.' He said that Henry knew his Latin declensions and conjugations and that he would fit right into the A-form. 'Here are the maths and Latin books,' he said, 'that Henry will need to peruse over the Christmas break to ensure he's up to speed with the new syllabus.' He tapped a finger on the two books that lay on the edge of his desk, one red, one black.

'We look forward to seeing him in January,' the headmaster added, smiling for the first time. It was a rather thin smile, as if it hurt him to give it. And then his mother smiled too, and Henry bowed, and they were shown out. It was over.

They were driving home, and his mother said she was proud of him. 'You sat so straight and answered so clearly,' she said. He nodded, then looked at the textbooks in his lap. The books had other boys' names blue-inked onto a slip of gummed paper inside the front leaf. He looked at the last one. 'Pupil's name: Ian Amble. Form: 4A. Book's condition: Poor.' Henry's name would be the next squiggle in that book. On the front was the statue of a man in a toga, his hand outstretched in formal salute. Henry knew he must become more like that statue if he was to do well at this school. He must be cold, commanding, and stone-like. That was how the boys and masters at the new school had looked.

He flipped through the book and stared at the tables of verbs and nouns, then tried to shape some of them with his lips. *'Silva, silva, silvam, silvae, silvae, silva'.* This word meant wood or forest, and they hadn't done it at his other school. He decided he liked the word *silva,* because it sounded like silver, and he could picture a forest silvery with frost, and a Roman legionnaire walking through it in his armour, his breath smoking with the cold.

Then Henry opened the maths book and looked at a worked example. *Divide 0.223 by 0.733 and write the result correct to three decimal places*. He looked at the rows of zeros and digits and decimal places. It was hard to like numbers, which combined and shrank in strange ways. They didn't need people to give them life. They bred amongst themselves in a world indifferent to human beings. They made their own sealed universe, one that Henry was locked out of. He hated maths. Maths told him that there was a world smaller than zero, which made no sense to him. Because zero was nothing, and how could you have less than nothing? It was as stupid as thinking you could have more than everything.

Chapter 27

About A Boy

It was to be his last Christmas before he started at his new school, and it was ruined by the two books he had to lug everywhere he went. All through the holiday he stared at the exercises with a sick feeling in his stomach. He feared he would never master the contents, the words and formulae which sometimes came out of the books and hung themselves over everyday objects, so that when they visited relatives in Bournemouth, the familiar scenery was draped in numbers that wouldn't resolve and verb endings that wouldn't conjugate. He knew then that he was a duffer and a fraud. He would be hated at his new school and exposed as an inferior mind.

Only on Christmas Day did he manage to forget. He was to receive a new bicycle and this was exciting, because he had never had a proper bike before. His mother was against it, of course. She said people were killed riding bikes all the time, and if they could be killed, Henry could, too. Nonetheless, his father had gone ahead and bought one, because a boy couldn't live without taking risks. His mother said it wasn't living with risks she worried about; it was dying from them.

His father wheeled the bike into the hall on Christmas Day. It had tinsel and ribbons on the handlebars and a freshly oiled chain that ticked when his father rolled it, on plump new tyres, across the carpet. The handlebars were curved downwards in the racing style, and it reminded Henry of a sheep or ram. It was like a living creature coming towards him with its head meekly lowered. Henry reached out and touched it, as if to make friends with something unfamiliar.

'Do you like it?' his father asked. He was wearing a blue crown from a Christmas cracker. The crown was lopsided, and there was a shine in his father's eyes from the wine he'd drunk.

Henry nodded. He had never seen anything so beautiful.

'Why not try it for size?' his father suggested.

Henry attempted to get his leg over the crossbar, but the saddle was too high, the bike tipping sideways. 'I can adjust it,' his father said. 'Let me fetch a spanner.' Henry waited for his father to return, holding the bike carefully, half-afraid it might run off of its own accord. His mother came out of the lounge with a yellow paper crown on her head, looking like a sad queen. She stared at the bike.

'You'll have to be very careful,' she said. 'The roads are so dangerous now. I think you should stick to the pavements.'

Henry didn't say anything. His father came back with the spanner and adjusted the nut, lowering the saddle by wrestling it from side to side. 'There,' he said, when the silver neck had slid down into its collared housing and the saddle was flush with the frame.

His mother looked at him, her mouth in a thin line. 'I just told Henry I want him to stay on the pavements.'

'Oh, he'll be all right,' his father said, tightening the nut again. 'He isn't a baby.'

'I don't want him riding to school.'

Henry stroked the handlebars. 'Oh, Mum. *Please*.'

'I don't see why not,' his father said. 'He won't come to any harm.'

His mother looked at them as if some fresh conspiracy had been hatched. 'How do you know he'll be safe?' she said. She turned. 'Henry, you must promise me you'll be careful.'

He promised, then reminded her that he'd done his cycling proficiency test back in primary school. He didn't tell her that all he remembered was a fat kid doing a wheelie on his Chopper and falling off.

So, despite his mother's objections, Henry would be allowed to ride his new bike to school. He must avoid the main roads, however. He could cycle in with John, who would show him the way.

It was a foggy morning and the cars had their lights on, making the water droplets in the air yellowish and smoky. Henry had no lights. He waited at the crossroads for his friend to arrive. He saw a twinkling light descend the hill, and then a flapping orange cagoule. The cagoule grew a head and gangly limbs and a shock of hair. It was only then that he recognised him.

'Hi, John,' he said. John stopped, pulling his foot out of the little cage-thing on the pedal and setting it on the ground. Henry's bike didn't have toe-clips.

'Hi.'

John was different, his hair longer, his body bent forward over the handlebars. 'Don't you have a proper top?'

Henry looked down at his blazer. It had the new school's crest on it: a blue and yellow chessboard but no chess pieces. His mother had sewn that on. 'No,' he said. There were beads of moisture on his blazer and he was shivering. He hadn't realised he was cold before.

'Well, you'll need one.'

'Yes.' Then he remembered. 'My mum says we need to keep to the side streets. The main road's too dangerous.'

John made a face. 'That'll take ages. We'll be late.'

'Oh.' No-one had told him that the quiet way was longer.

'The main road's okay. I always go that way.'

John fitted his foot into its little cage and rattled it impatiently. 'Okay, then?'

'Yes.'

They set off, John in front and Henry behind. They went along the road that buses and lorries and London traffic used. It was the same road Jesus walked along with bare feet and the cross over his shoulder. There was no Jesus today. John crouched low over his handlebars and began to pull away, cutting through the traffic. Henry had to pedal hard to keep up, because John was riding a Claud Butler, which was a proper racing bike, unlike Henry's Raleigh, which wasn't as good a bike as he'd first thought.

They cycled on. It was a kind of race now, and Henry was losing. His eyes were focused on his legs, willing them to pump faster. Suddenly, John flung out an arm and swept across the road, the tail of his cagoule flying behind him. Henry followed blindly, cutting a diagonal. He heard the beeping of a horn but ignored it. At the traffic lights, a car drew alongside him, and a woman rolled down her window.

'We could have killed you back there,' she said, stony-faced. 'You nearly went under our wheels. You pulled out right in front of us. You didn't signal.'

Henry looked at her and at the man sitting beside her. Henry was panting because of the effort of cycling. The man sat staring straight forward, holding the wheel.

'I'm sorry,' Henry said. His legs were trembling.

The woman shook her head, then closed the window. The lights changed and the cars moved away.

'What happened back there?' John asked at the next set of lights.

Henry shrugged. 'The people in that car said they nearly hit me when I changed lanes.'

John pushed the blond fringe out of his eyes. 'Didn't you look behind you? Didn't you signal?'

'No. I followed you. I thought your signal would work for both of us.'

John frowned. 'You have to *signal*, mate. The cars behind don't know what you're planning to do. They can't read your mind.'

Henry nodded. He'd been stupid, he saw now. He'd thought a kind of magic would protect him on his new bike and on his first day at school, but it wasn't the sort of thing you could admit.

They cycled on along a series of roads and junctions that Henry didn't know, and Henry was honked and shouted at several times. He was invisible without an orange cagoule, and he still wobbled between lanes because he didn't know where he was going, and John didn't wait for him. Then, suddenly, they were turning off the road and heading down a path lined by trees and spiked iron railings through which he saw the grey shadow of the school, half-hidden in fog. There was a rotten smell in the air that John said came from the sewage plant on the other side of the park. Then they had to dismount and push their bikes, because the spinney was crowded with boys dressed in the same uniform and with the blue and yellow chessboard on the front. Spinney was a funny word, Henry thought, as he hurried to catch up with John. It sounded the way his head felt after that car had nearly hit him.

They were going through a gate now and John was showing him the wide, rusting sheds where they could leave their bikes — the Claud Butler and the Raleigh Hustler. Then they were running to join the long trawl of boys who were dragging and pushing and elbowing their way into the redbrick building.

In all the classes he was the new boy, and all the masters said, ah, here's young Truffle, the bright new spark we've all heard so much about. Here's the one who's come to show you up. Then his classmates turned and looked at him and frowned.

The lessons began, and it was hard to know how make a good impression. There was art and Latin and English, and in Latin he saw the military man with neat tie and polished brown shoes and carefully parted hair that he'd met in his interview. 'Here's our new Latin scholar,' this man said. 'Let's test his mettle.' They were doing a translation, and he asked if Henry knew what 'they hurried' was in Latin, and Henry said 'festinaverunt' and the boys jeered because it was wrong. 'It isn't wrong,' the Latin master said, giving a little smile. 'Truffle's very clever. He has obviously learned a different verb at his old school. But he's quite right.' The boys jeered again.

And then it was breaktime and Henry went to the playground, which was a tarmacked square between the buildings. There was a tuck shop, and a railed-off area where some of the boys played football with a tiny, hollow, plastic sphere, swearing and shouting and dashing. Others hung around and ate crisps and chocolate bars. A gang of older, sullen-looking boys sat on a bench and stared at Henry because he was the new boy. They spat on the ground and contemplated their spit and then him, as if he was the same as the spit. One of the boys was small and thin and shaven-headed.

'That's Slaughter,' John whispered. 'You'd better keep out of his way. He's bad news.' Henry nodded. He'd never seen a boy whose name fitted him so well. Nor had he seen a boy whose eyes said so clearly that they wanted to kill someone as slowly and painfully as possible.

The bell sounded, and they went inside.

The day ground on. There were his new classmates to get to know, for not all of them mocked him or looked at him askance. Henry had a desk with an old, blue-stained inkwell, and was placed next to a boy who had braces on his teeth and watery eyes and fishy breath. All the boys were known by their surnames and this one was Goode. Goode was amiable like his name, and he explained that the school was all right once you'd got used to it. Henry looked around. He was grateful for the advice but was unsure if he believed it. The rooms he had been in so far were hot and airless and smelled of the teachers' sweat. The sash windows had flaky, yellowish paint on them, and strings that had frayed or snapped or dangled uselessly.

The day passed very slowly, and all the teachers singled Henry out for special attention. The PE teacher pressed his leg against him in the gym hall and held his face too close, so that his breath fanned Henry's cheek. He asked Henry which school he had come from and when Henry answered, this teacher ran his eyes over him as Henry stood shivering in his shorts and tee shirt.

'Truffle's found a boyfriend,' some of the boys said afterwards. 'Paddy's got a crush on you.' Paddy was the PE teacher.

Then in the next class, the history master pinched Henry's nose and said it was good to have a proper scholar in their midst at last. This teacher's fingers smelled of sweat because he kept them tucked under his armpits. All the boys stared at Henry and shook their heads, because that teacher didn't usually pinch anyone's nose in an affectionate way. In the science class, the teacher read his name from the register and said Truffle sounded like trifle, and was Henry someone to be trifled with? And everyone except Henry laughed at this incredible piece of wit.

Finally, it was time to go home, and he and John retrieved their bikes. They went to the public library because they had been set prep, and prep was homework, and it was best to do your homework in the library, John said. You would get extra credit for research.

They sat upstairs, using the reference books to add detail to their descriptions of how the Spanish Armada had been defeated by superior British tactics, and also by the weather, which John said was another tactic the British had up their sleeves to confound stupid foreigners.

'Why are you so late?' his mother wanted to know, when he came in tired with his bag full of new books. 'I thought you'd been killed!'

'We went to the library,' he explained. 'They set us prep.'

'They did *what*?'

His mother didn't know that word.

'They set us homework. John said he wanted to do some research about the Armada, and I went with him.'

His mother shook her head. 'I've been worried sick,' she said. 'You might have told me you were going off on a jaunt.'

'I didn't know before. John just suggested it. And it wasn't a jaunt.'

She put her hand over her eyes and took a breath. 'All right. How did you get on at school, anyway?'

He shrugged. 'All right, I suppose.'

'And how was it, riding your bike?'

'Fine.'

'You kept to the back roads?'

'Yes.'

'And do you like your new school?'

'Yes.'

'And were the other boys friendly?'

He paused. 'Yes.'

She seemed to be waiting for him to elaborate, but he said that he needed to do his Latin prep, because there would be a test in the morning. He didn't say that it hardly mattered whether he did well or badly. They would jeer at him either way.

Chapter 28

The Wheels of Chance

He rode his Raleigh Hustler to school each day. One afternoon, his PE teacher, Mr O'Neill, the one they called Paddy, the one who stood too close and sometimes put his arm round him, saw him pushing his bike towards the school gates. He sidled up, eyes twinkling. He had chestnut hair and a high forehead, and some people said he wore a wig.

'Nice bike, Truffle,' said Paddy, his brown eyes running over the bike and then up and down Henry, as if the bike and Henry were the same thing. 'Are *you* a hustler, then?'

Henry didn't understand this question. He looked at his bike, which had purple paint and silver chrome. He paused, suspecting the word 'hustler' might be a trap. It must have a double meaning he didn't know about. Most of what Paddy said had double meanings, according to the other boys.

'No,' Henry replied. He thought this was the safest answer.

'Jolly good, Henry. Just checking.' And then with a wink, Paddy walked away.

When Henry got home, he looked the word 'hustler' up. *Hustler, noun. Informal, North American. 1. A person aggressively selling illegal goods. 2. A prostitute.*

Henry knew he wasn't selling anything, so Mr O'Neill was asking him if he was a prostitute, which was another kind of selling. Henry didn't know why Paddy would ask him that, or why his parents had bought him a bike with a name that had a double meaning. They should have known. Parents were supposed to keep you safe from things like that. They were meant to protect you from ambiguity.

It wasn't only Paddy who had a problem with his bike. Sometimes, when he came to collect it from the sheds after school, he found it on its side, its purple paint scratched, its front fender dented. When he asked a boy who was standing next to it who'd done it, the boy said that it wasn't fucking well him, so Henry should stop suggesting that it was.

Chapter 29

Bartlett's Words to Live By

Henry clung on to memories of his former school, because it was, in some ways, still his. There were certain things he couldn't quite relinquish, the main one being Belinda Evans. Because after you've dreamed of someone, they aren't the same, and neither are you. They have entered your head and changed its landscape and left their footprints and fingerprints, their smell and their shed hairs and skin and twisted sweet wrappers, and you must collect these one by one, in an effort to find the person who has gone.

So, he cycled up the hill, riding his scratched Raleigh Hustler, to see the children streaming out in the uniform he used to wear, which looked so odd now, the jacket so blue, so bright, and that comical badge of sundial and shadow, as if that's all education was, illumination and the impression it made on a static object. The students he recognised, who had already changed a little, shouted greetings, and he stopped, asking where Belinda was, partly to avoid talking to those who already had the air of something half-forgotten. It was hard to find the rhythm of conversation, him straddling a crossbar and them going home with heavy bags, not knowing why he was here, unless it was that girl. But no-one knew where Belinda Evans was, so he cycled on, afraid of meeting her, and hoping that he might.

More kids streamed down the hill in an endless flapping blue wave. Each approaching girl, gangling, loping, dark-haired, pouty-lipped, briefly assumed her shape, and then, at the last minute, became someone else. In the end he cycled home, defeated; but at least he'd tried, and had demonstrated, perhaps only to himself, that the grammar school didn't own him, and that his heart was somewhere else.

No-one he knew had a girlfriend. In the view of Henry's classmates, it was silly even to want one. There was something unmanly about it, and boys in the A-form were supposed to be above such things. You could have grubby fantasies about females, but an actual girlfriend was impossible. The Latin master shared and encouraged the boys' scorn. He told them 'sweethearts' were a waste of time because they cost too much in lollipops. Girlfriends were useless things, like Violet Elizabeth Bott in *Just William*. They were creatures with insatiable appetites for lickable confectionery but nothing else.

Instead of girlfriends, the boys had prep and Latin cribs and cartridge pens. They had farts and insults and fighting. They gave each other dead arms and dead legs. They 'bundled' each other. They pinged each other's earlobes and punched each other's shoulders. They staged battles with ink-pens, flicking each other's faces and shirts. At breaktime, they would target a vulnerable boy and pin him to the railings, pulling his arms through the bars and holding him in place so the firing squad could do its work, the select group of four or five spattering the boy's face in an orgasm of blue and black ink. And although parents had written letters complaining about stained shirts and torn collars and pockets, no teacher ever emerged from the staffroom to put a stop to it. For the staff, breaktime was dedicated to drinking coffee and to the construction of a densely-woven tobacco-fog that leaked along the lower corridor. The playgrounds were the Badlands where the boys must police themselves.

Although there were no girls at Henry's school, there was a small band of female teachers. They were either shy, mousey, flat-chested women with spots, or large women resembling the figureheads of ships. Their English teacher, Mrs Bartlett, was of the latter type. She wore silk scarves in pastel shades that she tossed over one shoulder, as if she were standing on a promontory and facing into a headwind. She controlled the room by making it appear that she didn't control it at all. She dominated them by her goodwill and chatter, drawing out their opinions, bullying them into fluency, wheedling, flattering, and flirting. She treated them with more respect than they showed each other. Only occasionally, if there was actual rudeness, did she flush scarlet; her voice became a thin whisper, and then the boys would lower their heads until all was calm again.

She was not a beautiful woman. Her glasses were of a square and heavy plastic, and slid down the greasy stub of her nose as she spoke. With her tombstone teeth, prominent moles and rasping Northern accent, Mrs Bartlett was so far below their erotic ideal that she scarcely counted as a woman at all. She was large and indulgent and motherly, and it was for this reason that they dubbed her 'Ma Bartlett'. And, although they pretended not to, they loved her.

Chapter 30

Peeling the Onion

It was around this time that Henry stopped eating. When he took his sandwiches to the hall at lunchtime, he found he couldn't stomach them. He stared at the bread and ham his mother had given him and put the lid of his lunchbox back on again. Around him, other boys ate their food hungrily. It disgusted him to see their irrepressible appetites. Eating was a physical need as distasteful to him as going to the toilet; it should be done in isolation and with the door closed. He got up, walked over to the bin, opened his lunchbox and threw his food away.

That night, he asked his mother for a thermos of soup instead of sandwiches. When she asked why, he said sandwiches were boring. She nodded, buttering two bread rolls to eat with his soup and wrapping a piece of cake in greaseproof paper.

The following day, he sat in the lunch-hall again and sipped his soup while the others ate their sandwiches, crisps and chocolate bars. They looked at him with his thermos and his finger quirked in an odd way, and he looked at them.

'Why are you drinking that stuff?' a boy asked, after staring for a while.

'Because I like it,' he said. 'And it isn't stuff. It's soup.'

'It stinks of onions.' The boy wafted his hands to fan the smell away.

'That's because it's onion soup.'

'But where's your actual food?'

'This is food.'

'No, it's not. It's drink.'

'It's both.'

Other boys were listening now, staring at this freak exhibit.

'Anyway,' the boy went on, 'it's not enough. Are you on a *diet* or something?'

'Don't be stupid,' Henry said. He finished the soup, screwed the lid on the flask and walked out, throwing the bread rolls and cake in the bin, so his mother would think he'd eaten them.

The following day, he asked his mother for a piece of cheese and an apple instead of soup, because the boys had said his soup smelled. His mother had cheese and apple for lunch, and it was clean food; it was the kind of food women ate when they were slimming. Because that boy at school had been right. Henry *was* on a diet. It was horrible to sit on a chair and reach down and feel the fat that clung to the back of his thighs and calves: the heaviness of it, the slackness. It was disgusting to have a body that didn't conform to his mental idea. Better to be a starveling, or a gaunt priest in a horse-hair robe, or a pale popstar with bony limbs. Better that than a fat, gormandising fool.

Mark had eaten Edam cheese. Dutch things were healthy and stylish, Henry remembered. The past had been in colour. It had been a time of orange Volvos and orange women and football played on the green lawn, where he was England and Mark was Holland. Henry knew it was a world he couldn't go back to, but he could at least eat food that reminded him of it.

His mother nodded when he asked for a different kind of lunch but looked at him curiously. Then she cut off a hunk of Edam and found an apple, putting it all in a brown paper bag and passing it to him.

'I hope this isn't going to be one of your silly fads,' she said.

'No,' he said. 'Of course not. Anyway, you eat this for lunch.'

'But I'm not a growing teenager.'

He shrugged and walked away. He didn't want to be a growing teenager. He wanted to stay the same, or to shrink, just as she did. He wanted to become less than before, like Alice in Wonderland, because then he could go through the low door into the garden, wherever that was. And in the garden, like his grandma, he would be happy.

Throughout that day, he broke off pieces of cheese and slipped them into his mouth, holding them on his tongue until they dissolved. No-one saw him do it, and breaking school rules in this way was exciting; and although the adrenaline gave him tummy ache, eating Edam brought no guilt. He knew it was the least fattening of any cheese. His mother had a book that listed all the major foods with their calorific values, and it had replaced the book of etiquette as her personal bible. The book was a pamphlet grown tatty with use, and it had come free with a magazine. On the front was a picture of a strawberry, a slice of orange and a stick of celery, all misted with beads of water, as the naked women had been misted with water in the magazines he had seen. Only these weren't women. These were the virtuous foods, the Holy Trinity: all calorie-free.

Henry had noticed his mother keeping lists of what she ate during the day. In the evening, she totted it all up, and the sum was either good or bad. Bad meant more pounds on her hips, and more rolls of fat around her tummy when she sat in the bath. From this, he learned that there was another kind of maths, and it was the maths of food. His mother had taught him that, as she had taught him everything worth knowing. He wondered how he had never known before: how could he have been so ignorant?

Food was numbers and numbers were calories. An apple was 50

and a slice of cake 500. These figures filled his head when he tried to sleep, whirling and revolving and replacing the old counting games that had troubled him as a small boy. Instead of the voice telling him to count upwards to a certain point, now the goal was subtraction — to get the numbers down as close to zero as possible. Each night, he devised new stratagems for the following day. He could put water on his cereal so that he didn't need to use milk. He would eat Ryvita instead of bread. He would run around the edge of the carpet a hundred times to burn off more calories.

He lived with hunger now, but it was an enemy he could defeat by ignoring it. Its revenge was to deprive him of sleep. At night, he lay staring at the ceiling, a hollowness gnawing his insides. If he did sleep, he was plagued by nightmares. Often, he dreamed that he was at a banquet where he stuffed his mouth with cakes and pastries and pies, and woke in a misery of shame and guilt. He would have to go without food for days to make up for it. And then he realised hadn't eaten anything, and he'd been dreaming, and that it was all right. He hadn't polluted himself. To make sure, he ran his fingers over his belly and hips. He checked the rosary bones of his ribcage and found they were still there, just under the skin. He could have wept he was so happy.

He kept going, his days vague with lack of sleep, his buttocks sore where his sitting-bones had rested on the hard chairs, his spine red where its knobs and kinks had caught on the chair-backs. He lost more weight, noting the leftward slide of the red needle on the bathroom scales, pleased at the proximity of six stone. He gloated when he saw boys at school eating their breaktime snacks, because he knew how many calories they were consuming. By not eating he was keeping ahead of them — he was proving that he was better, superior, stronger. He was perfecting himself to a point of purity they would never reach.

His mother told him he was getting too thin, but he didn't feel thin. He still felt the flesh that clung to his thighs. He still saw a podgy, flawed boy in the mirror. And the more they tried to persuade him to eat, the more he resisted. He wouldn't let them break him, because if they did, he would be lost.

He remembered something his father had said once. Henry had been sitting in the lounge and listening to music. The hatch had opened, and his father's bald head had appeared. His dad was smiling. 'Having a session?' he said. His father had a stupid expression for everything.

'No,' Henry replied. 'I'm listening to music.' He wished the silly old man would go away.

His father didn't go away. 'If I listened to music,' he said, 'I wouldn't be able to control myself.'

His father remained there, his elbows resting on the countertop. He watched Henry, as if Henry would understand if he only waited long enough. Henry didn't know what he was supposed to say. Why would his father need to control himself when he listened to music? It made no sense. The point of music was that you didn't have to control yourself. It set you free.

Then his father had asked if Henry wanted a cup of coffee.

'I don't drink coffee,' Henry said.

'No,' his father replied, nodding as if he knew that. 'I didn't mean coffee. Something else, then? Hot chocolate?'

His father should have known he didn't drink stuff like that. Fattening stuff.

'No,' Henry said.

'Very well,' his father said, closing the hatch.

At school, Henry did not yield. He ate half his lunch and threw the rest away, or gave his apple to one of the wolfish boys who would eat anything. And if these other boys didn't respect him for being thin, it just proved how stupid they were. The truth was his skinniness just seemed to anger them. Once, when Henry walked into the lunch-hall, a fist struck him in the back, knocking all the air out of him. When he turned, there was a long queue of boys, and they stared at him blankly. It wasn't one of us, their eyes said. It was all of us. Henry didn't know how to fight a whole line of boys, so he smiled, pretending they hadn't really hurt him, and walked away.

'Poof!' someone shouted.

Henry began wearing a bangle to school. It was one of Alice's, and she didn't notice him taking it, she had so many. On one of her album-covers, there was a picture of a singer who had bracelets looped over his thin wrists. He wore a fur stole, and make-up, and long chandelier earrings, and he was more beautiful than any girl Henry had ever seen. Henry decided he wanted to look like that one day. He could at least wear a bangle for now. It would be a start; it would be a statement.

The boys mocked him when they saw it. Even the word they found ridiculous. When Mrs Bartlett asked what was wrong, they told her. 'Truffle's wearing a bracelet!' they said. 'He calls it his *bangle*!' They said 'bangle' in an affected way, flopping their wrists and fluttering their eyelids. When Mrs Bartlett asked to see, Henry offered his hand in limp apology. She stooped and inspected it, then pronounced her verdict. 'It's very nice,' she said.

'Only *girls* wear bangles,' they insisted, and Mrs Bartlett went red. She said they were being silly and should leave Truffle alone. Henry pushed the bangle back under the cuff of his shirt and didn't meet her eye. He knew Mrs Bartlett was just humouring him because he was a freak. 'Truffle's *queer*,' someone muttered a bit later. Mrs Bartlett didn't hear, or if she did, she pretended not to.

The rumours of his queerness spread. At breaktime, the boys on the playground wouldn't let him join their football game. The one who picked sides said he didn't want no effing poofs in his team. Henry said he wasn't one of those, but the game had already started, the boys chasing after the plastic ball with holes in the side. Their yells were loud, their shirttails hanging out behind like tongues. Every kick of the ball proved this was a game for men, not poofs.

He went to the perimeter of the playground to see if John was there. Sometimes John was on a bench, loitering with a group of other boys, the ones who were too cool or lazy for football. There was no sign of him. And, in any case, John had grown distant. He no longer wanted to associate with a boy who wore a bangle, and threw his lunch away, and couldn't play football because people thought him a poof.

Henry went to a corner of the playground where the drainpipes were, and where the weedy kids played the rooftile game. He watched them for a while. When they noticed him, they said he could join them if he liked. They explained the rules, which were very simple. You threw a ball onto the roof and watched as it trickled down. It hit bits of tile or guttering, jittering this way or that, and exited at a point you couldn't predict. It was a kind of rooftop pinball. A player had to stand underneath, and the challenge was to calculate where the ball would emerge and catch it. It was the kind of game only freaks and weirdos played, and Henry was welcome to join in.

Chapter 31

Becoming Henry Truffle

Henry decided to have a haircut, because this would be a statement to place beside his bangle and his thinness. It was the first time he'd gone to a shop to have his hair done. He no longer wanted his mother to do it, and when he'd seen a boy whose hair he'd admired, he asked where he'd had it done, and that boy had told him. The shop was called *Guise*, the boy explained, and the name was a pun. It was a salon for men or guys, but it would also give you a look, a disguise, or a mask. Henry liked the sound of that, so, that weekend, he got on a bus and set off for the distant salon in another town.

Guise was a parlour full of mirrors and sinks, and there were adjustable chairs with headrests, like at the dentist's. A young man in high-waisted trousers asked him what he wanted, and Henry pointed at a picture on the wall, and the man nodded. Henry sat in the chair while the man fussed around him. He made tiny snips of adjustment, sometimes misting Henry's hair with an atomiser. Henry liked being touched, adjusted, tinted, squirted and rubbed with scented wax that the man first warmed in the palm of his hands and then kneaded into Henry's hair and scalp. When it was done, the hairdresser showed Henry his head from different angles, and Henry saw that it was no longer a triangle to be mocked, but the skull of someone he didn't know, a person with cheekbones and new blond highlights. He decided he quite liked this person.

When his mother saw him, she cried, 'Oh my *God*, Henry!' and that was all he needed to know that it had been a success.

He wore this haircut to school on Monday along with the new platform shoes that would make him a little taller, because the other boys had begun to outgrow him now that he'd stopped eating.

When they saw his haircut they said, 'You look like a poof.'

Within a week, because he no longer applied the wax or styled the front of his hair into wings, his hair looked pretty much the same as anyone's else's. He let it grow until it became shaggy and shapeless, and he gave up caring about it.

Chapter 32

Naked Lunch

Now at lunchtimes, Henry escaped the torment of school and went to his grandma's. She lived nearby. It was a short bike-ride along a road of council houses and past a park called 'the rec', where bad boys went. Sometimes you saw the burned-out remains of a motorbike amongst the stinging nettles. His grandma lived in an upstairs flat above another one where people lived that she didn't like. They were called the Drennons, and she said they spied on her and complained if she made any noise. If she watched television, she had to keep the volume very low, otherwise the Drennons would hear and knock on the ceiling with a broom handle. Their name alone told you they were nasty people. It was a name that sounded like drains and dungeons.

If there was a vase in his grandma's window, it meant she was there.

'Come in,' said his grandma, for she was at home today.

His grandma looked different now. Gravity had bent her downwards and her legs had gone sideways at the knee. She walked up the creaky stairs, wheezing on each step. Henry followed, matching her slow steps. She had to pause for breath at the top, holding onto the back of a chair, for the stairs opened onto her kitchen. Henry looked around, because something was different. Her kitchen smelled of gas and cooking, and there was food frying in a pan. 'I'll get your lunch,' his grandma said. 'You go through and take a seat.'

'I just have two boiled eggs and Ryvita,' he reminded her, looking at the frying pan.

'Yes, dear,' she said. 'Go into the lounge.'

He walked through into the big room with the old television set and the heavy, old-fashioned dining table and the window overlooking the road. There were lace curtains and an electric fire with two of the bars burning red, because it was very cold today, and his hands were raw from cycling. Then he saw his mother sitting in a corner, turning the pages of a magazine. She wasn't supposed to be there.

'Hello,' she said, looking up.

He looked at her blankly. 'Hello.'

'I thought I'd surprise you.' She smiled, but he saw that she'd been crying.

Henry nodded and took his Latin books from his school bag. He had a test that afternoon. Boys were asked to give their translation of a section of text. Latin here differed from Latin at the comprehensive.

'How was school?' his mother asked. She held a scrunched-up hanky in one fist.

'All right,' he said. He wanted his mother to go away so he could concentrate on his Latin prep. She seemed to be waiting for him to say or doing something, but he didn't know what.

That morning he'd sat in assembly while the new Headmaster, whose fringe hung like a theatre curtain, had lectured the boys about falling standards, especially in matters of dress. He'd noticed boys altering their appearance and hairstyles to copy the current trends, and this must stop. Henry knew he was one of those boys. The headmaster had a quiet, civilised voice, but his face was pale and sweaty. He had dark, pouchy bags under his eyes, and looked as if he hadn't slept in a long time. Some of the boys said he was an alcoholic and probably a bender, and that he was sometimes found drunk on the floor of his office by the caretaker, so it wasn't for him to lecture them on standards. But lecture them he did, every morning.

Later, Henry had sat staring at maths questions, wondering why he couldn't understand them when everyone else could. Then, when they filed out of maths and entered the corridor, he'd got in Cole's way. Cole was from the year above and hung around with Slaughter. And because Henry didn't move, Cole shoved him in the chest, and before he knew what he was doing, Henry swore at him. Then Cole reached out and slapped him hard and everything went quiet. '*That's* what you get,' Cole had said, leaning forward. All the boys stared at Henry as the red handprint rose on his cheek. He didn't blub, though, so it was all right. It wasn't being hit that mattered. It was how you took it.

In science, the chemistry teacher, a slim man who dressed in neat suits, wore aftershave, and had metal things on his shoes that clicked as he swaggered down the corridors, shouted at him, because he thought Henry was talking in class. It was the boy behind Henry, but the chemistry teacher told him this was a poor way to begin, and he would have an eye on him from now on.

He couldn't tell his mother all that.

Then his grandma came in with a plate of food on a tray, all piled high and steaming. There were chips, beans, mushrooms and two fried eggs. Next to it was a plate of thickly buttered toast. She set it down before him. 'There you go, dear,' she said.

His grandma and his mother watched to see what he would do.

'I can't eat all that,' he said.

'Just do your best, dear. You're a growing lad.'

He looked from one woman to the other.

'All right,' he said, picking up his knife and fork. Then, very slowly and methodically, he ate his two eggs, going from the white and working inwards in tiny increments until he reached the golden yolks, which were his reward. And then, because they were watching him, he pushed the yolks to the side of the plate. He set down his knife and fork. 'I don't want any more,' he said.

His mother began to cry softly. 'Why won't he *eat*?' she said, as if he wasn't there.

His grandma took the plate away, saying he had wasted all those lovely chips. He said he was sorry, and then his mother got up and went out. She spoke quietly to his grandma in the kitchen, and then the door closed downstairs. It was quiet then, with just the sound of his grandma scraping the food into the bin and doing the washing up.

Henry finished his Latin prep. Then he cycled back to school on his purple Raleigh Hustler, the one the PE teacher had told him meant *Raleigh Prostitute,* the one the other boys sometimes threw on its side in the bike shed.

Chapter 33

The Boy on the Bus

Henry lay on his back, staring at the ceiling. His mother came in and looked at him. 'Are you okay?' she asked.

'I can't sleep.'

'I know,' she said, stroking his hair. 'What's wrong?'

'Nothing. I just can't sleep, that's all.'

'Just try,' she said.

He knew that it was pointless to try to go to sleep. The more you tried, the more impossible it became. Then his mother told him she'd read a book on relaxation that had tips in it. 'Imagine your legs are made of stone,' she said. 'Then your tummy, arms, neck, face: all of stone. You'll soon be asleep.'

'Yes, Mum.'

She stroked his hair some more. He felt the hardness of her wedding ring against his skull, but still, it was soothing.

'Are you sure there's nothing you want to tell me?'

He couldn't tell her he was hungry.

'No,' he said. 'Nothing.'

'All right, love. Get some sleep.'

She went away again.

For a while he tried to do what she'd suggested, imagining his legs as stone; but stone was heavy, and he didn't want to be heavy. He wanted to be light. When he pictured the word light, one went on in his head. All the corners of his mind were illuminated. He couldn't sleep then, because how could you sleep with the light on?

He waited, then crept downstairs when everyone was asleep. The kitchen jumped and flickered when he touched the switch. Above him, the family's laundry hung on the airer. The kitchen still held his father's cigarette smoke and the sweetish scent of his whiskey. The eye of the TV had gone out. He'd heard it through the floorboards and then it had stopped. His father had come stumbling upstairs, and there were bathroom sounds and toilet sounds, and into-the-bedroom sounds, and then silence.

He looked around the kitchen. It was strange to see a room that was usually busy become empty and dead. The room made him feel he had no right to be there. He looked around. The dogs lay on their sides, moulded around each other like a black yin yang symbol. Anna raised her head, looked at him sleepily and thumped her tail. Even she knew he shouldn't be there. Her muscles tensed and strained as if she might get up. 'No,' he said gently. 'Stay.' She sighed, shook herself and sank down.

Henry went to the pantry, opening the door and turning on the light. He looked at the tins and bottles, the sauces, the vinegar, the vegetable oil. At eye-level, he saw the bright squashes: orange, lemon, tropical fruits. The lower shelf was tins: beans, alphabetti spaghetti, the plump hearts of tomatoes, Jolly Green Giant sweetcorn. Then there were the bottles of preserves with fruit in suspension, the Kilner jars of pale, drowned strawberries and the floating laboratory organs of plums. Meanwhile, on another shelf, lay the remains of a joint of lamb: congealed globules of fat sitting on grey meat. The dogs would get it tomorrow. Next to the lamb was an apple pie with a border of crinkled pastry, the whole thing dusted in sugar, and with two nostril vents to let the steam out when it was hot.

He ignored it all. Instead, he opened a tin and looked at the biscuits in their cellophane wrappers. He breathed in their odours, the vanilla of the custard creams, the chocolate of the Bourbons. Then there was the toasted smell of the sugared rusks that he'd sucked on as a baby and that his mother now used for trifles. There were malted milk biscuits with pictures of cows on the side. He prised out the wheel of a chocolate digestive, raised it to his lips, inhaled, put it back. Then he closed the tin, turned off the light and left the pantry.

He didn't cycle to school now. On the bus they couldn't get at him, and it was warm on the bottom deck, and safe. He didn't go upstairs because that was where the bad kids went, the smell of their cigarettes drifting down, along with the sound of laughter and swearing.

Henry liked to sit with the old people and the women with baby carriages. He felt at home there, because they were quiet and thoughtful. As he sat, he looked out the window. It was a rainy day, the brake-lights of the cars blurring their reds and oranges. When the bus reached a stop, the pneumatic doors opened with a bang as the door folded against the sides like a wing. People got on, showing their passes or shelling out coins, tearing their tickets from the drum's metal teeth.

Sometimes he sat next to a small boy and talked to him. The boy had a green school uniform and cap. He had a button nose and freckles and wore shorts, even on a cold day. Henry didn't ask which school the boy went to and he didn't recognise his badge. They talked about the weather and sometimes the boy asked questions, such as why waterdrops dripped the way they did on windowpanes, moving up and down and sideways in mazy patterns, sometimes looking like blind tadpoles fumbling through space. He asked why the bus doors hissed when they opened. The boy had noticed how, when it rained, the big windscreen-wipers cut semi-circles on the dirty glass but never touched the triangle of dirt in the centre. He wanted to know why that was. Henry tried to explain about the wipers' fixed arcs and the places they couldn't cover.

Sometimes there were boys from his school on the bus and they looked at Henry as they came down the steps from the upper deck, laughing and dragging their bags.

One day at school, a kid with a shaved skull came up to Henry. It was on the lower corridor, near the staff room with its smell of pipe smoke and coffee. The boy was Mugford. He wore drainpipes with braces and white socks and heavy Dr Marten boots. He had a slow-witted brother who was twice his size and dragged behind him like his shadow. The smaller brother was Andy; the taller one Dave. Dave sometimes took his cigarettes out and would be about to light one when Andy stopped him. 'Don't be an idiot,' he would say. 'We're in school.' Dave would blink and look around him and put the cigarettes back.

'We saw you on the bus this morning,' Andy said. 'And what we want to know is, who's the little boy you were hanging out with? Is he your boyfriend?'

'No,' said Henry. He tried to move past, but Dave was blocking the way.

Andy laughed. He turned. 'Listen, Dave, Truffle's into little boys. Sits next to them on the bus and touches them and stuff.'

'Pervert,' said Dave.

'I'm not,' said Henry. 'I don't.'

'Little boys,' said Andy, shaking his head.

Dave turned and looked down the corridor. 'Where?'

'No,' said Andy, touching his arm. 'I don't mean here. Never mind, Dave.' He turned back to Henry. 'We'll be keeping an eye on you from now on, Truffle,' he said. 'Now we know you're a kiddie fiddler.' Then he winked and walked away, his tall brother loping after him.

The next day, Henry got on the bus as usual. When he reached the place where he normally sat, the boy in the green cap removed the bag that was reserving a seat for him and smiled. Henry walked past him and sat at the very back, turning his head to look out of the window where the rain wasn't making tadpoles anymore, but was just rain.

Chapter 34

Shunbathing

Paul Kingly was a horse-faced boy with a muscular body. In the showers, he stood revealing himself to whoever dared look. All around him were lesser boys, shyly shielding themselves and turning their bodies into the fan of cold water, then moving quickly to the security of towels and clothes. Kingly made no attempt at concealment. Some even suspected that he chafed his privates to make them larger. He looked around, defiant. Sometimes he picked on an undeveloped boy whose manhood was lost in rolls of puppy fat. 'Good God, what's *that*?' he laughed, pointing and showing his yellow teeth.

Everyone turned to look. The undeveloped boy put his hands over himself. Some people whispered that he had a micro-penis, nodding sagely as if this were a well-known affliction to put beside the other boys with evident defects: Drew, with his harelip; Drain, with his tongue-tie; Stevens, with his hammer toes; Wilkes, with his corroded, rust-coloured hair. Truffle, with his effeminacy.

Henry stood in a corner, shivering in the wind that came through the open door. Outside was concrete and railings and the closed iron shutter of the tuckshop. He could see the bin full of wrappers of the kind of food he didn't eat: Curly Wurly and Mars and Salt and Vinegar crisps and Crunchy and Turkish Delight. The wrappers stirred and shifted in their metal cage when the wind blew. The door had been propped open onto the bitter cold and the smell of the 'marshes' that was really the sewage farm beyond the park.

The PE teachers said fresh air would toughen them up, saying this from the security of their warm tracksuits.

Henry hated the cold, the gooseflesh and hair that stood up on his forearms and made him look like a chicken. He hated the icy showers that never grew warm, and the PE teachers who watched, arms crossed over their ample bellies, instructing them to 'wash the smelly bits.'

All the boys had nicknames. The one who didn't keep his hair clean was Greasy Jim and the short Italian one was the Cockroach. The boy with lush pubic hair was Mark 'Jungle' Jackson.

Jackson was one of the boys who had developed earlier than anyone else, and if it was a source of pride for Kingly, it was the source of shame for Jackson. He turned to the wall in the shower-block, and that was when one of the boys noticed the bronzed buttocks amidst the row of pale moons. 'Hey, Jackson, how come your bum's got a suntan?' the boy asked loudly. Jackson said nothing, but the tightness is his shoulder-muscles gave the game away. He left the showers, then tried to dry and conceal himself with a towel at the same time, which was impossible.

But the others had seen now.

'Yeah, you're brown all over. How come?'

The chant went up. 'Yeah, Jackson, how come?!'

They hounded him, and one boy tried to pull his towel away. Jackson snarled and snatched it back, telling them to get lost. His eyebrows squirmed, his hands fumbling with his clothes. Then, because they wouldn't leave him alone, he suddenly cracked. He told the truth, which was that he spent his weekends at naturist meetings. On sunny days, he and his family took their clothes off and played tennis with people like them. 'There's nothing weird about it,' he mumbled.

'Taking your clothes off to play tennis?'

'Yesh.'

Jackson had a speech impediment, which was a recent development.

'And there are women there and everything?'

'Yesh.'

'And you don't think that's weird?'

'No.'

'You bloody pervert!'

'Lucky sod, more like.'

Someone decided to spread the news. 'Hey, listen everybody! Jackson's a bloody *nudist*!'

A crowd of half-dressed and dripping boys gathered round him.

'Does that mean you get to look at naked girls?' someone asked. 'For free?'

'It ishn't like that,' Jackson said, tightly. 'Now go away.'

But they wouldn't go away. The boys speculated about what they would look at if they were at a nudist camp, and what they would do if they became aroused amongst so much naked female flesh. What did *Jackson* do, they asked? Hide it behind the handle of a carefully angled tennis racket? Jackson had had enough and wouldn't answer. He got dressed without drying his hair. It dribbled onto his collar as he hurried off, shoes untied, bag unzipped.

Jackson couldn't run far, however. He was a marked man now and went into a decline. His speech defect got worse; his words slurred through a tightly wired boxer's jaw. In class, his head twitched and jerked and turned around, as if he feared someone might creep up behind him and stick a piece of paper on his back with the word NUDIST on it. He kept glancing at his watch even though he'd just checked it. He fiddled with his pen, spinning it, dropping it, picking it up again.

Then, one day in an English class, someone blurted it out:

Jackson was a nudist.

'No!' said Mrs Bartlett, her mouth dropping open. Jackson's shoulders bulked forwards and he muttered something. Mrs Bartlett, who didn't understand shyness, wasn't to be put off so easily, because everything must be shared in a spirit of friendly confederacy.

'Really!' she said, staring through her square-framed glasses. 'But what do you *do* there, Jackson? I've always wondered. Do tell us.'

After contemplating his watch and fiddling with, dropping and picking up his pen, Jackson finally spoke. 'We shunbathe,' he said, chewing his words like Sean Connery. 'And play tennish.'

'What, with all your bits jiggling about?' Kingly said.

'That will do,' said Mrs Bartlett. She paused while the class calmed down. 'But *do* you, Jackson? Play naked tennis?'

'Yesh.'

'Oh, *my*.'

The students roared and Jackson lowered his head.

'New balls, please,' someone said.

Mrs Bartlett told them to grow up, but they didn't.

Things changed after that. They had discovered a new way of getting at someone. You didn't have to punch them in the back or throw their bike on the ground in the bike sheds. You could use words and banter and joshing, and it was all schoolboy japes and innocent fun. And no-one could punch you for it, because it wasn't bullying.

Chapter 35

The Rebel

John, Henry's ex-friend, the one who'd turned his back on him when he'd needed him most, went around with a new friend now. Francis was a tall boy with large front teeth and red cheeks. He wore shoes with two-tone heels and was confident and always smiling as if life was a joke only he got.

The other boys had faces that twisted into grins when they heard a dirty joke or a dig at someone else's expense, and then they cackled and leered but didn't smile. They had grey skins and matted, oily hair. Their noses were too prominent, the knuckles of their hands too big and their feet too long. They had spots and disgusting things like wank-hankies they left under their beds and that went rigid with dried semen.

Francis was different. He didn't have any disgusting habits that you could see; he didn't jeer, mock or hate anyone. His skin was clear and his hair clean. He held his head high, but wasn't arrogant. He had a kind of natural aristocracy, although he spoke with a rough south London accent. He was in the A-form, but he wasn't the kind of boy who worried about grades. He wasn't deformed by intellect, as many of them were, and he wasn't a rugger-bugger. He played sport but didn't care about it much. He was a dilettante, accomplishing things with the minimum of effort, doing just well enough to avoid notice. Overall, he acted as though nothing mattered much, especially schoolwork, and he gave the impression he thought people who agonised over such things were a bore.

There was something appealingly rough about Francis. He wasn't the son of a doctor, bank manager or accountant, as most of them were. He lived on a council estate, a place where scruffy house-fronts had graffiti on the walls, where NF was sprayed on phone boxes and tyreless cars sat on bricks. He had no dad, and no-one asked why, although he probably wouldn't have cared if you had. He broke rules whenever he wanted to and got away with it, and he respected others who broke them too, because what were rules, after all? And who decided they *were* rules, anyway?

Someone said his family were Irish and that Francis had the luck of the Irish. No-one knew for sure if he had Celtic blood, but Francis wrote his English essays in flamboyant turquoise ink, and green was the colour of Ireland, so maybe it was true. He certainly had the raw-boned look of an Irish ruffian combined with the swagger of a Dublin dandy. On the school noticeboard were pictures of famous writers, and Francis looked a bit like the young Oscar Wilde, only not as camp, and with short blond hair instead of long, brown, writers' hair.

Francis was creative in his own way, however. In English, he once composed, in his signature green ink, a story about a toothless greyhound running its final race at the dog-track and dying at the end in a sprawl of tangled limbs. For this absurd and sentimental tale he was awarded an A, not because the story was any good, but because Mrs Bartlett, like everyone else, loved him. They loved him because he was irresistible.

Henry, however, resisted him at first. He was suspicious of the friendship between Francis and John. John was posh; his family had a boat and they went sailing at weekends. They played golf, and lived in a big house opposite a green where John practised his chipping with a nine iron. Francis, on the other hand, was common. He had no dad, no boat and no golf clubs. Instead, he had a mum who smoked cigars and ran her own business. Some people said his mother swore and drank wine in the afternoons. Strange men were always round her house, they said.

Henry didn't know about that. All he knew was that Francis was a conundrum. He conformed, but broke the rules. He was intelligent, but not academic. He was articulate, but mangled the pronunciation of basic words, saying 'beeth' instead of 'beef'. He wore brightly coloured nylon jackets when not at school, the kind that Henry's mother would think vulgar and 'too American'.

He was also a prankster. He recorded his voice on a tape machine and hid it in a cupboard, so that it came on half-way through a maths lesson, confusing their master with hooting sounds and ghostly warblings. This was the maths teacher whom Francis called 'Daddy Stump', because he said Mr Stump resembled his deceased father. Mr Stump was huge. He had a shapeless body and wore an equally shapeless suit, riding a bicycle to school and wobbling between the lanes so that the traffic backed up behind him. It was odd that Francis needed to torment someone who resembled his dad, as if he were enacting revenge on his father for dying like that, yet living on as a ghost. Francis was also the one who had tied John up on his birthday, leaving him trussed on the floor of the classroom for the cleaners to find at the end of the day, the apparent victim of a satanic bondage ritual. No-one else in the A-form did things like that. No-one else would have dared.

And because Francis was big and strong, and because this drew the favourable attention of his classmates, Henry began to feel that his own dedication to starvation was futile. When he looked at Francis, so manly and confident, he thought that being a boy wasn't so bad after all. Being strong and capable wasn't pathetic or boorish. Maybe humour and facetiousness were more reliable methods of survival than earnestness, introspection and worry? Maybe being thin wasn't everything.

The next day he asked for a cooked breakfast. His mother accepted this in the same way she'd accepted his request for Edam and onion soup; that is, with mild exasperation. When he asked for eggs on toast, she said that was all right, but that she wished he'd told her earlier, because then she could have made sure she had enough eggs in the house. Why did he always have to spring things on her like this? He might have given her some warning.

It was clear to him then that he could never win, and that whatever decisions he made in life, they would always be wrong.

Chapter 36

Dead Dads Club

One night, the calm of Henry's house on the hill was disturbed by a phone-call, which his mother took in the front room. Henry stood outside the glass-panelled doors and listened. He heard the sound of a muted conversation, but not the words. After a while, he wandered off, because it was nothing to do with him.

When his mother came to find him in his room, she was very serious. 'That was John's mother,' she said.

'Yes?'

'She said John's father died last night.'

'Died?'

'Yes.'

He looked at her. 'How?' he asked. It was the only question he could think of. John's dad was a tubby man who drove a yellow Fiat that was too small for his body. A slightly pompous man with too many chins. He couldn't be dead.

'Heart attack.'

'All right,' he said, although it wasn't.

'And John's mum was wondering if you could go into school with him tomorrow, for moral support.'

'Okay,' he said, shrugging. 'But I catch the bus now, remember? I don't cycle.' He thought this might put John off.

'Yes, his mother knows that. But tomorrow you can walk, can't you? John will meet you in the usual place.'

'Okay.' His voice was flat. He didn't know how to react to news of someone's death. He'd had no practice.

She looked at him. 'You don't sound very keen, Henry. He needs you. This is a terrible time for him.'

'I know.'

'Is that okay, then?'

'Yes. I just don't know what I'll say to him, that's all.'

She sighed. 'You don't have to *say* anything, Henry. He's your friend. Just be with him. That will be enough.'

The next morning was cold and foggy. There was a light, mizzling rain. John had his hood up like a monk.

'Hello.'

'Hello.'

They nodded to each and set off down the road, because moving was better than talking.

'Don't say anything to anyone,' John said after a while. 'About, you know — what happened.'

'No,' said Henry. 'I won't.'

They went on in silence, their footsteps sounding on the wet pavement. John looked straight ahead, staring at cars, motorbikes and house-fronts, but not appearing to see them.

'Shit weather,' Henry offered, because you had to say something.

'Yeah.'

'You okay, then?'

'I'm okay. You?'

This was a strange question. Henry's father hadn't died, although part of him wished he had.

'Oh, I'm okay.'

'Okay, then.'

They walked on, their legs falling in and out of rhythm, which was what their friendship was like. They maintained their silence, looking at things and not looking at them; everything the same and not the same; the dead man they couldn't talk about hiding behind every house and traffic island, and no dead man hiding there at all, because once you were dead, you were dead.

At school, Henry did as he'd promised; he told no-one about the death. And no-one knew or guessed, because John looked and behaved just the same. And then a week later, a boy called Cornwall asked John why he was so tall and lanky. 'Is your dad a giant, or what?' he asked, with casual insolence. Henry made a signal for Cornwall to shut up, but Cornwall didn't notice. Like most of the boys, Cornwall had the sensitivity of a cricket bat.

'My dad's snuffed it,' said John.

Henry thought this an oddly dismissive way to talk about it.

'Oh,' said Cornwall, mildly curious now, and not in the least put off his stride.

'He wasn't tall, though. Average height, I guess.'

Cornwall considered this new bit of evidence. 'So, how come you're such a lanky git, then?' He raised a satirical eyebrow.

John shrugged. 'Dunno,' he said.

Cornwall nodded, but wasn't satisfied. 'Jammy bastard,' he added as an afterthought.

And that was how it became known that John's father was no longer alive, and that John had no right, genetically speaking, to be as tall as he was. It also became a source of commonality to unite John and Francis: the fact that John's dad was no more, and that John, like Francis, was a now fully signed-up member of the Dead Dads Club.

Chapter 37

The Queen of Sheba

At lunchtimes, the three of them — John, Francis, Henry — went to Francis' house. Henry had become Francis' friend too and, although there was some rivalry at first, John had accepted it.

Henry was plumper and taller now and not so easily bullied. In fact, he bullied others whenever the opportunity arose. Chiefly, he bullied John, because John was an easy target and didn't fight back. Also, John had betrayed him when Henry was thin; he hadn't protected him as a friend should have done. A part of Henry would never forget that, and that part wanted revenge. He would pick his moment.

Despite these grudges, they were older now and generally accepted each other's imperfections, except when they picked on them. Triangles never worked for lovers, but their three-way male friendship seemed just fine.

They went to Francis' home because it was close to school. Hanging around the playground was for little kids, and a bore. Henry no longer spent lunchtime with his grandma. She had moved to a new ground-floor flat in a modern apartment block, because her asthma was so bad she could no longer manage the stairs. She had left the old flat that smelled of drains and cooking and the gas-heaters that popped and roared and threatened to blow the place to smithereens when you washed your hands.

Francis' house was as different as he was. It was a terraced council property that hid behind a high wooden fence, as if it thought it was a cut above the other houses on the estate and was keeping its distance. Inside the fence, when you opened the large wooden doors, sat two enormous white vans, each with the legend *Sunshine Cleaners* stencilled on the side. This was the company that Francis' mother ran. A large Airedale was there, and it turned its great, square-shaped head to look at you. The dog had a slow, regal air. After a while, it might allow you to stroke it, but as if it were doing you a favour, and only tolerating your touch as a concession to civility. Its rough fur felt like steel wool or tightly coiled Brillo pads, and stroking it made your hand oily, so you had to use soap to get the smell off, or you would carry it for hours afterwards. Francis' house was a bit like that. It left something on you that lingered, not unpleasant but not quite wholesome either.

Sometimes a brown poodle came out and looked at them. It had a skin condition with bald patches and a raw pinkness under its tattered coat. It didn't want to be stroked but stood with planted feet, snarling.

The huge Airedale was called Sheba, a name which made her sound like an exotic Queen. There was nothing exotic about the big-headed dog with shaggy eyebrows and a stiff stub of a tail that seldom wagged. She gave half-hearted woofs, as if she were only doing it because it was expected; she was quoting other dogs and finding it tiresome. Her woofs were questions. 'Woof?' she said, looking away as if she'd lost interest in the reply. The poodle was called Otto, a name which made him seem like a German count, the kind who clicked his heels and had a monocle and ended up being a Nazi in war films. His barks were commands and exclamations. 'Yap!' he said. 'Yap! Yap!' When Henry squatted and spoke to Otto, he bristled and growled, even though he had met him before. He didn't bark at Henry, but at someone he appeared to see behind him or through him, which made you think he was psychic and able to see ghosts. Henry's mother had once said dogs could do that, and this was called clairvoyance. The mangy poodle didn't seem very spiritual, but you never knew.

Whoever had named Otto and Sheba had ideas above their station, because they were self-important names and too big for the creatures that owned them. At Francis' house, people were trying to make things bigger and better than they really were.

Francis' mother was often there, walking from room to room, speaking in her fake-posh Margaret Thatcher voice and waving a copy of *The Times*. She looked like a woman who'd once been pretty but wasn't any more. Her blond hair was cut in a schoolgirl bob. She was small and slim, and she wore leather boots, narrow skirts and too much pale-blue eyeshadow. 'Who are you?' she said, when they met her for the first time, 'and what are you doing here?'

When Henry said they were there because Francis had invited them, she slapped him around the head and called him a cheeky young bugger. Then she waved her hand and told Francis to get them drinks and whatever else they wanted, because they were welcome.

After that, she left them alone, because there was 'a businessman upstairs' who needed 'attending to', which sounded, even to them, like a euphemism. When she'd gone, they listened to Ian Dury and drank coffee. Francis put eight sugars in John's drink, and John didn't notice until he tipped the cup to drain it and found himself chewing on a slurry of undissolved grit. Then the businessman came downstairs. He winked at them and told them as he left to be 'good, but not too good', which was difficult advice to follow. Finally, Francis' mum came down, adjusting her hair. She asked them again what they were doing there and told them to clear out. Which they did, trudging back to the comparative boredom of a school afternoon.

Chapter 38

Dead Souls

School would have been all right if it hadn't been for the staff. The teachers were mainly men of the unkempt, cigarette-reeking, sweat-stained variety who kept their hands under their armpits or suggestively in their pockets, fiddling with the stem of a pipe or, possibly, something worse. They would swagger over to pinch a favourite's nose, so that the boy of their choice might savour the odour of their oniony, unwashed bachelordom.

Most of their teachers were freaks. There was the music teacher, Mr Bone, for example, who was a tall, moustachioed man who looked like a pale, fleshy mushroom. He waved his arms expressively as he explained the constituent parts of a fugue, something that had little relevance to boys obsessed with punk music and prog rock. In his armpits bloomed a pair of greenish stains, which grew as the lesson continued. He was telling them about Saint-Saëns, a subject that caused him unseemly excitement and made him sweatier than usual. The album he played, the vinyl crackling and burping and rumbling on the rickety turntable, was *The Carnival of the Animals.* The boys weren't that interested in guessing which animal Saint-Saëns was evoking by using the double bass *in allegro pomposo* or the glass harmonicas and *glissando* piano-runs. None of this compared to ELO's *Out of the Blue,* a record that had a *Close Encounters of the Third Kind* spaceship on the front, or David Bowie's *Diamond Dogs,* where the cover showed a beautiful half-canine creature. Half-boy half-dog was how they felt, but Saint-Saëns hadn't written any music about that, just silly old fish and elephants and donkeys. By the time the lesson ended, Mr Bone's personal stink had filled the room, and they ran gagging for the exits.

All the teachers stank. The dwarfish men who taught French and history, so alike they might have been twins, had tobacco-kippered complexions and a smell of pub ashtrays. They had hair side-parted over flaky scalps and a vocal delivery that was all throaty cackles and leering Sid James innuendo, their unfunny quips emphasised by jabs of their short, yellowing fingers. When they left the room, they left their smell behind them, a reminder of what not to become when you grew up.

The boys saw their teachers so often that they had become as familiar as members of their own dysfunctional families, tolerated, ignored and hated with equal vehemence. Teachers could be as withering as a father and as long-winded as an uncle. Some lied, as parents did. Others pretended to like them, like aunts and cousins. You had no choice but to put up with them, because however hard you wished for it, they wouldn't go away.

Mrs Bartlett was still their English teacher, following them from year to year, like a conscience. She was a little fatter now, a little greyer, but still well-meaning, and still annoyingly keen for them to succeed. She fed them her worms of knowledge as if they were baby birds. Unlike the male drill-sergeants who were intolerant of their slackness, doziness, stupidity and laziness, she still believed in them, and in the dormant souls inside them that she might one day reach. Most teachers had no interest in their souls, because a schoolboy had acne and a habit of seeing double meanings in perfectly innocent words like 'titular'. A boy was, as a species, singularly deficient in the soul department.

Mrs Bartlett disagreed. She cared in the way the men did not.

She was the one who actively *liked* them; loved them, perhaps, even though they had no desire to be loved. She turned every lesson into an earnest conversation which the boys resisted, because speaking was a weakness and unnecessary exposure, and their tongues were fluent only in the language of oaths and expletives. Most of their education had led them to believe that showing your emotions would only lead to humiliation, but suddenly they were supposed to express their ideas with freedom. 'Share your thoughts,' pleaded Mrs Bartlett. Or: 'What do you think? Let me know what you feel about this!' She would point at her book, expecting the hulking brutes before her to *emote* about Winston Smith or Caius Cassius or Billy Casper or Philip Pirrip. And they couldn't. They understood these characters well enough, so why torture them into expressing it all over again in far less elegant a way than the book had done? It made no sense.

So, the boys refused to share their thoughts just as they refused to share their food, their shaming fantasies and their sordid peccadilloes. Sharing was not what boys did. They cuffed, bundled and insulted each other, throwing fists and half-eaten sandwiches at friends and rivals alike. To show affection to another boy wasn't allowed, but you could thump him on the shoulder and numb the muscle; or raise your knee and give him a dead leg; or spatter his face with droplets of ink, just as you had when you were younger. These things didn't get old, and the syntax and vocabulary of male affection remained the same. You couldn't hug another boy or smile at him except in mockery, but you could steal his food, taking the limp strip of ham from the sandwich he'd left unwisely in his desk, and inserting a piece of paper on which the phrase 'IOU pig-meat' had been scrawled in wobbly pencil. Or you could put drops of sulphuric acid on his lab-coat and feign innocence when it began to disintegrate. You could clap the back of a friend's head with an open palm in which you'd concealed a pre-masticated wad of chewing gum, so that your friend had to cut out the matted hairs that night with his mother's sewing scissors. If there was a bald patch on his head when he came in the following day, one that had convinced his mother he was suffering from a mysterious bout of alopecia, that was funny; that was a good laugh, and he was a good chap for not taking it seriously. And that's what friendship was: causing each other the maximum of discomfort and embarrassment to your own delectation and mirth; it was hurting someone, but in a friendly fashion. That's what the boys meant by loving your neighbour as yourself. You despised yourself, so why not treat others the same way? This was their logic, their schoolboy code of misconduct.

But Mrs Bartlett persisted. She radiated Northern grit and gumption, and she wasn't going to change her mind in a hurry. She smiled, showing her snaggled assortment of teeth, and inviting the class to join in the warm hug of learning and mutuality. She failed to understand that there was no emotional socialism in the boys. They were loners and natural aristocrats; they were scoffers and scorners. Grammar school had bred the spirit of competitiveness in them, so it was irksome to be expected to behave now as if education were a matter of collaboration. Few of them did anything communally, apart from sport, where they hated their own side far more than the opposition, because their team was made up of ball-droppers, fatsoes, milksops, cowards, and liabilities.

Experience had taught the danger of openness. Some of the boys supported Crystal Palace and went to football matches at weekends. If cornered in a carriage by fans of the opposing team they were sometimes beaten up, their faces punched, their scarves thrown from the window. The message was clear. If you had loyalties or loves, it didn't pay to declare them.

But Mrs Bartlett wouldn't relent. She viewed them as if they were still what they'd been in the third form: lovable scallywags, amiable rogues who could be shamed with a disapproving look, or laughed at, or teased, or cajoled. But they were neither amiable nor lovable. They were hostile and venomous — great sprawling youths stupid with hormones, their hair heavy with grease, their faces and shoulders spattered with acne. Their trousers were too tight in the buttocks and too short in the leg. Their thick wrists obtruded from frayed cuffs. Their voices cracked and wobbled, fluted and violined, before settling into a guttural drawl. They exhaled cynicism and stuffed their faces with tuck-shop junk. They farted poisonous fumes, so had no sympathy when a soldier died from Chlorine gas in a weedy pacifist poem by Wilfred Owen. According to Owen, the dying soldier had 'a devil's face sick of sin'. Well, big deal. They had much the same faces, their complexions haggard from wanking and poor rations, their nostrils bothered by each other's stink, so what was all the fuss about? They were in the trenches too, but at least they didn't whine about it.

Chapter 39

The Power and The Glory

Even though the teachers tried to stop it happening, anarchy came into their classrooms. It entered like the bees that blundered though the windows in summer, an event that caused a havoc of swatting books and flapping gym towels and muttered oaths. But if the normally indolent boys panicked in the presence of a bee, they scarcely reacted to the far more dangerous world outside. It was hardly their fault. They'd been taught that all that mattered was getting the grade, and remembering the facts they'd been stuffed with — the elements in the Periodic Table, the ablative absolute in Latin, the major features of conurbations in the Ruhr valley. Their world was turned inward, each teacher claiming that his or her subject was all that mattered. The outside world wasn't really there — or, if it was, it was to be resisted or ignored unless it was part of the syllabus. The boys mustn't be distracted. Instead, they must focus on themselves and their futures, and on the subject each teacher claimed would save them from the abyss. The boys knew this was a lie. They knew the teachers were justifying their miserable jobs by pretending each subject was all-important, when it wasn't.

Outside the window, the other world was still there. It was a world of power cuts, and punk; a world of strikes and the IRA. Bombs were everywhere: in pubs, letters, packages, carrier bags, pillar boxes; in tube stations, trains and litter bins. There were fire-bombs and nail bombs, car bombs and boat bombs. All this was in the air and on the radio and on the TV in the living room, but the boys hadn't been taught to take an interest, and these events might as well have been happening in another country. It wasn't the past that was another country; it was the present. Because nothing exciting or dangerous ever came to their town. No-one they knew had been blown up. And if Francis really was Irish, he showed no sympathy either way when another IRA bomb went off and innocent people were blown to pieces.

This stuff was just news, and the news was boring. The things that really bothered you weren't the violence on the football terraces, or someone being kneecapped in Belfast, or the Yorkshire Ripper killing another woman with a hammer and a sharpened screwdriver. It was the lights going off at 7pm in the middle of a Norman Wisdom film. *That* was annoying. Then your mum would go groping for candles, and you were suddenly helpless, plunged into a world before electricity, a world of voices and hard edges in which the house became a Gothic mansion no less eerie than Satis House in *Great Expectations*.

When there was a power cut, the house first went dark, then became a thing that quivered in a candleflame. Henry tried to read a book or complete his homework or brush his teeth in a wobbly cave sculpted from the wider darkness. Sometimes a person came out of a wall with a firefly or will-o'-the-wisp, but it was only himself in a mirror. He got lost, because the house had changed shape. In the dark, it was a place of invisible ceilings and unguessable distances. People changed, too. Henry's sisters became characters in a nineteenth-century novel: pale, ghostly shapes that moved from room to room, trailing long shadows. And then, without warning, the power came on, and the candles were blown out, and the magic died, and it was the same old house again, and his sisters the same boring girls they'd been before.

There was always sex to distract you from the tedium of the old routine. On TV there was *Pennies from Heaven* and *I, Claudius*, the programmes where you were always guaranteed a bit of nudity, something that was justified by the context of ancient Rome or music-hall decadence. Seeing a real naked woman was an idea too fanciful to be imagined, so the boys found compensatory activities. One kept a list of celebrity deaths, another of serial killers. Others remained fixated on women, if only in the pictorial form.

At the back of the classroom, they stuck up photos of topless models torn from page three of *The Sun*. It became their household shrine, and the girls their personal deities. The teachers seldom, if ever, came down the aisle between the desks, and it was just as well. For one boy had discovered a way to rub out the contours of the women's breasts so he could draw much larger, shapelier ones. His classmates wanted bigger portions of everything, and so, with a soft-nibbed 4B pencil and the cartoonist's slow diligence, Brian Chiles, classroom artist, obliged. He gave women the desired augmentation, and soon he was accorded a respect he'd never had before, because he was the keeper of the vestal altar where the *Page Three* Girls lived with their alliterative names — Debbie from Derby, Laura from Liverpool, and Paula from Paignton.

Chapter 40

Things Fall Apart

O-Levels were suddenly upon them. It was O for ordinary, O for emptiness. The years were ticking down to the zero hour of exams, and there was a new briskness in the teachers' manner. They had taken to threatening them with time. 'In a year's time,' they said. 'Next summer.' Or 'In June.' Deadlines crept closer. Soon, A-level choices would have to be made, their destinies plotted.

The boys didn't believe in destinies and did their best to ignore these requests to rouse themselves and stir from their torpor. The future was as unreal as the past, as unreal as the world outside the window, as unreal as the present they drifted through. They felt they were falling apart, just when they needed to cohere.

As if in sympathy with their predicament, their Latin teacher fell to pieces. He went off sick and was away for months, replaced by a small, keen woman whom they largely ignored. None of them had liked their Latin master, but they respected his cruelty, his inflexibility and rigour. He was the same Latin teacher they'd always had. They missed old Mr Skelcher, because familiarity had bred acceptance, not contempt. What they loathed, above all things, was the shock of the new, and that keen woman waving her Latin textbook and exhorting them to learn even more words from a useless dead language, was the new.

One day, and without warning, Mr Skelcher was back, if only after a fashion. For the man who returned to them was an impostor

— an older, greyer version of the man they'd known before. Mrs Bartlett told them that he'd an operation to remove several feet of his lower intestine and to repair what was left. This was hard to imagine. Henry pictured yards of white, blood-stained tubing in a galvanised bucket, the doctors endeavouring to patch it, as he had once fixed a puncture. Mrs Bartlett had organised a whip-round and sent Mr Skecher a book about the Romans, but whether this had improved his stoicism in the face of cancer they were never told.

At breaktime, Mr Skelcher wandered the playgrounds in his uniform of tweed jacket, pressed beige trousers and highly polished brogues, the bowl of his pipe obtruding from his breast pocket like a small periscope doing a recce. He had the manner of a confused major inspecting his troops — troops who, in his absence, had grown beyond recognition and become, by some twist of fate, the enemy. He looked them up and down and shook his head. In the end, he wandered away, as if he thought he might have come back to the wrong school, after all.

In lessons, he began as usual, but when he tried to select a boy to do the translation, he faltered, his finger hovering, his eyes clouding. 'Um — you, boy. Let's hear your version.' There was a silence and an exchange of glances, because they knew what had happened. Old Skelcher couldn't remember their names — he, who never forgot anything and had a mind like a knife. The boys lowered their eyes, embarrassed. This was the teacher who, in the past, had offered no sympathy if they forgot a verb form, or misconstrued a passage from Caesar, giving them a 'kiss', his term for a cross or fail, and marking it in his register, his ledger of judgment. Sympathy, he'd taught them, was for weaklings. And because he'd never extended it to them, he couldn't expect it now. The truth was, the old fool had lost it, and they couldn't pity him. Indeed, they despised him.

It wasn't just his failing mind that was the problem; there was also the smell. The boys had only a vague notion of what a colostomy bag might be. All they knew for sure was, at a certain point in every Latin lesson, an unbearable odour filled the room. The boys at the front slumped over their work, as if overcome by weariness. They were the dying canaries in the coalmine. They were the sign that Old Skelcher, colonically at least, had reached the point of no return.

When the air got too poisonous, Old Skelcher would hoist himself to his feet, lurching towards the door with a curt, 'Carry on, chaps. Back shortly.'

They waited, the room humming in its brown gauze. The boys by the sash windows winched them up and gulped fresh air. And then they heard it — the slow clump-clump of his returning shoes. The windows were hastily closed, the boys resuming their translation was if nothing had happened, although Old Skelcher's face, when he finally heaved himself back into his chair, showed that something clearly had.

Chapter 41

To Sir, With Love

A year before their O-Levels, Mr Muldoon replaced Mrs Bartlett as their English teacher, and he couldn't have been more different. Whereas Mrs Bartlett had come to lessons on time, bustling in with boxes of novels or plays, plus a selection of hats to wear so they could assume different roles when they acted out scenes, Mr Muldoon arrived late, sweeping into the room like an actor who'd delayed his appearance in order to bring his audience to a pitch of expectation, but had failed to notice that he'd succeeded only in bringing it to a pitch of indifference. He was so tall his head almost brushed the top of the doorframe. He brought nothing with him but the gift of himself, and a thick volume which he held under one arm. When he reached the desk, he flung his book down as if he had nothing but contempt for it. 'All right, lads,' he said, in a voice like a sneer. 'Get out your Dickens.' This was not a euphemism. As they were to find out, Mr Muldoon had no truck with that debased form of wordplay. He permitted ambiguity only when they were engaged in poetic analysis, but the tiresome business of schoolboy *double entendres* was not to be borne. 'And be sharp about it,' he added. The boys' smiles faded, and they got out their books as instructed.

Mr Muldoon wasn't like the average teacher. He made an impression. He was a glamorous figure who brought into the classroom the odour of foreign cigarettes, Old Spice aftershave and hair tonic. He had dark ringlets, high cheekbones and a splendid physique. The boys knew this because they'd spotted him in the gymnasium after school, clad only in shorts and trainers. Here he lifted dumbbells in the company of one of the PE staff, and the boys, who'd pressed their noses to the windows, had been surprised to discover that he had, under his formal clothing, an athlete's body, roped with muscle. For a man who earned his bread teaching poetry, he hoisted heavy weights with admirable virility.

In the classroom, however, he favoured a flapping pinstripe, the trousers of which ended two inches above the ankle. His hair might be dark and curly, but it shone wetly, as though he had just walked out of the shower. His skin, meanwhile, still bore the traces of teenage acne. Moreover, his face had a faint sheen, as if he'd sat up too late reading Yeats, drinking moonshine whiskey and writing a tortured sonnet sequence. If Francis was fake Irish, Muldoon was the real thing. It was disappointing, then, that when he finally spoke, it was in the rounded vowels of Cambridge University.

On his first day of teaching, whereas Mrs Bartlett had handed out lollipops, he laid down the law. He did this in the form of a short speech. 'The more observant of you will have noticed that there are bookshelves at the back of this room,' he said. 'These shelves are full of books, and these books are my own. They are not to be touched or tampered with in any way. Is that clear?'

'Yes, sir,' they said, looking at each other. It was unpleasant to be mistrusted so early in their relationship.

'Good. Then we understand each other, don't we?'

'Yes, sir,' they said, annoyed at being forced to respond like first formers.

And thus the lessons with Mr Muldoon began. Many felt that, as an introduction, this did little to advance the cause of mutual confidence. Some began to yearn for the good old days of Ma Bartlett, with her bad teeth, warm vowels and attempts at cosy debate. They even missed her fishy odour, resenting the new smell of bars and male beauty products, something that confounded their notions of what a man was.

Mr Muldoon's teaching style came as a shock. He didn't require debate. What he required was an attentive audience. He found this, above all, in Henry, who hung on every word of the English master's quasi-Shakespearean soliloquies. Francis, on the other hand, found him boring. 'He's so patronising,' Francis observed after a couple of lessons. 'How can you respect someone who looks down on you?'

Henry wondered, on the contrary, how you could admire someone you didn't look *up* to.

The other boys didn't like him either. It was his sarcasm that rankled most. When Mr Muldoon returned their essays, he flung them back, all disfigured by his emendations. 'Trite!' he wrote in large red letters, or 'Clichéd!' or 'Melodramatic to the point of hysteria!' The boys grumbled, puzzling over the comments and bitter marginalia. But before they could figure out what Muldoon meant, he'd launched into his lesson, reading from a novel, or a poem, or Shakespeare, doing all the accents and characters like a one-man show, with no instruction as to what they should write down, or which quotes they should memorise. He didn't ask them to put on hats or read out roles. He performed. Their task was to listen and be silent; his to impart wisdom. What they made of it was their own affair. And finally, when he grew tired of teaching, he set an essay, rapping out a title and expecting them to complete it in twenty minutes flat. After that, he slumped in his chair in a fit of profound Celtic melancholy.

Grudgingly, the boys wrote their essays, knowing their work would only be covered in more of the acerbic one-liners after they'd handed it in. But they complied, because they were a little afraid of

Mr Muldoon. They suspected that, like the be-stubbled Irishmen they sometimes saw on TV, something dangerous lay under his wit, despair and lyricism — something explosive.

Chapter 42

*The Subtle Art of Not Giving a F****

Disturbed by the spread of profanity, Henry and his friends began to keep a swear box. It was always crammed with coins and IOUs because, despite loving literature and high culture, their minds were irredeemably infected with smut. They stretched innuendo to breaking point, and that included the word innuendo itself. In their conversations, a pen was never a pen, for its shape and seductively lonely monosyllable invited them to add the verb 'is' to release its comic potential. An old inkwell, meanwhile, was a Freudian hole, dark with possibility. They couldn't help themselves.

In the gaps between their swearing and obsessively sexual allusion, Mr Muldoon read them *Tess of the d'Urbervilles*. It was as if the mad evangelist, the one who daubed words in red paint on walls and fences, had been in their school, but instead of warning against the evils of sensuality, had painted primary-toned reminders of it. For they saw sex in every book, film, and gesture, in every banal and innocent object. A pen sliding into a pencil case. A banana being slowly unpeeled. A boy taking off a ring and pushing his finger into it again. Everything was sexual. The rest was window-dressing.

'The pen is red,' said Cornwall one day, holding up a biro.

Boroughs was indignant. 'Put 2p in the box, you bastard!'

'Why the *flaming fudge* should I?'

His verbal dexterity was to be admired, because Cornwall had tiptoed past obscenity, although *fudge* was pushing his luck.

Burroughs wasn't to be deflected. 'Because *the pen is red* is just an anagram of *the red penis,* and you know it!'

'Oh, come *on*!'

'Hey, you said *come*! 4p in the box!'

'I wouldn't touch your dirty little box if you paid me.'

'Another 2p! That was a filthy innuendo!'

'I wouldn't put anything in your endo, either, you dirty, pillow-biting little sodomite.'

'8p!'

And so it went on.

It was clear, however, that a few boys had gone beyond the world of smut and glossy centrefolds. Some had begun actual dating. Pornography was obligatory, but a girlfriend was still considered *risqué, outré,* and other French words that required an accent and a raised eyebrow. Even that hopeless case, John, had confessed that he was 'dating' now, and they plagued him for information about the girl — not about her appearance, although they were curious to know what she looked like and would've been angry if a total waste of space like him had bagged a beauty. No; their real interest centred on the parts of her anatomy that she had revealed to him, and which they hoped, in time, he would reveal to them by virtue of a full, technicolour confession. The female anatomy was still *terra incognita* to most of them, and they had never touched anything other than the dream-girls of their fantasies. Magazines were commonplace, but a two-dimensional image gave you no idea of the real thing, which had bumps and sheltered sylvan nooks they could only half imagine.

This was the time when the word *clitoris* hung in the air like an exotic fruit or a fantasy archipelago, and it seemed an important clue to the mystery that was womankind. Few knew of its fabled location, and John's explanations weren't helpful. 'It's in a fold,' he said vaguely, scratching the mole near his nose. 'Sort of at the top. On the outside, though, not up the, ahem, you know, hole.' He waved his arms as if that might help them picture it. 'It's a bit like the beak of a baby bird,' he added. He mimed the latter with his hand, opening and closing it.

This wasn't helpful either. They were pretty sure a clitoris couldn't open and shut like that. They'd read in *Cradle of Erotica* all about the *vagina dentata*, but that book had said firmly that no actual vagina came replete with teeth. This was a comforting thought, although it planted a seed of doubt. Now, John had planted another one, for a vagina was beginning to sound like a triffid that might consume you. John might be bluffing, of course, or deliberately laying a false trail to confound them. They would have to find out.

'Where is it really?' they insisted. 'What does it look like?' Clitoris was the word The Stranglers had inserted into the song *Peaches*, so it must be important.

'I just told you where it is,' John said wearily. 'It's in a fold. A sort of flap at the front.'

They touched their own bodies to orientate themselves. 'What, like, under the belly button? Like a joey in a kangaroo?'

'No, you idiots!'

'Where, then? Draw us a picture!' They pushed an old envelope and a biro at him.

With a sigh, he obliged. What he drew looked like an elevation on an Ordnance Survey map: a lonely promontory, surrounded by wrinkled contour lines.

'What's the hell's *that* meant to be?'

'A clitoris! What the hell do you think it is?'

'Liar! You're taking the *piss*!' They snatched the paper away and tore up his drawing, throwing it into the air. 'Don't bloody bother,' they said. 'We'll find out for ourselves!'

They knew they had no way of doing this, however, and John

knew it too. His smug face declared as much.

They went back to class. In the Biology lesson, they had to blow through tubes into tanks of water and then work out, by measuring the displacement of liquid, the capacity of their own lungs. Miss Macpherson, who was coldly Caledonian in her white coat, didn't mention the clitoris once, which just went to show how utterly useless biology lessons were.

Secretly, though, they were in awe of John. He was the boy you would least expect to be an initiate in girl-lore — the rank outsider who'd won the Grand National. And because they were jealous, they required revenge. All they needed was the name of his girlfriend, and once they finally discovered it, they scrawled it on the walls of the private study room for all to see.

Jenny for a penny: call me!

Ring Jenny for a good time!!!

Jenny services all your requirements!!!

In this way, they cheapened the thing they wanted. Nonetheless, it was one in the eye for John, the pith-helmeted explorer who'd discovered the *non plus ultra* of gynaecological topography.

'And did you wear a *rubber johnny*, Johnny?' they taunted. 'Last time you were on the jobby with Jenny?'

He told them, quite correctly, to piss off.

At lunchtimes, the three of them went to Francis' house and drank coffee. They listened repeatedly to *New Boots and Panties* by Ian Dury and the Blockheads, and the song *Billericay Dickie* was their favourite. They loved Ian Dury. Here was a singer whose mind was as filthy as their own. The suggestively named Dickie seemed to be both an animated penis and an alias for the singer himself, a cockney chancer who bedded as many women as he could, and anywhere he could. What Ian Dury's songs taught them was that women were up for it too, as long as you gave them drink or drugs first and you had a car, preferably a Ford Cortina, to stand as a proxy for a bedroom. Under those circumstances, women might consent to have sex with you. Otherwise, it seemed wildly improbable.

But John was having sex already, and he had none of these things. He was a tall, gangling, spotty disaster. He didn't have Ian Dury's gift for wordplay: he blundered his way through sentences that seldom reached the end. He had a push-bike, a mild stammer and a face that was an open invitation for a punch.

Despite John's increasing exasperation, the inquisition continued. 'Where do you *do* it?' they asked, when they had him alone at lunchtime. 'When does it happen?'

Francis swung the Anglepoise so that it shone in John's eyes.

'I told you. When her parents are at church. Hey, you're dazzling me!'

They pushed the light closer. 'Stop whining and just answer the bloody question!'

'I have!'

'You're shagging your bird while the parents are *praying*?' They moved their faces closer, their voices assuming the metallic edge of German officers in *Colditz*.

'Um, yes.'

'You dirty, depraved, deceiving, Gottless bastard!' They said 'Gottless' because it sounded more Hun-like.

John gave a nervous laugh, but didn't refute the accusation.

'And does Jenny get down on her knees, like in church?'

'What?'

'Do you give her a little cushion to kneel on when she's, you know, praying to the Great Pink God?' They opened their mouths in a manner suggestive of sword-swallowing. 'Or Tiny Pink God, in your case.'

John shook his head. 'Oh, give it a bloody rest, will you?'

'You should give *her* a rest, more like.'

'Yeah, a headrest, to stop it bobbing back and forth when she's fellating your filthy trouser-snake.'

'Shut *up*.'

'What's it like, anyway?'

He shrugged. 'Well, what do you *think* it's like? It's great.'

They hated him for that word more than they could say.

'Don't her parents *suspect* anything?'

'No. We just have to be quick, that's all. You know, get it done before they get back from church.'

'*Get it done*? It isn't a bank job, you unromantic bastard!'

'Yeah, yeah.' John glanced at his watch. 'We'd better go, anyway. We'll be late for history.'

As they trudged back to school, that was how they felt. That they were late for history. Time had passed them by, and they had missed the bus, and that skinny git John had got there first. They hated him. They hated Jenny. There was more revenge to be had, because that was all they could hope for now. Meanwhile, they must bide their time. If they could ruin John's relationship and have him as their mate once more, they would do so, because then it would be like the old days. They would be the Three Musketeers again, and all would be for one, and one for all.

Chapter 43

The O-Gape of Complete Despair

O-Levels were upon them: days of sitting in serried ranks while the clock ticked and sweat ran down their backs and teachers patrolled the aisles, doling out extra paper for those who needed it. It was too hot, and their trousers pinched, and the hall was silent, save for the turning of pages, the rapid scribble of pens and the occasional cacophonous hay-fever sneeze. Henry copied some of his maths answers from the clever boy, Wilkes, who sat diagonally in front of him a bishop's move away. It was multiple choice, and the letters Wilkes had shaded in were different from Henry's, so Henry erased his own. He didn't approve of cheating unless he himself was doing it, and in any case, no-one saw.

Then it was chemistry. Halfway through, Henry sniffed too hard, and blood burst from his nose, spattering his exam paper. The invigilator, Mr Colyford, came clicking across in his high-heeled shoes. He dropped a scented handkerchief on Henry's desk, then walked away without saying a word. Henry didn't use it, because he had a pocket crammed with tissues. He couldn't get his blood on Mr Colyford's dandy accessory; it was too intimate, too shaming an act. Instead, he plugged his nostril with a twist of paper that rapidly became a sodden tampon and fell with splat on the desk. He repeated the process until the blood had stopped and the final tissue solidified into an iron-hard ingot. His desk was now a battlefield where he had fought the Periodic Table and lost, which just went to show that it did have something to do with the menstrual cycle after all.

After the exam, they had to fill in an incident form. Henry hoped the blood would conceal his weak answers and show his examiner that he had literally bled for the cause of chemistry. Mr Colyford said, as he picked up his unused hanky by the extreme edge, that Henry had presumably jumped to the end of the paper and answered the high-scoring questions first, to ensure the most favourable result. Henry nodded, although he hadn't done that and hadn't even thought of it. He'd probably failed, and there went his career as a doctor, along with the chance of sharing the healing touch that had once cured his mother of her terrible migraines.

Then it was Latin, and Latin was good, too, because Old Skelcher had trained them to be like officer cadets, practising self-discipline and rigour and drilled to perfection on the parade ground of his classroom. Don't write anything for the first fifteen minutes, he'd commanded, just plan your answers; and they had done that, to a boy. The invigilator, the geography teacher they called Brian the Snail on account of his small size and sleepy manner, sat at the front. He panicked, because the boys were just sitting there motionless like petrified statues of boys, not living ones, and not one of them was writing a damned thing. He whispered to the bearded teacher (Mr Dore, history) who, knowing better, shook his head, and smiled. Because Brian the Snail, who was really Mr Deards, didn't know about battle tactics, or that the Latin students were a garrison of men equipped with shields and body armour, and with the ablative absolute amongst their weaponry. It was only after they'd planned all their answers that they finally picked up their pens and began to write, and at that point, Mr Deards could breathe again. And it was only then the boys realised how good a teacher Old Skelcher had been, and how wrong they'd been to hate him, and now it was too late to say thank you.

The best exam was English because that was easiest, as you could express what you felt, not just what you knew. Henry wrote about Estella in *Great Expectations*, feeling as he wrote that he was Pip, and that he had great expectations too, although he didn't know whether they were his or had been foisted upon him by others. As he wrote his answers, he glanced up and saw that John, who was sitting in front of him now, was writing at a feverish pace. The skinny kid was doing it again, excelling at a subject he'd always been average at. For six months he'd slumped against a wall in English lessons, looking as if that succubus Jenny had drained him of all his bodily fluids. Now he was on fire. But not everyone was. In the distance, across the exam hall, Henry could see the humped shape of Francis. He was fiddling with his pen and not writing, just tugging pensively at his lower lip and staring into space. He had evidently forgotten everything Mr Muldoon had ever taught him.

When the final exams were all over, they left the darkened hall and entered the sunlit playground reborn as almost-men. However well or badly they'd done, it was over now and too late for worry. They had a summer of idleness ahead, with only the prospect of the results-envelope to cast a shadow over things. And then it would all begin again, with A-levels as the next obstacle in an endless series of hurdles that extended beyond view.

This was too much to think about. It was the holidays and a time for celebration.

The three of them packed their things and cycled into the Kent countryside where Francis' mother kept a caravan in a farmer's field; and for a few weeks they swore and played football and explored the riverbank like the Famous Five minus two boring and unimportant members of the gang. Jenny was forgotten, school an irrelevance, families a mere footnote. It was the three of them, just like the old days. There were no rules. They sat up until 3am, playing cards and calling each other all the foul names they could think of. They ate burnt fry-ups and toast and shop-bought cakes. They went into a newsagent and made John buy a copy of *Men Only* because he was the tallest. They wrestled in the hayfield and threw straw at each other. They played Pooh Sticks in the river and relieved themselves in the chemical toilet. Then they began to stink and to tire of eating chocolate for breakfast and baked beans from tins for their tea. They tired of cowpats and barking dogs and each other's lame jokes. In the end, they admitted that they were homesick, so they loaded their panniers and cycled home again, standing up in their saddles and pedalling the thirty miles that seemed mainly uphill now, keen to get home and keen to get away from each other, for it had been too much of a good thing.

And then, a few weeks later, the letterboxes flapped and there were their results on the doormat. And would you believe it? That skinny bastard John had done the best.

Chapter 44

The Ballad of Joey

In the sixth form, they had to choose between arts and sciences. They couldn't do both because the timetable didn't permit it. In this way, Henry's dream of being a Renaissance man, a doctor who removed tumours while quoting Keatsian odes, went up in smoke. Suddenly, the division between destinies became as clear as the Berlin Wall, and you were on one side or the other. Henry chose arts and Francis and John sciences. His friends were to be vets, apparently, while Henry was to be some indefinable thing for which a job description had yet to be invented.

Meanwhile, their lives as sixth formers began, and they no longer shared classes. There was a certain, inevitable cooling between them. Henry now spent time with a religious boy who wore green shirts, read Oscar Wilde and did competitive speed-walking, wiggling his buttocks in a provocative way, in pursuit of something only nominally a sport. John and Francis, on the other hand, hung out with the bodybuilders and science nerds and rugby thick-necks. Henry, Francis and John looked at each other's new friends with suspicion.

But although things had changed outwardly, in other ways they remained the same. The Three Musketeers still met at lunchtimes, and Francis and Henry still quizzed John about what he'd been up to in the bed department. John still told them to 'grow the hell up' when they asked for more precise anatomical details, and they still maintained he was a tight bastard who was shutting them out. He said they were losers who took their frustrations out on him.

It was true that, though they invited John's confidences, they didn't respect them. One day, they wheedled out of John the juicy titbit that he and Jenny had a pet name for John's penis, and this was 'Joey'. It was the same name as John's dog, an ugly and bad-mannered mongrel that had come from a rescue centre, and that sniffed your crotch with rather too much enthusiasm when you entered John's house. Apparently, John and Jenny had written letters to each other using this nickname, which they believed a code uncrackable even by a member of M15. According to John, Jenny's letters contained such euphemisms as 'longing to take Joey out for a walk' and wishing to 'stroke Joey's head and tickle his ears.' John confessed it all one day in the stark light of the Anglepoise lamp, after swallowing too much over-sweetened coffee, and once it was out, there was no taking it back.

This information was gold. It was too hilarious a secret to be kept for long, and by the following day, every boy in the sixth form knew. Kids who barely recognised John came up to him and asked him how old Joey was, and if Joey had chased any pussies up a tree recently. Someone else wanted to know whether Joey had to wear a 'muzzle' in public places.

That lunchtime, over coffee and *Young Americans* on the 8-track, John told them they were utter bastards for telling his secret to other people. Henry and Francis shrugged. They said that John couldn't complain, because technically the information was in the public domain, and such things must be disseminated in the interest of wider transparency. That's what Ma Bartlett had taught them, after all: to share and share alike. John said he would never tell them another thing because they were bloody effing shits, and they said that was fine by them, because they were sick of hearing about John and that miserable old whore Jenny. Then John slammed down his coffee and went out, banging the door behind him. The other two looked at each other and nodded sadly, for the Three Musketeers were no more. and that had proved it. D'Artagnan had stormed out.

And then, the next day, John said they could come round and meet Jenny that weekend, and everything changed.

It was a sunny Saturday and Henry and Francis waited awkwardly for John to answer the doorbell. A dog, presumably Joey, barked in a distant room. The boys exchanged grins, for they foresaw much mirth and ribaldry at John's expense. They would make fun of him and his girlfriend, and the lovers' relationship would come crashing down around their ears.

The door opened and John came out, blinking and squinting like a reluctant politician come to face the press. He seemed very tall, his long neck stretching above his collar. He grinned. 'Hi,' he said. Then they saw a movement behind him and through the doorway stepped Jenny. She was small and smiling, and as soon as they saw her, all their carefully prepared jokes withered and died. Jenny took John's arm at the elbow and looked up at him. She was normal and natural, and they looked right together. It was Henry and Francis who were the spare parts. It was they who were the gormless ones. This was not how it was supposed to be.

For a while, they followed their original plan, however. They made fun of John's tee-shirt and the wispy bumfluff on his chin. They punched his arm and called him a stupid old bastard. They went through all the dumbshow of embarrassment. To Jenny, however, they were formal and polite, even courtly. Then they ran out of quips, because they found that she was human. In their imagination, they'd made her into something monstrous that reality couldn't sustain. But she was just a girl. She wasn't clever or pretty, or sexy or devious. She was shy, with a spatter of freckles across the bridge of her nose. She had an asthmatic laugh. She wore sensible girl-next-door clothes and giggled when they attempted a joke. They rather liked her.

They went for a walk in the park with Joey, and did not once refer to his role in the lovers' correspondence. They simply speculated about whether people grew to be like their dogs or the other way round. Then they came back for tea. They asked Jenny about her school and her A-level choices but didn't listen to her replies, because they were too busy thinking up the next joke to impress her and make her laugh. Every now and then, they looked at her breasts and tried to imagine her naked, but found they couldn't. And then, when they'd finished the tea and eaten all the biscuits, and when the silence of yawns and creaking sofa-springs had become too much, they made their apologies and left.

After this visit, they pledged to find girlfriends of their own, because being an eavesdropper in another person's relationship was pathetic. But this was easier said than done.

And then, one day, Chloe, who was fourteen now and all grown up, removed Henry's photo from a family album and took it into school. Henry was in swimming trunks, his eyes crinkled in the sun's glare. Behind him lay the beach, with deep shadows under sun-umbrellas and windbreaks checkering the yellow sand. It wasn't a picture Henry was particularly proud of, and when his sister told him what she had done, he was annoyed. Then she added that it had created some interest among her school friends, who wanted to meet this boy with muscles and a suntan. Henry didn't know what to think about girls he'd never seen ogling his picture, but he didn't mind really, because left to his own devices, he was never going to meet anyone. The photo was a start. Maybe something, or someone, would come of it.

Chapter 45

The Hunting Party

In the sixth form there were parties and, having little else to do and no other way to meet girls, Henry went to them. He met a few of Chloe's friends this way, but none interested him much, and none of them seemed to think he lived up to the promise of his photograph. 'You're shorter than I thought,' said a giraffe-girl from the vantage point of her heels, before stalking away to get off with Gordon Vane, the tallest boy in their year. Things went downhill, altitudinously and morally, from there.

These parties usually occurred in dimly lit rooms where music pounded and the air was thick with cigarette smoke. The girls wore fashionable styles and looked with disdain at the grammar-school boys who didn't. The boys favoured shapeless trousers, rugby shirts and unbranded trainers, their faces running the gamut of lantern jaws and smashed pumpkins and acne battlefields. Their hairstyles were ragged bowl-cuts and their bodies unimpressive: all slouches, chicken chests and scholar's humps.

The music served to drown the social awkwardness, but it only created an awkwardness of another kind. The boys watched the girls as they danced with each other, and these girls watched the boys watching them, as they moved their white stilettoes and ballet pumps in complex patterns and held their lit cigarettes at acute angles to their bodies.

These were girls of different types, sophisticated and frightening.

There was a stout girl in a tight-fitting cocktail dress and elbow-length black gloves who danced jerkily to Madness and The Selecter and The Beat. There was a 'mod' in a parka with braces on her teeth and a WW2 target symbol on her back. A drunken Henry aimed himself at that target and snogged her in a corner before realising, after snagging himself painfully, that he was in imminent peril of razoring his tongue. He retreated, injured, from the field of conflict.

Finally, the boys tired of this, and someone put on 'Go Buddy Go' by The Stranglers. Then the boys did the pogo, because the only skill required in this non-dance was the ability to jump up and down with your hands at your sides. They were like salmons leaping vertically and trying to swim up a waterfall to their spawning ground. Henry grew hot and took off his shirt, and this excited interest from no-one except a girl who tried to dance with him and labelled him 'slippery'. Meanwhile, Francis, who prided himself being elusive and what he called an '*eminence grise*,' sloped off to find another party that was rumoured to be happening nearby. Then John went home early because he was missing Jenny, and he didn't see the effing point. Then someone disappeared to vomit in a toilet and someone else broke a handle off a door and then the parents came in and turned all the lights on, because wasn't it time everyone went home? The father stood with the broken door fixture in his hand, and he looked at them as if wondering whether it had been worth fighting a world war for this bloody shower.

Chapter 46

Troilus and Cressida

Henry wasn't quite the novice he pretended to be. There'd been an encounter with a girl at the end of the Christmas holidays that he'd told no-one about, because he was ashamed and knew that, like John, he would become a laughing stock. Angie was more than a girl, and less than one. She was a cousin, aged seventeen, with brown hair, a chubby body, and a lecherous gap between her front teeth that made her resemble a young version of the Wife of Bath. So it was almost, but not quite, incest.

She'd come round with her parents, Uncle Leslie and Aunty Jean. Before they'd arrived, his mother had flown into her habitual panic of hoovering, dusting and baking. She'd made meringues with clotted cream. She'd got out the best china and polished the floors and tables. She would have polished the children but Chloe and Alice were out, and Henry was supposedly doing an essay, although he was, in fact, standing in the kitchen with a cup of coffee. He'd begun drinking coffee because he believed doing so made him an intellectual. In fact, it only succeeded in making him jittery and giving him heartburn, but still, he thought, one must suffer for one's art.

Henry's father had lit a cigarette and was shaking his head at the fuss. It was only Leslie and Jean, for God's sake, not a Papal bloody delegation. There was no need to hang out bunting for people like that. 'Les won't care,' he said, putting out his unsmoked cigarette as the hoover zoomed near his ankles. 'It isn't as if they live in a palace.'

This was beyond dispute. Les and Jean occupied a tiny, terraced house that smelled permanently of cabbage or bad plumbing. The lounge had a view of the gasworks, which his father called a 'room with a phew!' because it stank.

'Leslie might not care, and you mightn't,' his mother said, unplugging the hoover and rubbing at a grease-mark on the wall, 'but I do.' She turned to Henry, who was moodily nursing his heartburn. 'And *you'll* need to make a bit more effort, mister. Try to be sociable for once. Don't just skulk off and hide in your room like you normally do.'

Henry didn't like being characterised in this way. He wasn't a mister, and he didn't skulk, because that was a cheap dismissal of his profoundly existentialist gloom. 'I have that essay to finish,' he reminded her.

She flung the cloth into the sink. 'Oh, you *always* have an essay to finish!' This, of course, was an outrageous lie.

'I want you to make an effort, for once,' she went on. 'You can finish the essay any time.'

'It's due in on Monday,' he pointed out, quite reasonably. 'Which is, like, tomorrow.'

'Oh, tomorrow and tomorrow and bloody tomorrow!' She wrapped the cable around the hoover as if it were a rope around someone's neck. It was usually his father who swore, but his father wouldn't have bothered to quote *Macbeth*. Her reference to tragedy was overdoing it rather, Henry felt.

'Just be nice to Angie, please,' she said. 'And no fighting.'

'I'm not *six years old*, Mum.'

'Physically, no. Mentally I'm not so sure.' She frowned at him. 'Anyway, it's only Angie. No Daniel this time. He's at football.'

She said this as if it made it easier, but it didn't. Henry liked Daniel, who was a younger, more vulgar version of himself. Daniel dressed flashily, spoke cockney and reeked of aftershave and cigarettes. He wore clunky signet rings and bracelets, told dirty jokes and shared titbits about his love-life, which usually involved clinches with receptive girls in unreceptive places. Porches. Broom-cupboards. Lifts.

Henry scanned the horizon, taking in the lie of the land. He thought he might risk a second coffee, now his mother was no longer armed with a dishcloth. 'You know I never have anything to say to Angie, Mum,' he said, speaking quietly so as not to raise her ire, 'and she never has anything to say to me.'

His mother put her hands on her hips in her warrior pose. 'Don't be stupid, Henry. How hard is it to talk to people? Just try for *one afternoon*, can't you? We'll probably go for a walk anyway, and that'll use up some time. I don't know why you always make such a song and dance about things.'

Henry thought about improvising jazz hands and attempting a soft-shoe shuffle but decided against it. He glanced at his father, because for once they were confederates in the face of attack. Their shared look took in the immaculate kitchen, the meringues, the expensive biscuits. It wasn't *them* making the song and dance.

'But I do need to finish that essay,' he said gently.

'Henry.'

'Oh, all right.'

The kettle came to the boil as his mother soon would, so he made his coffee quickly, feeling again the vague dyspeptic burning in the pit of his stomach. One day, he would have an ulcer. It was something to aspire to, now that the age of Keats and tuberculosis had gone.

'Put that cup on a tray, Henry,' his mother said, wearily. 'Or I'll find a line of drips all the way to your room.'

Henry felt the line of drips somehow included himself.

He sat at his desk. His coffee cup was empty, while his *Troilus and Cressida* essay lay half-written in a pool of light. He needed the light on during the day because his father, in a frenzy of DIY enthusiasm, had built the desk behind a panel that blocked the window, thereby creating a dark but oven-like solarium. It was a kindly gesture that had gone badly wrong, as his father's gestures invariably did. The 60-watt bulb was making Henry sweat, but despite this, he tried to focus. He ran his eyes over his work. He'd been contrasting the idealism of the Trojans with the cynicism of the Greeks. He had to discuss how love was presented in the two camps and determine what a contemporary audience would make of it. Shakespeare seemed to be suggesting that, while some men hopelessly overvalued the women they were in love with, idealising them into goddesses, others — the pimps, pragmatists and clowns — cynically *under*-valued them. Henry had to decide who was right. Love was either delusional or transactional. There seemed no other choice on offer.

After a while, he heard the crunching of a car on the drive, then dogs barking, and finally the jollity of doorstep greetings. He abandoned his work and trudged downstairs. Any excuse to get away from that burning lightbulb and the conundrum of love.

They were all in the lounge, where the best cups sat on wooden coasters. His father had put a pop-classical album on the stereo.

Angie was looking at the bookshelf and turned as he came in. 'Oh, *hello*, Henry.' She said it archly, as if he had been keeping her waiting. She was in jeans and a pink cardigan, and she looked different from how he remembered. She had a rounder shape and a new boldness of manner.

'You look bored,' she said, helping herself to a biscuit. '*Tu as l'air de t'ennuyer*.' The use of French was unnecessary, but she was the academic in her family, everyone said. His mother said Angie had pretentions of grandeur.

‘I’m not bored,’ he said.

She nibbled her biscuit, negligently dropping crumbs and disdaining the bourgeois vulgarity of a plate. ‘Daniel couldn’t come, by the way. He’s playing football.’

‘I know. I heard.’

‘It’s a game for thugs,’ she said, raising an eyebrow and expressing a tired exasperation at the limitation of brothers. ‘You’ll have to put up with me on my own.’

‘Yes, I know.’

‘Charming.’

‘That’s not what I meant.’

‘It’s what you *said*, though.’ She winked, or squinted; it was hard to tell. Her mouth, meanwhile, was full of biscuit.

‘No, *you* said... Oh, never mind. *Sorry*, then.’

They stood in silence and watched the adults talking with false heartiness.

She swallowed. ‘It’s awful, isn’t it?’

‘What is?’

‘All this.’ She made a grand gesture that included the room and the act of polite conversation with coffee, biscuits, doilies and occasional tables.

‘I suppose.’

She yawned, her teeth prettier than he remembered. No gaps now. She’d had those braces, he remembered, that had made her lisp. She raised her cup and sipped her coffee contemplatively. ‘Your mum said we’d be going for a walk later on. After coffee and stuff.’

‘That’s the plan.’

‘So, there’s a *plan*?’

‘Oh, yes.’

She sighed. ‘Me, I hate plans.’

‘Me too.’

She looked at him. 'Let's just do our own thing, then, shall we?'

He shrugged. 'That'll be hard. It's all mapped out like the D-Day landings. Rendezvous on Omaha Beach at 1500 hours.'

She rolled her eyes. 'Oh, great. Are you going, then?'

He raised one shoulder. 'I have an essay to do, but I think Mum's going to force me.'

She looked at him. 'Oh, those *mums*.' She said it as if they were a breed apart. 'What's the essay on, anyway?'

He told her, although he knew she didn't care.

'Toilets and Crevices?' she echoed with a smile.

'*Troilus and Cressida*.'

'Ah. And that's...?'

'It's about the Trojan war. You know, one of Shakespeare's problem plays.'

'The problem being it's *boring*, I suppose.' She set down her cup. 'Well, sorry to break up our scintillating conversation and everything, but mother nature calls. It's the only mother I listen to, personally.'

She walked away. Henry stood holding his cup and nursing his heartburn. He watched, vaguely, the sashaying of his cousin's hips, the cleft between her buttocks visible through the fabric of her jeans along with the proffered fruitlike plumpness. Through the door and out. His mother caught his eye and announced that this was the perfect time for them to have their little walk, seeing that the weather was so lovely and everything.

Then there was a general bustle of activity in which they all began to prepare themselves. Jackets were found and put on. Lipstick was reapplied. Dogs were gathered and tethered with collars and leads. As they waited in the kitchen full of noise and the slavering of dogs, Angie reappeared, looking pale. 'Headache,' she said, tapping her temple with a finger. 'Bad one, I'm afraid.'

Henry's mother frowned. 'Oh dear! That's *horrible*, Angie. I get headaches too.' She paused. 'Look, you'd better stay here, then. You can keep Henry company.' His mother glared at him. 'You've got schoolwork to do, haven't you, Henry?' She said this fiercely as if he were trying to deny it, then turned to Angie, lowering her voice as if he were no longer there. 'I think it's an excuse, myself. Still, I'm sure he'll be glad to catch up with you.'

As if they were running a race, and Henry had been left far behind.

'It's been a while,' his mother added, 'since you last saw each other.'

'Yes,' Angie nodded. 'It has. But to be honest, Henry doesn't really look as if he needs any company right now.' She took a pill from her handbag, half-closing one eye, as if the migraine were making her wince or she were taking aim at someone.

'Oh, take no notice of him.'

The dogs had begun to run about now, barking, tongues lolling. His mother turned. 'Take care of that headache, Angie. And Henry, get her a glass of water, please, so she can swallow that tablet. And *do* be sociable. Angie, feel free to *force* him if he resists.'

'Oh, I will,' she said, winking, or squinting.

'I do have an essay, Mum,' he said, feebly, as they trailed away in a cacophony of dogs. 'I can't talk and write an essay at the same time. I'm not Superman.'

But no-one was listening and the door banged, and suddenly the house was empty. Just the two of them, and *Troilus and Cressida* waiting upstairs, that awkward couple in the bedroom.

'No, you're not,' said Angie.

'Not what?'

'Not Superman. You're too weedy.'

He looked down at his skinny arms. He was thinner than in the photos his sister had shown the girls at school. 'Oh, thanks a lot.' There was a silence. 'Well, I'd better get on with my homework, then. That's all we non-supermen are good for, apparently.'

She shrugged. 'Okay, student boy. I'll sit down here and read. You're not the only intellectual in the family, you know.'

He saw that she had nothing with her: just a handbag.

'Read what?'

'Oh, one of your mum's books, I guess. She's got loads, hasn't she? I'll pick one.' She wandered back into the lounge and selected something from a shelf, then folded herself up on the settee. 'Happy writing. Don't bother about me.'

'I won't.' He walked away, then turned back, remembering. 'How's your headache, by the way?'

'My what?' She looked up from the pages of *Fat is a Feminist Issue*.

'Headache.' He tapped his skull.

'Oh, *that*,' she said. 'You know.' She raised an eyebrow.

He didn't know, but it was the kind of thing women said that didn't require a response.

'All right, then.'

He sat at his desk under the hot light and tried again to think what and how to write. He swivelled his wheeled chair and rolled back and forth to get the precise angle of attack required for essay-writing. Then he picked up a pencil and began drawing a man, sketching the muscles the way Leonardo da Vinci might have done. He fancied himself as an artist and had toyed with the idea of doing A-level Art. He did the shading and cross-hatching to make the figure look three-dimensional, then sat back and looked at it. Not bad. Not bad at all.

'What are you doing?'

He turned. Angie was watching him. He hadn't heard her come in.

'Writing my essay, what does it look like?'

'No, you're not. You're doodling.'

'It's not doodling,' he said, trying to hide his picture under a piece of ruled A4. 'It's art.'

She came and stood beside him. He could smell her perfume: sweetness with an undertone of sweat. 'I don't know why you're hiding your picture of a naked man,' she said quietly. 'This is the modern world. No need to be ashamed of male nudity in this day and age.' She paused. 'Anyway, it's not really *art,* is it? Or Shakespeare.' She made a pretence of remembering. 'Not — what is it again? Toilets and Cesspits?'

'Troilus and Cressida.'

'Yes. It's not *that,* is it?'

He fiddled with his pen. 'Well, I got a bit stuck with my essay, to be honest. I was just gathering my thoughts.'

'Or wool,' she said. She yawned, stretching her arms over her head. Her breasts bulged, threateningly. 'Why do you have to write it *now,* anyway? Oh yes, don't tell me. You've got a deadline.'

'Yes.'

'Oh, God save us from deadlines!'

He didn't know what that meant. What deadline was she working to? He cleared his throat. 'Well, I prayed to God earlier, but the deadline's still there.'

'God? No, He's no good,' she said dismissively. 'It's no use praying to Him. Anyway, you can't write an essay if I trap your arms, can you, student boy?'

'Pardon?'

'I said you can't write an essay if I trap your arms.'

And before he could move, she'd spun his chair round and slid her hands through the crooks of his elbows. He wriggled, but she was too strong for him.

'Get *off*, Angie.'

'I've been told to keep you company, remember? That's what I'm doing.'

'No.' He struggled. 'You're *hurting* me, that's what you're doing.'

'Oh, boo-hoo!' she mocked.

'Anyway,' he said, wrestling ineffectually, 'you've got a headache, remember. You should be resting or something.'

She laughed. 'I haven't got a headache. I was lying, you dumbo.'

He went limp and tried to turn his head. 'You what? Why?'

'*Why*? Who wants to go on their stupid walk, anyway?' She gave his arms a tug and the chair rolled backwards on its little wheels. Then she tugged again and again, inching it backwards in tiny increments. '*Walks* are stupid. *Dogs* are stupid. *Parents* are most stupid of all.' Tug, tug. 'You found a ruse to get out of it, didn't you, so I found another one. A loophole, *si tu veux*. I used my head, you see. That's a pun, by the way. Pun for punishment.'

The chair rocked, the wheels rucking up the carpet, snarling it, bunching it.

'Be careful,' he said, wobbling now, because he was travelling backwards towards her, advancing in a helpless, widdershins fashion.

'Why?' she teased.' Are you *scared*, student boy?'

She tugged harder, and the chair caught on a new wavelet of carpet. It tilted, poised, then went over backwards. Henry's head hit the carpet with a thump, and he lay there, dazed.

'Whoops,' she said, looking down at him with her ugly, upside-down face. 'Silly me.'

Before he could get up, she'd moved the chair out of the way and was crouching over him. 'Anything broken?'

'No.'

'Pity.'

'Thanks.'

'Shall I call an ambulance?'

'Don't be silly.'

'Your mum?'

'Shut up.'

'Air-sea rescue?'

'Give it a rest.'

'Give it a rest?' she laughed. 'Where did you buy your idioms, in the junk shop?' Then she was straddling him, squatting on his chest and kneeling on his weedy arms. 'It's exercise you need, not a rest. A Jane Fonda workout.' She slapped his face, making his ears ring.

'Ow! What are you *doing*?' His voice sounded feeble in his own ears, but the power had drained out of him. That bang on the head. The way she was sitting pointedly on his crotch.

'What am I doing? What does it look like? Taking advantage of you, that's what.'

She bent lower over him, so he felt her breath fanning him. Coffee and biscuits and peppermint toothpaste. She was too heavy, and he could hardly breathe. 'Why would you do that?' he protested.

'Revenge,' she said. 'And because you lied.'

'Lied? No, I didn't.'

'You did. You said you had an essay to write, and I find you drawing porny pictures of naked men.'

He squirmed. 'That's not what they are. Anyway, *you* lied about your headache.'

She smiled. 'Well, that makes us equal, doesn't it? A pair of liars.' She slapped his cheeks again in a series of gentle cuffs. 'What's the compound noun for that, I wonder? A largesse of liars?' Slap. 'A duplicity of deceivers?' Slap. 'A barrow-load of bullshitters?' Slap, slap. Then she began tugging at his top.

'Please stop, Angie.'

'No.'

He tried to fight her off, but his arms were trapped. Her sharp knees bit into his biceps. Her bottom bumped on his balls. Then his tee-shirt was rumpled up and round his neck like a scarf. She pinched his nipples and held them, tweezering them with her fingertips, twisting and twisting.

'You're *hurting* me.' His voice was hoarse. The pain was a pleasure, but he couldn't admit it.

'Oh dear. We can't have that, can we?' She twisted them more, then dug her nails into his chest and scratched it, cat-like, with her talons.

He shuddered. 'Ow!'

'*Ow*?' she echoed. 'Is that the best you can do? Is this an episode in *The Beano* or what? Are you Walter the Softy?'

She rolled off and watched him as he lay there panting. She was leaning on an elbow and inspecting him as if he was an exhibit in a museum of freaks. 'You're bleeding, you know.'

'I know,' he said, dismally.

'It's your fault for being so thin-skinned.'

'Thanks.'

'Never mind. Mummy will make it better.'

Then she reached out to him. When she touched his belly, he didn't resist. She moved her hand softly up and down and his breathing quickened. 'Do you like that, student boy?'

'Please don't call me that,' he whispered. His throat had thickened and talking was difficult. 'You need to stop now.'

'I can't. You know how it is, student boy. I've started, so I'll finish.' She looked at him as her hand stroked him. 'I'm powerless to resist. Or you are.'

'You can't,' he said.

'But I can. I am.' Her hand moving and moving.

Blood burned his face. Humiliation, shame, joy. It couldn't be all of them, but it was.

She paused and unbuttoned her pink cardigan. 'My, it's hot today. Now, what have we got here?' She removed the cardigan and pulled off her tee shirt with a flourish. 'A right pair of unlikely characters.'

He could see her nipples, pink and hard, poking through the bra's lacy fabric.

'Don't,' he said. 'It's wrong.'

'Oh, do shut up,' she smiled, unhitching the bra and letting it fall. 'Don't be such a prude. Now, what have we got *here*? Is this a good example of pathetic fallacy?'

Her hand, travelling south, found something, and, at first gently and then steadily, began to work.

They were downstairs by the time everyone came back.

'Are you two all right?' his mother asked, full of outdoor freshness.

'Of course we're all right,' Angie replied, with a sleepy half-smile. The buttons of her cardigan were done up wrong, but no-one seemed to have noticed.

His mum appraised them. 'Well, that's good. And your head?'

'My...?

'Migraine,' she prompted.

'Ah, yes. It's calmed down now. The pill helped.'

'Oh, that's a relief. And your essay, Henry?'

'Yes,' he said, flushing. 'It's, well, it's coming along nicely.'

Angie looked at him. 'I think he had trouble at first, but we got there in the end, didn't we, Henry? He did, I mean.'

His mother looked at her and nodded. 'Oh, well, that's good, then. All's well that ends well. Now, who'd like a nice cup of tea?'

She moved off briskly to organise the cups, saucers and plates of meringues for those who might be peckish.

When the guests had left, Henry wondered whether his mother had noticed the buttons or Angie's flushed cheeks. She probably had, because she noticed everything. But whether she had put two and two together, he would never know.

Up in his room there were scuffmarks on the carpet. On his desk lay the picture of the naked man. Meanwhile, the metal housing of his desk lamp was very hot because he'd left it on. He looked at his essay, abandoned mid-sentence. He had a pain and three scratch-marks where Angie had raked her nails over his chest, drawing blood.

He sat down and picked up his pen. The essay was asking him who was right in their conception of love. Was it, as the Trojans thought, a kind of divine transport that lifted you above the sordid conflict of tribal rivalry, or, as the Greeks believed, a delusional lapse into animal cravings? Henry still wasn't sure, but at least he had an idea now what he might say.

Chapter 47

From Russia with Love

Parties were such sweet sorrow. You had to become a better version of yourself. You had to force yourself into a pair of tight corduroys, styling your hair so it hid your spots, using your sister's deodorant so you smelt of something less offensive than the usual schoolboy funk. You also needed alcohol. And this meant asking your father, who was the gatekeeper to the adult world, for the substance without which you would fail.

His father had a drunk's unquestioning faith in the efficacy of booze. He thought drink an essential lubricant for the functioning of polite society. Humans couldn't communicate without it; love couldn't be made; babies couldn't be born, or treaties signed; friendships couldn't endure. The fact that he himself had no friends and became a monster when he drank entirely escaped him. So, when Henry announced that he had another party to go to, and that he was supposed to take alcohol and couldn't just drink his friends,' his father nodded, opening the doors of the liquor cabinet as though they were the doors to manhood itself. 'That should do you,' his father said, taking out a half-bottle of vodka and a bottle of a pink mixer called *Russchian*, a brand that had a certain Cold-War frisson to it. 'Don't tell your mother,' he added, tapping his nose conspiratorially.

Henry didn't.

And that was how they communicated now. Henry ignored his father except when he needed money, alcohol or a lift, and at that time his father would do what was required. If he didn't, Henry would become sullen and withdrawn. Henry made it plain how it would be from now on, because there was a Cold War on between them, too, and an emotional realpolitik held sway. If his father wanted any relationship at all, it would have to be like this: transactional.

To Henry's surprise, his father complied. He became a man who peeled off five-pound notes when Henry needed funds; a man who drove him places at improbable times and picked him up from unlikely locations. Even in the small hours, he would be there, sitting in the darkened car, waiting. Sometimes, when it was very cold, his father would wear his commissar's fur hat, the one that made him look like one of the stony-faced men in Red Square, those party faithfuls who stared impassively as the phallic warheads trundled past. And that was fitting, thought Henry, staggering out of a party happily drunk at 1am. All night, he'd swigged vodka and the vaguely communistic mixer his dad had given him, and here was his father come to collect him in the fancy-dress of the Russian Politburo. He was Leonid Brezhnev in a clapped-out Ford.

Henry, meanwhile, flying on booze and in love with the person that alcohol had made him, had decided that he approved of the world after all. Girls had loved him at that party, and now he loved his father, the one who'd given him the magic panacea of vodka and Russchian. His dad, with that funny hat perched on his bald head, was a friend at last, a comrade in arms.

'How did you get on?' his father asked, as Henry fell into the car and fumbled for the seatbelt.

'All right, Dad,' Henry slurred.

'And did the vodka help?'

'It helped.'

'That's good.'

Henry's brain was spinning, and he was finding the catch on the seatbelt an impossible puzzle. 'Thanks for picking me up.'

'That's all right.'

His father looked at him and nodded. He didn't ask who he'd met, or what he'd done, or how much he'd drunk, as Henry's mother would've done. There was no interrogation, no leading questions, no disapproval. He simply started the car and drove away through the vaguely Russian fog, while Henry lowered his head and, after a mile or two of attempting conversation, fell asleep.

Chapter 48

Les Misérables

At the next party, Henry met a girl who was very particular about her name. It was Karen as in 'car', not Karen as in 'carrier bag.' Karens were vulgar and commonplace; Kaarens were not. She wished this distinction to be understood, and Henry nodded, meekly.

'Kaaren as in car,' he mumbled, looking at her correctly-dressed form and doing a mental checklist: neat clothes, court shoes, hair centrally parted; make-up in primary colours from a child's paintbox. She didn't look much like a car. If she were a car, however, she would be a Daimler or a Rolls Royce. You couldn't put your feet on her velour-seating, or push a lolly stick into her ashtray.

It was not surprising that she objected when Henry, full of alcoholic bravado, took liberties. 'No, no tongues,' she said, pulling away. Henry withdrew his head and brought her face into focus. She looked like a sad Linda McCartney. He would have to behave more like a Beatle from now on if he was to have a chance. Then Henry remembered that he'd never wanted to be Paul; it was John he admired. In that case, he would need to woo a Yoko, but there were no Asian girls amongst the English dumplings, Celtic maids and Germanic giantesses at this party.

'What A-levels are you doing?' she asked, because they were having a conversation now. They were holding hands and, for some reason, this was an intimacy she didn't object to.

'English, French, and history,' he said. 'And art.' He added the latter even though it wasn't true. 'I may be an artist when I'm older. My mother's an artist.' This wasn't true either, obviously, but truth was for pedants.

Karen's eyes widened. 'Is she? What's her name? I might know her.'

Henry tried to remember. 'Rosalind Truffle,' he said. He noted the frown. 'Oh, she's not that famous in England yet. She's, um, French.' He knew one should always lie in multiples of three. It was in *Macbeth*.

'Your mother's *French*?'

'*Oui*,' he said, 'but not so you'd notice. She's lived here so long she speaks English like a native. Like you, in fact.'

'I'm half-German.'

'Oh.'

Karen frowned at a new thought. 'You must be fluent, then.'

'Pardon?'

'I mean, I'm surprised you need to study French for A-level, if your mum's French.'

He gave a Gallic shrug, wishing he had a cigarette to do something expressive with. 'Well, yes, French is easy for me, I admit. That's why I'm taking art as well.'

She nodded. 'Okay. And, um, what do you draw, or paint?'

He considered this carefully. 'Nudes,' he said, drawing a cello-shape in the air.

Karen nodded, then stared into the middle distance. She unstuck her palm and looked at her watch. He saw that the face of it was very small, and wondered if time was less important to girls.

'I need to be going,' Karen said, touching her hair.

He looked at her blankly. 'What?'

'My father's picking me up,' she said. '*Mon père*,' she added, helpfully.

'Your father?' He paused. 'Is he French?' He'd noticed that her accent was better than his.

'What?'

'I mean, there's no need to go so soon. The night is young.' He tried to remember the French phrase. *'La nuit est jaune.'*

She frowned. 'That means the night is yellow, doesn't it?'

He belched softly. 'Exactly. It's an idiom. A yellow night is like a blue moon. It doesn't happen very often. It's a time to drink and *faire l'armoire.'*

'L'amour.'

'That too.'

A distant bell rang, a blast of cold air entering the room. A booming voice, then a bulky form hovering beyond the frame of the door. 'Karen?'

'Coming, Dad.' She stood up and straightened her clothes, which didn't need straightening. 'Bye,' she mumbled, patting Henry's hand.

'Au reservoir,' he said, watching her walk away.

He found his dad's car under a streetlight. Henry's steps were unsteady. He saw that his father was still wearing the commissar's hat, but the hat was wrong now, because love was French, not Russian. His dad should have worn a beret. He already had the moustache and air of tired cynicism.

'How did you get on?' his father asked, as Henry opened the door.

'Oh,' Henry said, fumbling with his seatbelt. 'Not good.'

'Not good?'

'Non.'

'Why's that?'

Henry gave up on the seatbelt, which wouldn't click together. 'Oh, you know. The vodka didn't seem to help, somehow.'

His father nodded. 'Well, maybe vodka's not your drink,' he said, starting the car.

'What do you mean?'

'Only that you could try something else next time. Whiskey, for example.'

'Okay,' said Henry. 'Would it make any difference?'

His father shrugged. 'Try it and see.'

Chapter 49

Telephone

Henry stood in the room with the paintings of horses. It was always cold in there, whatever the season. It was the cold of candelabras and old wax candles and green embossed wallpaper. As he stood, he noticed that his hand was shaking. Despite this, he dialled the number. His mother had told him that a faint heart had never won a fair lady and he must grasp the nettle. So here he was, grasping it. Here he was, willing his heart not to be faint.

The phone rang for a while and there was a voice. It was an adult's voice: a mother's.

'Hello?'

Henry rushed out his words before he lost his nerve. 'Can I speak to Karen, please?'

The voice sounded cautious. 'Yes. Who's that, please?'

'It's Henry. Henry Truffle.' Mums were gatekeepers, he knew. They needed surnames, and one must be formal at such times.

'Just a minute,' she said. 'I'll see if she's free.'

He heard whispers in the background, then footsteps and the jostling sound of a phone being picked up.

'Yes?'

Her tone was cool and preoccupied, as if he'd interrupted something.

'It's Henry.'

'Henry...?'

‘We met at the party.’

‘The party?’

This was understandable; she must go to so many.

‘At Chris’ house. We spoke French. Um, my mum’s an artist.’

There was a pause. ‘Oh, yes. I remember now.’

There was static on the line. He pictured her hand holding the phone. Nail varnish of chipped avocado green.

‘I wondered if you wanted to meet up or something?’

There was another pause, as if this were an outlandish proposition. ‘Meet up?’

‘Yes. You know, the two of us. Meeting somewhere.’ In space and time, he mouthed.

Another pause. ‘Why?’

‘*Why?*’

‘I mean, what for?’

His heart did something strange in his chest. ‘To chat. You know.’ What did people normally do on dates? Eat lobsters? Knit cardigans?

‘Um, well, I’m quite busy with schoolwork at the moment,’ she said.

‘Yes, of course. I get a lot of homework, too.’

‘So, I don’t really have the time.’

This was perfectly understandable. The face of her watch had been so tiny. You couldn’t fit much time on it. But he wasn’t very big; she could fit him in.

‘Maybe next weekend, then? I’m flexible.’ Invisibly he mimed it, his infinite flexibility.

‘I have a hockey match.’

‘What, the whole weekend?’

‘Training one day, a game the other.’

He paused. ‘So, you’re not free at all?’

‘No.’

‘Not *ever*?’ He tried to laugh.

‘Not really. I’m so busy.’

‘Okay.’

He waited for some new idea to come; none did.

‘Sorry,’ she said, filling the silence. ‘It’s just not that convenient, what with hockey and everything. I don’t have the time to go out.’

‘And you’re sure?’

‘Quite sure. Sorry.’

She hung up.

Chapter 50

The Rosy Crucifixion

His mother had a collection of pills. There were sleeping pills, headache pills, anti-constipation suppositories, indigestion tablets and antidepressants, the doses written in pen on the boxes' sides. For years, doctors had dealt with her illnesses, real and imagined, and these were the remnants of her aborted courses of medication. There was enough here to kill an army, and Henry wasn't that. He took the ones he thought he needed: sleeping pills, paracetamol, the ancient pack of blue Valium.

He sat in his room, at the desk where he did his homework, and started his note. 'I don't want to go on,' he wrote, and looked at it. This was not a good way to begin, and Mr Muldoon wouldn't have approved. Where was the originality? Where was the spark of wit? He scratched it out, because he couldn't die on a cliché or mimic the phrasing of a dumb teenager in a film. He was aiming at pathos, but the words kept coming out wrong. 'My life's a failure,' he wrote next. 'It's all hopeless.' He watched the pen shape the feeble, shop-worn phrases, and as the phrases shaped him, he realised he'd become as laughable a cliché as everyone else. This didn't make the pain any less real. He finished his note and folded it, placing it in a plain envelope with 'Mum' on the outside.

He was allowing twelve hours; he would be dead by the time they found him. He would swallow all the pills. Twenty should be enough to do the job. He had his glass of water ready. His glass had always been half-empty; soon it would be completely so.

His mother's voice, interrogative, edged with irritation, came from downstairs. They didn't usually receive phone calls so late at night; it was an unwelcome intrusion of the outside world. Who would be so rude as to disturb them at this hour? He remembered the call that had announced the death of John's dad. Then it came again: the downstairs voice.

'Henry? It's *Francis* on the phone. Are you asleep?'

He set down the pills. His mother didn't like Francis; that much was clear from the way she inflected his name. Henry couldn't say he was asleep, because saying so would disprove it. If he remained silent, his mum would come clumping upstairs to check on him, and then she would discover what he was doing, and he would be undone. She would take the pills away and he would be forced to go on living, and he didn't want that.

'All right,' he said, putting his note and the pills in a drawer, closing it and going downstairs. 'I'm coming.'

He stood in the morgue of the front room. It was the best room, yet they hardly ever used it, and it never changed. There was an aura of trapped time. A silver candelabrum on the beeswax dining table. Jacobean chairs with uncomfortably knobbly backs. Half-burnt-out display candles. A second stereo, on which Joni Mitchell's *The Ladies of the Canyon* lay, silent. He'd left it there, forgetting to put it away last time he played it.

He held the white bone of the telephone to his ear. 'Hello, Francis,' he said.

The deep voice on the other end of the line was matey, its modulations oddly like his own. It was sometimes hard to work out who had imitated whom.

'All right, mate? What you up to?'

He took a breath. 'Nothing much. I'm just going to bed, actually.' Henry put his finger inside the curly telephone cable, its multiple rings encircling it.

'Bed? It's 9.30, you berk!'

'I'm tired.'

'Not surprised, mate. I've heard you've been pissing it up all over town. I'm just calling to see how you got on at that party.'

'What party?'

'What do you mean 'What party?' The one you went to, and I didn't. Chris Whatshisface's birthday, or whatever it was.'

'Oh, that.'

'Yes, *that.* Meet anyone nice?'

'Yes. No.'

'It can't be *both,* you moron. I bet it was crawling with nymphos.'

'No. Not exactly.'

'Well, who did you get off with, then? Not another girl with braces on her teeth?'

'No.'

'A dribbler? A boobless plank?'

'Nope.'

'A paraplegic in a wheelchair?'

'They were all out of those. I did try.'

'What, then? Not a paper-bag job? That must be it! A girl so pug-ugly you're ashamed to tell me!'

'No.'

'Who, then?'

Henry paused. 'No-one really. Just a girl who said 'No tongues' when I kissed her.'

'Oh, man!' Francis blew air into the receiver. 'Was she a nun or what? Or a lesbian? Or both? It goes with the word nun, as in 'none'. No sex. No touching. No tongues. It's in the catechism.'

Henry considered. 'Well, she was wearing a cross round her neck. She wore flat shoes and sensible clothes.'

'There you go! I told you, she's a bloody bride of Christ! A lesbian for Jesus! I've read about them. You've got no chance with that type, trust me.'

'Maybe not.'

'So, fill me in on the details. No-one's told me anything.'

They chatted then, and Henry began to laugh at the usual stuff boys laughed at. They made jokes about girls with bad nail-varnish; girls who didn't fall for you just because you'd decided they should; girls whose names must be pronounced this way and not that, or who fenced you off with crucifixes as if you were Count Dracula. Girls who preferred a hockey stick to you, and had homework, and tiny watches, and no time for the love-god that was Henry Truffle.

'She sounds like a joke, mate,' said Francis, sighing. 'No wonder she prefers her hockey stick. I expect she mounts it at bedtime. Is she a looker?'

Henry paused, inspecting the white rings of the telephone cord around his empurpled wedding finger. 'I'm not sure. She looks like a sad Linda McCartney.'

'A *what*?' He blew out more air. 'I thought you always fancied yourself as a John Lennon sort of geezer?'

'I do.'

'Well, then, Linda isn't for you, is she? You need to find a Yoko, mate.'

'I know. There weren't any at the party.'

'Go to more parties, then. You'll meet one in the end. Law of averages, man.'

They laughed. It reminded Henry of his dad. If vodka doesn't work, try whiskey.

In the end, Henry hung up and went back upstairs. He opened

the drawer and took out his note and the pills. He stared at them for a while and tried to remember how he'd been feeling before the phone call but could not. Then he picked up the pills and went back to his mum's room, replacing them in her medicine bag. Back in his room, he re-read his note and shook his head, as Mr Muldoon would have done, at the hackneyed phrasing. Then he tore the note into small pieces, and put them carefully in the bin.

Chapter 51

The Idea of Perfection

He met Jacquie at another party. She was fifteen, conventionally pretty and, it transpired, pretty conventional. She had blonde hair, a slim body and the face of a slightly idiotic doll. She was imprecise in some ways but not in others. She pronounced government as 'gover-ment' and called a library a 'lie-berry', but was strangely pedantic about the spelling of her own name. This, she explained when they first met, sitting against a wall as drunk kids reeled past them and *The Day the World Turned Dayglow* hammered from distant speakers, was spelled with a 'cq' instead of the usual 'ck'. 'Jackie with a k' was vulgar, whereas her own name, derived from the French, was *debonaire* and classy. Henry nodded. Jacquie with a cq; Jacquie Sea-Cucumber. It reminded him of Karen-as-in-car and was a worrying sign, but there was no crucifix around Jacquie's neck to ward him off. Besides, she seemed to like him. There would be no excuses about hockey and homework with this girl. He knew this because, after they'd talked and sipped warm, overly sweet wine, she'd let him kiss her, using his tongue. They spent the rest of the party doing little else. In the brief interlude in which Henry came up for air, he made up some nonsense about having Viking ancestors who'd come across the sea with horned helmets on their heads and hornier habits in their pants, a flight of fancy inspired by the fact he was wearing a pendant with a longship on it. Jacquie listened and smiled and pretended to believe him.

Meanwhile, the noise and stupidity of the party went on around them. At one point, a drunken 50cc biker boy called Stu came bumping down the stairs on his backside, drink in hand. At each step, beer foamed out of his can in frothy, ejaculatory jerks. Henry and Jacquie watched in silence. It was depressing to think anyone could get that drunk, and Stu seemed to think so too, for his face wore an uncomprehending look as he sat on the bottom step and looked around him.

Stu, who was at Henry's school and had once thrown Henry's Raleigh Hustler on its side, scratching the paintwork, had a huge scar on his face where he'd driven his bike through a plate glass window. This was karma, Henry felt. The boys had thought it funny ever afterwards to ask him if he'd cut himself shaving, to which he had only one response: piss off, you fuckers. At this party there was a rumour that an inebriated girl had canoodled with Stu in a darkened room, and that she had mistakenly kissed his scar instead of his mouth. Without corroborating evidence this was hard to verify. Then a drunken girl walked past with a bit of toilet paper skewered to the heel of her shoe, and someone said *she* was the girl who'd kissed the scar, and it all made sense.

Henry and Jacquie sat against the wall and drank their wine and watched the human zoo parading before them, and it was funny for a while — until it wasn't. Then Henry began to think that, like Jay Gatsby in the book he'd just read, he was outgrowing the need for parties. He had his Daisy now. It was time to move on. He must only hope that he wouldn't end up dead in a swimming pool.

On their first date, he went to the terraced house where she lived with her parents. He wore jeans and a white hooded jumper with holes under the arms. He hadn't made much effort because Francis said trying too hard on a first date was a mistake.

Jacquie had tried harder than him. She was in neatly pressed jeans and wore her freshly washed hair in springy clusters. She smiled like an estate agent as she showed him around the house. She had a mole on her face like Marilyn Monroe in *Some Like it Hot,* but there the similarity ended, unless you counted her breathless laugh.

Her parents were out. This was a good thing, because Henry wasn't keen on parents. You had to woo them as well, and he didn't want to do that yet, not when Francis had said he shouldn't even woo Jacquie. He should just play it cool.

Henry stood in the lounge and looked around him. There was an illuminated tank in which tropical fish flickered back and forth. Henry observed that most were flat and had eyes on the side of their heads. He realised he had never really looked carefully at fish before. He saw that some had frills and trailed lacy bits. They were fussy in a flouncy, feminine way, while others were like tiny restless sparks. 'Nice fish,' he said. Mr Muldoon had told them never to use the word 'nice' because its real meaning was 'precise', but Muldoon wasn't there now.

'Yes,' said Jacquie Sea-Cucumber. 'We like them, anyway.'

Henry looked at the ornaments and pictures on the walls. They were mementoes from Spain and Greece: sad-looking donkeys pulling carts; novelty ashtrays; objects made from shells with eyes on stalks. It was difficult to talk about things bought without any taste or discernment, but one mustn't be snobbish on a first date. Tropical fish were easier.

'Is that an angelfish?' he asked, turning back to the tank.

She smiled. 'That's a neon guppy. And that's a cory over there. That yellow one with bulgy eyes is a goby.'

'I thought the Gobi was a desert?' he said.

'No, it's a fish. Different spelling.'

'Ah,' he said, nodding.

They watched the mindless circulation of fish.

'Can we feed them?' he asked after a while.

'I've done that. If you feed them too much, they die.'

'Oh.' He pointed to a fish at random. 'Um, I like that one best.'

'Yes. It's another goby.'

'A desert fish,' he said.

She ignored his joke.

'Some gobies camouflage themselves. Others have suction pads on their bodies and can stick to a rock. One type makes a clicking sound by grinding its teeth together.'

'My dad does that at night.'

'If you look,' she went on, 'you can see that some move about by using their fins, not their tails.'

'Ah.' Henry wondered what the human equivalent of moving with your fins would be. Whatever it was, Francis did it. Moving without appearing to try.

'If you have several in a tank, the weaker ones seek protection from the dominant one. They're quite territorial.'

'Are they?'

'Yes. They're a bit like people.'

'My mouth doesn't gulp like that,' he said, nodding, 'unless I'm drinking.'

'But that's what they're doing. They're gulping water. That's how they get oxygen.'

'Oh, right.' He stretched his arms over his head, for this was boring. Later, he would have to tell Francis that there'd been no sex on their first date. Instead, Jacquie Sea-Cucumber had given him a lecture on fish.

'You've got holes under your arms,' she observed.

He'd forgotten. 'Oh, yes,' he said, lowering them. 'It's my mum's jumper. I borrowed it.'

She frowned. 'You wear your mum's clothes?'

'Only some of them. Her jumpers fit me. She's quite tall.'

'Oh.'

The clock on the wall ticked louder than before.

'I'll make us a drink,' Jacquie said. 'What would you like?'

'Coffee, please.'

'Coffee it is.'

Henry waited in the lounge and listened to the kettle roaring. The house smelled of ready-rub tobacco and furniture polish. There was a packet of St Bruno tobacco on a table. Henry's father smoked Embassy No. 5 with the coat of arms on the front, or Benson and Hedges Special Filter in the gold packet. Embassy was like the place his father worked, and number five reminded him of his mother's bottle of Chanel perfume. Gold was the salary his father brought home. Ready rub was for people who put their cigarettes behind their ears. Jacquie's dad was a bus driver. Henry had never met a bus driver, except the man who'd driven him and his grandma to the whist drive when he was a boy.

Jacquie came back with the drinks, and they sat and sipped them. She asked about his A-levels and he asked about her O-levels. He didn't lie this time. He didn't say his mother was French or an artist. He was trying to be real.

'Can I use your bathroom?' he asked after a while, because real people did that.

'Of course. It's upstairs. You can't miss it.'

He went up to the landing and missed it, because all the doors looked the same, and he opened one that was a bedroom. Then he found the door with a wooden plaque that said YER TIZ. The door was ajar, and he saw the base of a sink and a pink, fluffy mat. The toilet had a knitted cosy on top. Henry lifted the seat the way his mother had taught him, and urinated. Then he flushed and washed his hands, looking in the mirror. He practised a few expressions in the glass, but none of them was particularly convincing. Then he saw the toothpaste. He took the cap off and squeezed some onto his finger and rubbed his teeth with it. Then he gargled, slooshed and spat. Just in case.

When he went downstairs, he asked Jacquie what the plaque on the toilet door meant. Jacquie's parents had things on their walls from Greece, Turkey and Spain, and he thought it might be a phrase translated from Arabic or Moorish. 'Yer Tiz? Oh, you know. "Here it is."' She pronounced it in a West Country accent.

'Oh,' he said. He knew what his mother would think of people who had a plaque on their toilet door bearing a phrase like Yer Tiz in phonetic English.

They went to a park where the river sparkled, and dogs yapped, and a toy sailboat on a lake floated over its own reflection. Henry and Jacquie held hands. Her hands were manicured and had clear varnish over filed, shapely nails. She had small hands with shop-girl nails. They were travel-agent nails; secretary-holding-a-phone nails. Nonetheless, her hands fitted his perfectly, just as she, with her smallness and slightness, fitted him.

Over the next few weeks, he found out about her life. She had a part-time job in Woolworths. She worked there on Saturdays, eating in her break the sort of food he didn't approve of — pork pies, Mars Bars, potato crisps. She loved her parents and doted on her dog, a Yorkshire terrier who had a habit of getting grass seeds wedged up his penis when he went for walks in the park, a misfortune that necessitated endless visits to the vet. Henry had almost made a joke about needing to visit the vet himself because he had seed wedged up his own penis, but he thought better of it. It was the kind of joke he would have told Francis.

Chapter 52

Sidekick

Francis was curious about Henry's new relationship, and Henry was happy to talk about it. He sometimes preferred his description of what had happened with Jacquie Sea-Cucumber to the event itself. Things that had been dull or humiliating achieved the high gloss of hilarity in the retelling. Henry kept nothing back, and it was odd, because he'd never liked sharing in Ma Bartlett's lessons. Between friends, however, anything was possible.

Henry told his stories and Francis listened. The stories gave Henry a power over his friend, as if their roles were reversed; and if the stories weren't quite the truth, it didn't matter, because no story could ever be.

Henry told Francis about Jacquie Sea-Cucumber.

He told him that it was lovely to peel her from her underwear in the creaking-floorboard silence of her room. It was lovely to taste her cold, salty, goose-pimpled, sea-green flesh while her parents were downstairs watching TV, knowing nothing but suspecting everything. Her father, Henry explained, was a bald and sun-baked bus-driver who made oddly Shakespearean comments whenever Henry left the room. 'I'll see you *anon* then, Henry,' he said, winking, for it was one man of the world speaking to another. Her mother, however, had the red nose and sour face of the Queen of Hearts. She turned to stare at Henry when he left the room with Jacquie, because Henry was the Knave of Hearts, stealing the tarts and taking them up to the bedroom to eat in private, while the stereo played to cover the movement of the bed. And if the Queen didn't demand Henry's head as he rose to go to that room to 'listen to music,' she did give him one of her 'looks,' because she knew a ruse when she heard one. The father merely smoked his fag, rubbing his bald forehead with a gnarled, bus-driver's hand before going back to the TV, because there was nothing new under the sun, and Jack must have his Jill, and naught must go ill.

It was all right once they were upstairs. There, the nice and dutiful daughter became Jacquie Sea-Cucumber. She was as cool as one, and when she'd disrobed, she smelled of the sea and sea-urchins and rock pools and the inside of a crab's pink shell...

Francis sighed. They were in his lounge and the anecdote had taken an unexpectedly long-winded turn. 'Enough of the literary bollocks,' he said, removing the cushion from his lap. 'Get to the point! Did you do it or not? *That's* the question.'

Henry blinked. 'No, of course not.'

'Why not?'

'Um, well, I couldn't exactly do it when the parents were there, could I? They would've known. And the Sea-Cucumber wouldn't have allowed it.'

Francis sighed. 'Bummer, man.' He paused, frowning. 'When am I going to meet her, anyway, this girlfriend of yours? It's all very well *describing* stuff, but I don't even know what she looks like.' His face was vaguely aggrieved; however much Henry shared, it would never be enough.

'This weekend,' Henry said. 'We can meet up then.'

'All right, mate,' Francis said, smiling. 'Now we're in business.'

They met at Francis' house, and they soon fell into an easy rapport. It was another triangle, another three without jealousy. Francis hugged

Jacquie and she was almost crushed by his towering, bear-like form. Then they laughed and sat on the sofa and drank tea. After a while, to escape the prying eyes of Francis' mother who was hovering nearby, they went for a walk in the park, the three of them strolling arm in arm, with Francis' dogs off their leads, the big lumbering Airedale in the distance, the tiny poodle at their heels. And it worked, this *ménage a trois,* because Jacquie was both catalyst and aphrodisiac. The friends were more attractive to each other when Jacquie was there: the conversation sparkled; the wit flowed. And Henry knew Jacquie was happy, because those words almost rhymed, and because she smiled, playfully cuffing Francis' arm whenever he said something rude. Francis flirted with her, and that was all right, and she flirted back, and that was all right too. Two into three did go, and there was no remainder.

One day, when it was just the two of them, Henry told Francis about how men had once sworn fidelity to each other in a blood-brotherhood. Henry had found this idea in a book by DH Lawrence, and it had appealed to him, this pledge between men, this pact that was solemn and formal and like a sexless marriage. Henry and Francis were in the park again with Otto and Sheba, the latter cantering like a warhorse around the park's perimeter.

'Explain,' Francis demanded. 'You realise that Lawrence was a nutter, don't you? Although I enjoyed watching *Women in Love* on TV. You know, the Ken Russell thing? Mad movie. There's this huge scene where two men wrestle in the nude in front of an open fire for like half an hour. It's totally insane.'

Henry nodded. Then he told him how the two characters in the book had discussed cutting their arms and rubbing the wounds together, because that would make them one blood. Lawrence had called this a *blutsbrüderschaft.*

'You'd get septicaemia,' Francis said, frowning. 'That's all that would happen there. And you'd probably die.'

Then he went off to hunt for Sheba, who'd disappeared into the undergrowth. He whistled and called, whacking the nettles with a stick. Sheba was a loner like him, but she always came back in her own time. And that was why Francis cried when, six months later, Sheba fell ill with cancer, and he had to take her to the vet to be put down.

Francis' mum, who was unsentimental about dogs, refused to do it. 'You take her, Francis,' she said. 'She's your dog. You sort her out.'

Francis put the old Airedale in the van sloshing with great drums of cleaning chemicals and drove her to her appointment with doom. Henry was there too, because even though it was a school day, that's what friends were for. You had to be there at the bitter end, even if the end was a dog's.

When they arrived, they were shown through to the surgery. Francis lifted Sheba onto the steel table, and she stood with her tail between her legs and her shoulders hunched. 'It's all right,' Francis whispered, patting her. Then the vet shaved a patch on the dog's leg and slid the needle under the skin. The dog yelped in indignant surprise, then her legs buckled, and she slumped onto the table. As she lay there, a slow flood of urine came from her rear end and formed a widening puddle. 'I'm sorry,' Francis said.

It wasn't clear who he was talking to.

The vet nodded. 'Oh, that's all right. It often happens. We'll clear it up, don't worry.'

The boys patted the dead dog for a while, then thanked the vet and went out. They paid the girl in reception and went back to the van. It was parked on the narrow road, two wheels up on the kerb. It looked a bit like a dog lifting its leg and pissing. Francis bent over the wheel cried quietly, while Henry sat there embarrassed, because he'd never seen his friend, who was so big and manly, weeping like this. 'I'm sorry,' he said at last. Then a car went past, and the van rocked in the wind. There was a thump and a clatter and after a while they realised what had happened. The car had hit the wing mirror and broken it, and wires were hanging out. 'Shit,' said Francis.

When they got back, they had to explain to Francis' mum how the mirror had got broken, and how it wasn't their fault, because they were just sitting there doing nothing when the accident happened. And the mother looked at them as if she regretted not taking the dog herself, because you couldn't trust two boys to do a thing properly.

The next day Henry was given a detention for his unauthorised absence. He tried to explain but they weren't interested. Going to the vet with a friend in school time wasn't moral support, they said; it was truancy.

Chapter 53

Binocular Vision

Her parents were going away, so Henry and Jacquie would finally do it.

It was a fact that Henry's knowledge of sex remained painfully small. Apart from his singular encounter with Angie, it was limited to what he'd read about in books or seen on TV. In the few magazines he'd looked at, there was no actual sex, just static models in postures of lonely abandon. The absent man was the viewer, the one whose actions must be imagined and manually simulated. What happened when bodies came together in space and time was a mystery of mechanics beyond Henry's imagining. On TV, it was suggested rather than shown: in the bouncing of a car's suspension and the fogging of its windows; in giggles under blankets and the coy slow-fade; or the grimmer realities depicted in the black and white films he watched at weekends: the women who got pregnant in *A Taste of Honey* and *Saturday Night and Sunday Morning*, and who explained, by the factory gates or in the shadow of the gas works, that they would have this child anyway, and to hell with the consequences. Because that was the other thing about sex: unless you were careful, it produced unwanted babies. And that was why Henry had in his pocket now the items that had cost him a world of suffering to get hold of.

'Have you got them?' Jacquie asked, as she opened the door. She was dressed in her weekend-schoolgirl garb: narrow-fit, stone-washed jeans, thin sweater, small gold chain. She had a spot on her chin and her skin was greasy. Her hair was full of its usual idiotic blonde bounce.

'Yes, of course.'

'Did it go all right?'

'Yes.'

He stood in the hallway that smelled of ready-rub tobacco and the sweetish scent of laundry. It was her parents' smell, for he was in enemy territory, armed only with a plan for seduction and a packet of condoms.

'You sure you're okay?' She touched his arm. 'You got them all right?'

'It was fine. No problem.' He tapped his pocket.

'You weren't embarrassed?'

'Of course not.'

The truth was that he'd spent thirty minutes in the chemist filling his basket with things he didn't need — shampoo, soap, vitamins, a large bag of wheatgerm — to cover the packet at the bottom. He had to hide his intentions, because there was nothing more humiliating than a teenager in search of sex and the products to make that sex possible. Despite hiding the condoms under other more humdrum items, he was convinced the other customers knew what was there and what he planned to do with them. His face was hot, his heart jittery. He had already made many needless circles around the shelves, and people were looking at him strangely. He needed to act.

He was at the counter, and the girl on the till was pretty, which made it worse. She rang up the items, tapping the keys with a pianist's elegant fingers. She had slender arms and a silver bracelet on her wrist. Her hair was ash-blonde, and she wore it loosely over her shoulders. In her white pharmacy jacket, she looked pure and unruffled. He looked at her for a moment and took in her cool beauty: the high cheekbones with a faint scar on one of them; the knowing look in her grey-blue eyes. Finally, she stooped into his basket and prised out the object that had become snagged in the mesh. He glimpsed the swell of her breast and the top of a lacy bra. Jacquie Sea-Cucumber didn't have breasts as nice as that; she had measly schoolgirl breasts, and pimples on her chest. Henry watched, his cheeks burning while the counter-girl tugged at the thing that was stuck there. When it came free, she placed it on the countertop and rang it up on the till, then said the amount in a matter-of-fact voice. She put the condoms in the bag along with everything else. Her eyes rested on him for a moment as he fumbled for the money in his jeans pocket, then her gaze shifted away; it was nothing to do with her what he bought, or what he intended to do with it. This was a commercial transaction, that was all.

He paid and left the shop, and it was done.

He cycled up the hill to Jacquie's house, thinking about the things he'd bought. The toothpaste and other items he could stuff in a cupboard and hope his mother didn't notice. Then he thought of the condoms. He'd only seen used ones, because you could hardly not see them. Rubber johnnies were everywhere. You found them in hedgerows, in gutters, and at the foot of walls; you found them in parks and laybys; or draped limply over the back of public benches. They were dirty ice-pop wrappers; seedy, amputated glove-fingers. And now he had a pocketful of fresh ones.

'Shall we eat something?' Jacquie asked, as he stood in the hallway, thinking this would be his last night on earth as a virgin. In a few moments, he would walk through the portal dividing boys from men and know what everything had been leading to up, everything the poets and novelists and movie-makers had told him about for as long as he could remember. He would be joining that ragged brigade of young seducers: Paul in *Sons and Lovers*; William Fisher in *Billy Liar*; Troilus in *Troilus and Cressida*. It was oddly surprising to him that the house didn't reflect his excitement and sense of occasion. There was no bunting, no Christmas lights. Jacquie hadn't even showered or done herself up. She looked tired and uglier than usual, with her exhausted Saturday-shopgirl face. He caught the faint odour of sweat and money.

'I've had dinner,' he said, because he had.

She nodded. 'Well, I haven't. I've been working all day. I haven't stopped.' She made a tired gesture with her hand.

He nodded. 'All right,' he said.

'Are you sure you don't want to eat anything?'

'I'm sure,' he said.

'Okay, then.'

He stood in the overly lit kitchen of scrubbed zinc draining boards and worktops while she made herself salad, carefully slicing the cucumber, tomatoes and celery and then washing the lettuce in a colander. Then she removed a pork pie from its plastic wrapping. He gritted his teeth. She ate far too many pork pies for his liking, and had the faintest shadow of double a chin. In thirty years, she would look like her mother. He was irritated by what she would be in the future, because it was a future he might be part of.

'Come on,' she said when she was done, as if he were the one holding her back. 'Let's go through to the lounge.'

They sat in front of the television while she ate. She chewed each mouthful carefully and minutely and, as she did so, her cheeks bulged like a hamster. She was making her food last as long as possible, eking it out. Finally, she could delay no longer. 'Would you like coffee?' she said, setting down her knife and fork primly, like a pair of metal legs together at the ankles.

'No, thanks.'

'I'm having tea.'

Jesus, he thought. 'All right, then.'

She brought in the mugs and set them on coasters. Then they drank their drinks, and she made that hollow swallowing noise she always made when she was nervous. It was a sound he hated. Finally, she set her cup down. 'Shall we go up?' she said.

She lay on the bed, cold and naked as an offering. When Henry tried to pull the curtains, she said no, because then the neighbours would guess what they were doing. Her neighbours knew everything, she said.

'What neighbours?' He stood at the window, peering out.

'The people over the way. Don't stand there, or they'll notice you.'

He could see no-one, just a quiet road of cats and parked cars.

He turned. Her body was unappealing, lying on the bed like that, stiff and pale. He thought of cod on a slab. 'Do they spy on you, then?'

She shook her head. 'No, but they know Mum and Dad are away for the weekend, and your bike's outside. If the curtains are pulled, they'll guess what's happening.'

'Okay, then.'

He took his clothes off, keeping to one side of the window. Then he crawled over to the bed on his hands and knees. If he stood up, his naked back would be visible to some imaginary man with binoculars.

It was cold in the room and the beam from the streetlight came in and made a yellow patch on the carpet. It made a path towards the sacrificial victim. He sat on the bed and took the thing out of the box. He used his teeth to break the sealed foil, then pulled out the slippery ring of rolled-up rubber. It had a droopy teat at one end. Then he slid it on and adjusted its position, following the instructions on the box, leaving a space at the end for his ejaculated seed. Then he smelled his hands. They stank of surgical rubber, and he remembered fixing punctures on his Raleigh Hustler. He looked at his manhood in its comical disguise: a villain with his nose snubbed in a woman's stocking.

'Have you put it on right?'

'I think so.'

'Make sure it doesn't come off inside me when… you know.'

'I'll try.'

'Come on, then.'

He leaned across and touched her with his evil, rubber-smelling hands.

She winced. 'Your hands are so *cold*!'

'Sorry.'

'Blow on them, then.'

He did so, chafing them on his legs. 'I think they're okay now,' he said after a while, knowing it had made no difference.

'All right,' she said, her face set, stoical.

They struggled for a while, but she was as stiff and lifeless in his arms. If there was a portal in her body's lower half, he couldn't enter it. Someone had sewn it shut.

After a while, Henry rolled off. 'It's useless,' he said, lying back.

She cried gently in the dark. 'I'm sorry,' she said.

'It's not your fault,' he said, although it blatantly was. That nonsense about the window. Her insistence on lying on the bed and not in it. The open curtains and the yellow stripe of the streetlamp.

Henry closed his eyes. He thought about the till-girl in the chemist. She'd been a pretty girl with nice breasts and a lacy bra. It would have been easier with her, he knew. Because Jacquie wasn't what he'd imagined. She wasn't cool as a cucumber. She was scared of her neighbours and of her parents finding out. Her room still had kids' toys in it: unicorns and teddies and old dolls with staring eyes and fixed grins. And that was where it had gone wrong. She was a child.

Henry cycled home through the night streets, standing on the pedals and pumping his knees, riding recklessly and swerving around parked cars he almost hit in his blindness. He was full of rage and passion on account of the sex he had not had and would probably never have, and he swore into the dark and cursed condoms and girls and neighbours with telescopes and the TV and books that had said it would be different. When he got home his mum was still up and hovering in her dressing gown as if she knew what had happened. When she asked if he was all right he said of course he bloody well was and walked straight through the kitchen and up to bed.

Chapter 54

Fat is a Feminist Issue

After the disaster, Henry avoided both Jacquie and Francis for a while. He stayed at home, sulking, eating his mother's food, and doing his homework. Having a girlfriend hadn't solved everything. It hadn't solved anything.

He consoled himself with food. If once he'd denied himself, now he over-indulged, and his mother welcomed his return to the fold. He'd been 'a stranger' for a while, she said, always out, always brooding and never wanting his dinner. Now that he was around the house again, she had someone to cook for and could resume her culinary obsessions. So, she cooked, and they ate, and it was wholefoods one week and fancy desserts the next; then it was soups or casseroles, or vegetables cooked in the hissing time-bomb of the pressure cooker.

Then his mother read a book by Germaine Greer and everything changed. Suddenly cooking was a matter of oppression and exploitation. It exasperated her now, because there were so many other things she could be doing with her life, like walking the dogs. She bought time-saving gadgets in solidarity with the sisterhood. A freezer, she decided, was the first thing that would set her free. And for a while it did, the family dutifully eating warmed-up chicken pies, cod fillets and parcels of yellow goo called crispy pancakes, things that took minimal effort to prepare. Instead of fancy desserts they had rock-hard ice-cream, their spoons glancing off the lunar surface of the raspberry ripple and peach melba. They ate Arctic Rolls and frosty Black Forest Gateaux. Everything seemed Germanic or Nordic. The future, it seemed, was frozen.

Then a microwave joined the freezer. Raw potatoes, wrapped in paper towels, revolved on the illuminated plinth, wobbling unsteadily and emitting an ominous hiss. Ten minutes later, there was a ping, and the door flew open on a cloud of steam and potatoes that were almost edible. 'We need to turn them over,' his mother would say, touching them with her nail before popping them back. She smiled and patted the microwave, as if it signified that the old way of cooking was over for good.

Despite these changes, his mother wasn't happy, and the migraines returned. Her fits of dieting, where she subsisted on packet soups, explosive bran-and-prune mixture and salads, returned. If she was on a diet, they were, too. 'It's important not to be full after eating,' she declared in a new spirit of evangelism, when they complained they were still hungry. 'A meal isn't supposed to fill you up.' They looked at each other quizzically, because everything she said was a paradox now. In the past, a meal wasn't over until you loosened your belt and pushed back from the table with a groan. Now she'd changed her mind. 'You should leave twenty percent of your stomach empty,' she advised. 'That's how they eat in Japan — and they know how to eat over there.' She had begun to threaten them with cultures that weren't their own. 'You never see a fat Japanese person,' she added.

'What about Sumo wrestlers?' their father said, poking at an unappetising salad with his fork. 'They're huge.'

'Yes,' his mother said bitterly, 'but they get fat on purpose.'

And because this was irrefutable, and because none of them could be bothered, this ended the argument.

Sometimes, because she felt misunderstood, Henry's mother

threatened them with the prospect of divorce. She would pack a bag, run from the house and head for Grandma Ivy's, only for Henry's father to go out in the car and bring her home. She would come back with her face set in the expression of martyrdom. This was the look she wore in restaurants when the food wasn't to her satisfaction, but their father refused to complain. She was powerless, her face said. She had only come back for the sake of the children. Let them be grateful.

His mother's outbursts formed part of a pattern. She'd begun returning to shops the things she didn't like. She would refuse to leave, even though the shopkeeper ignored her, or said no refund could be made for goods that weren't faulty. But she had listened to radio programmes about consumer rights, and she demanded satisfaction. The stand-offs usually ended with their mother walking out of the shop with her nose in the air; because even if she hadn't got her money back, she'd scored a moral victory. No-one was quite sure what this moral victory was, and it was around this time that Henry began to hear the word *menopause* spoken, as if that explained it all.

His father didn't believe in the menopause, or if he did, didn't think it could be used as an excuse. He began to rebel against their calorie-free cuisine. Every night, he nibbled his snacks of crisps and peanuts, consuming them along with his mugs of whiskey. As a consequence, he grew steadily fatter, as Henry knew to his cost. On a recent holiday, they'd been forced to share a room, and one morning he had seen his father's naked body. His flesh, as he hopped on one foot attempting to pull on his too-small Y-fronts, was flabbily elastic, his chest breasted around a central draggle of hair. His belly was a pale dome, his red penis hanging down like something in a primitive cave-painting. It was pitiful.

But if Henry could pity his father physically, he couldn't in any other way. Once, when Alice came back late at night, she made the mistake of entering through the kitchen where his father sat with his whiskey and snacks. From his bedroom, Henry could hear his father's voice, his vowels honied with booze, his sister's replies in weary counterpoint. Then he heard the door close and his sister's feet coming slowly upstairs. Finally, there came the bellowed word, 'Bitch!' resounding through the house.

Alice was engaged to be married now. She was working in a bank in London, her long Alice in Wonderland hair replaced by a feathered crop with brassy highlights. Her voice had changed, too. Now she spoke a form of flattened cockney, an accent she deemed more 'real' than middle-class English. She had taken up smoking, along with a boy called Keith who was training to be an electrician. He was to be her husband, because although he looked like a boy, he was in fact a man of twenty-one.

Henry wasn't sure he liked Keith. He had bog-brush hair, a prominent Adam's apple and a nervous swallow. He'd begun to hang out at Henry's house, sitting in a chair in his platform shoes, open-necked shirt and medallion. Keith drove a car and could fix engines. He played Alice Cooper on his car stereo and flung empty cigarette packets from his car window, spinning them so they travelled far into hedgerows and gardens. He was practical, common and a bit of a yob. Henry wasn't sure he wanted him as a brother-in-law.

Keith and Alice would sit up late in Henry's lounge watching TV. Once, when Henry opened the kitchen hatch to offer them coffee, he saw Keith's feet hanging off the end of the sofa, toes downward. Then he saw that the feet were moving.

'They're doing it,' Henry thought, closing the hatch. 'Right here in my own house. And I haven't even gone to bed.'

He knew he shouldn't hate his sister for that. Alice was only doing what he'd tried and failed to do in someone else's house. But he did hate her. His sister was cheapening herself. And if she was cheapened, Henry was cheapened, too.

'That Keith boy isn't of our class,' said Grandma Ivy, expressing what everyone except Alice thought. 'He's not suitable.'

But Alice and Keith didn't care what Grandma Ivy thought. They wanted to get married, and nothing, and no-one, would stand in their way.

Chapter 55

Zero Shades of Grey

Television could still bring them together as nothing else could. Henry and his sisters were watching *The Waltons*, a programme that depicted a family as unlike theirs as they could imagine. They liked *The Waltons*. Their favourite bit was the theme tune and the ending where John-Boy summed up the events and added his own homespun moral to the day's proceedings. The programme always closed on a picture of the house, with a window glowing and the stillness of the evening and the throbbing of crickets. Then came the goodnights, the names double-barrelled and strange in their Americanness:

'Goodnight, Jim-Bob.'

'Goodnight, Mary Ellen.'

'Goodnight, John-Boy.'

This was followed by two fluted notes on a mouth organ and three high ones on a glockenspiel — ding, dong, ding. These sounds were the sonic equivalent of the stars that hung in the idealised sky.

Their mother loved *The Waltons* too, and liked to mimic the southern accents in her *Gone with the Wind* voice, but she wasn't there. Grandma Ivy had phoned complaining of breathlessness, and their mother had gone to visit her. This was the sort of thing that happened now, and it was better it happened at Grandma's than at theirs, because there was nothing you could do when Grandma had attacks like that.

In the TV show, when Grandma Walton had had a stroke, she had come back almost as good as new, just slightly damaged with her facial expression a little frozen. Their own grandma had survived two World Wars and was strong. She would be okay.

The programme ended and the phone rang. After a while, the hatch slid back and their father's bald head appeared in the gap. 'Mum's just called,' he said in a TV announcer's voice. 'She says Grandma collapsed after an asthma attack.' He paused. 'And she thinks she's dead.'

He looked at them, and they looked at him, but didn't say anything else; there was no elaboration, just the headline. Then he closed the hatch, and they went back to watching the television.

It was *The Black and White Minstrel Show* now. White men in makeup were pretending to be black men. One was kneeling and singing about his Mammy. His white gloves were like the ones Grandma wore on hot days. Mammy, the man sang. My dear old Mammy. My heartstrings are tangled around Alabammy. The white gloves quivered and his mouth made an upside-down shape and you could have sworn he was crying even though his make-up wasn't running. When the programme ended, the children looked at each other again but still didn't say anything. There was too much to say and nothing to say at all, and in any case that black and white man's face had said it for them, so they turned the TV off and went back to their rooms.

Chapter 56

The Beautiful Room is Empty

His mother told them how it was. His grandmother blue-lipped and staggering to the car, a look of terror in her eyes. Can't breathe, she'd said. Oh dear. Then sitting in the car and grabbing his mum's hand, then slumping as if something had snapped or broken inside her. Then his mum driving through rush-hour traffic to the hospital with the dead woman sitting beside her. His mother could have spared them that picture, but she wasn't one to stint on details. What she had suffered, they must suffer too.

When Henry heard all this he went and sat in his bed and read *Murder in the Cathedral* by TS Eliot. Meanwhile, the females in the house made tea and talked in the kitchen. And then, Oh my God, where's Henry? they wondered, finding him at last in his place of refuge. We suddenly realised you were all alone up here, they cried, not understanding that this was where he wanted to be. They thought you absolved grief by talking and talking, but he just wanted to be left alone with the silence and TS Eliot, who expressed pain better than all their witless witterings. That was what literature was for: to say what stupid people could not.

Like the women of Canterbury, Henry wanted to pass unobserved and grieve in that way, but it wasn't allowed. Everything must be made public. Maybe that's why his father had disappeared, going for a walk in the dark God knows where. He couldn't stand it either.

Henry helped his mother empty his grandma's flat, although he did more watching than actual helping. He tried not to breathe, because the air still bore a trace of his grandma's smell, a smell of cooking and lavender. That smell scared him now. He didn't want the odour of the dead inside him.

The home of a dead person was different. It was emptier and colder, the walls further apart. Everything had a defunct look, and the shine had gone off things. The TV looked as if it had never been turned on. The corridor was wider without his grandmother's broad shape occupying it. Her trinkets — porcelain horses, a miniature wheelbarrow holding ceramic flowers, photos of forgotten relatives in silver frames — all sat meaninglessly on shelves. It didn't seem polite to look at them.

As they tidied up, Henry saw that the dead lived on in the stuff they left behind. A comb with white hairs caught in the teeth. A toothbrush with a reef of dried paste on the handle. The drawers and wardrobes full of clothes, all smelling of an old lady – faded floral dresses, frumpy cardigans, outmoded jackets. Henry followed his mother, trailing behind her with the dustpan and brush, or dragging the hoover on its long cord. There were things to be vacuumed away, or put straight, or erased. White hairs on a pillowslip. An upside-down slipper. The phone pulled to the edge of the table. Half a cup of cold tea with a scum on top. An address book on the floor, its pages sprawled open after that last desperate phone call.

The kitchen looked wrong, somehow. The saucepans and kettle stood awkwardly while the clock drew circles in the air, as if waiting for something. There was a folded J-cloth on the edge of the sink, and half-empty jars of tea and coffee on the worktop. You didn't want to touch any of it now. It would contaminate you.

His mother had brought her own flask of coffee, because she didn't want to drink a dead woman's Nescafé, even if it was Gold

Blend. 'Don't you want anything?' she asked.

No, he said. He didn't. He just wanted to go home, but that wasn't allowed. Respect must be paid, duties performed.

They saw to all the things that must be done: putting the rooms straight, wiping surfaces, stuffing clothes into bags. You couldn't keep them, his mother explained. He looked at all the clothes, useless on their hangers smelling of mothballs, the boxed and bracketed shapes of the person who wasn't there. You could only get rid of them. You couldn't keep a dead person's relics in your house. It would drive you mad.

Then, because his mother was tired, she asked him to deal with the food and kitchen stuff. This meant throwing more things away. Henry opened cupboards and biscuit tins and looked at the flapjacks, brandy snaps and fig rolls. He was hungry but couldn't touch them. Instead, he tipped them all in the bin. He opened the cutlery drawer and bagged up the stainless steel, the small knives with handles of yellow bone, the nutmeg grater, the hallmarked silver. There was a set of fish knives and tiny mustard spoons, all museum pieces and junk-shop curios, all bric-a-brac for jumble sales.

Henry picked up his grandmother's address book. He opened it and turned the pages. Names and numbers had been scribbled out and new ones written above. He didn't know who any of these people were. His grandmother's life branched off in too many directions for them to follow, and most of the people in that book were dead now, his mum said. Put it in the bin, she told him, so he did. There were things written on bits of paper — shopping lists, library books to get out, reminders. *Ask milkman for extra pint. Send Mim card. Make doctor's appt about knee. Anything by Catherine Cookson.* He noticed that her calligraphy was loopy and old-fashioned because someone had once taught her copperplate. Henry thought about keeping these written things as souvenirs, but his mother had said they must be ruthless, so the scraps of paper joined the address book and the fig rolls in the black bin-bag.

Then his mother came in and gave him a damp cloth. She reminded him of the dustpan and brush. He mustn't stand around gawping. So, Henry made himself useful. He swept the dead bees and flies from the shelves. In the bathroom, he placed in another bag the pink flannel, loofah and cake of amber-coloured soap with his grandmother's silver hair stuck in it. In the bedroom, he found her shoes: brown leather, the cream interiors with the maker's names, the sweetish smell, the heels a little worn down. 'Charity shop,' his mum said, standing outside the room because she didn't want to look at them. Henry put the shoes in another black bag his mother had labelled for that purpose.

Slowly, they stripped the flat of the grave goods, performing the last of the obsequies. In some cultures, people honoured the dead and lived amongst them; in theirs, they tidied them up and sponged away the last remaining signs that they had been alive. There was only rubbish now and Henry looked at it. An old pink nail brush. A chipped Chinese vase. A wooden fruit bowl with a stain on the bottom. Ventolin inhalers held in an awkward cluster by the shackle of a rubber band. Handbags with stiff clasps that contained boiled sweets and out-of-date pension books. And, on a small table by an armchair, a copy of the *Radio Times*, the programmes circled in blue biro.

'Put it all in the bin,' his mum said. 'Get rid of it all.'

Chapter 57

Normal Rules Don't Apply

The priest, in his long white vestments and purple stole, shuffled his notes together and mounted the step to his lectern, his bald forehead shiny with sweat. The music was still playing. It was a mournful piece on an oboe, something discreet and classical that his mother had chosen to convey a refined kind of grief.

The oboe wailed on so long that people began to shift in their seats and wonder if something had gone wrong. Eventually, the music faded. The priest blinked, stared at his notes, cleared his throat and began, his voice sonorous with holiness. His speech went on and on as the oboe had done before him, and it was full of bland piety. Henry had given him a list of facts about his grandma, but the priest didn't refer to them. Instead, he mentioned the love we feel for the departed, and the mortality we all must face, for in the midst of life we are in death. The dead live on in the children and grandchildren. The dead are not dead; they have gone on to a higher form of life. 'And, so, we remember her,' said the priest, who had never known her.

Afterwards, they stood in a courtyard behind the crematorium. It was minimal and discreet. There were empty benches and tastefully raked gravel. Thin saplings stood in wire-mesh cages. The mourners walked among the wreaths.

At last, they found the one they were looking for.

'Here we are.'

They stood around and read the inscription. 'Ivy Wilton: 1902-1978. Much loved mother and grandma.'

While the family grieved, the other mourners admired the flowers: the sprays and the lilac hearts, the white wreaths and lemon-blue sheafs, the ones in the shape of a cross or mounted on a mossy pillow, for death was a sleep and a forgetting. Chloe, who had ignored their gran for years, stood sobbing and inconsolable. Then the sun came out.

Alice was under a tree. His father joined her, and the two loitered in the awkward confederacy of smokers.

'I think that music went on too long, don't you?' his mother said. She was beside him now, awful in a black hat.

'No. It was fine.'

'Did you really think so?'

'Definitely.'

She considered this. 'I just wish someone had actually spoken about Grandma. Everything the priest said was so general. It was all so anonymous. I didn't feel Grandma was in it, anywhere, did you?'

His mother called her Grandma, because they did.

'No,' he said, looking at her.

'I *had* hoped that you would write something,' she added.

He took a breath. 'Well, I did.'

'That you'd read it out, I mean. Because the vicar just waved your piece of paper in the air and never referred to it once.'

'I know. I'm sorry'

She sighed. 'Well, it's too late now.'

'*You* could have said something,' he ventured.

She shook her head. 'I would have been too upset. And too embarrassed.'

'Yes,' he said.

'And just think,' his mother went on, adjusting her hat. 'It'll be

Alice's wedding soon. Grandma would've loved to have seen that.'

Henry turned and looked at Alice, who was still smoking under a tree. Behind her, the crematorium chimney belched black soot. Ashes to ashes, dust to dust. Then he remembered, his grandma had disliked Keith and disapproved of the match — had his mum forgotten that? She would have hated to be there. Overall, he thought, as the mourners began to leave the cemetery and drift back to their cars, and as new mourners arrived along with a fresh hearse, his grandma had timed her death rather well.

Chapter 58

The Robber Bridegroom

Henry stood in his ill-fitting jacket between his two ill-fitting sisters. He tried to smile but couldn't. Alice, a skinny bride in ivory satin, was making her usual rictus. Only Chloe seemed genuinely happy.

The bright sun made Henry squint.

'You're looking tense,' said the photographer, lowering his camera.

'You' meant Henry.

'Why won't he smile?' asked his mother, inviting those nearby to join in her condemnation of Henry's poor behaviour and the general delinquency of sons. The audience of inquisitive faces smiled politely.

The truth was that Henry was trying very hard to smile, but his face wouldn't comply. He hated people taking pictures of him. He hated the falsity of posing. He hated the bullying photographer and the people in stupid hats and suits with stupid white flowers on their stupid bloody lapels.

'Why does he always have to ruin photographs?' his mother asked.

No-one knew the answer.

Their father had vetoed a wedding car. It was an unnecessary expense. He would drive.

Alice smoked all the way to the church.

'A wedding's a big day for a woman,' his mother said, when

Henry complained. Alice drew on her cigarette. The car window was open, blowing smoke into Henry's face.

He, his mother and Chloe were squashed in the back. 'Stop moaning,' his father said. 'This day isn't about you.'

Henry said nothing. Alice's wish had come true, he saw: she was bony in her wedding dress. She had knobbly shoulders and the vertebrae in her neck were visible, as if displayed as a sign of her virtue. She had short, dyed, burnt-looking hair and everything about her was brittle or singed. Even her voice was hot and ashy. 'Get over it, Henry,' she said, when she heard him coughing behind her. 'Stop making such as bloody fuss.' She was allowed to swear on her wedding day.

He didn't say anything, just opened his window. Then Alice complained that she was cold, so he shut it again.

Before the wedding, Alice had to go on a diet, because she must be slim in her wedding dress. It was the most important thing in the world. So she began smoking more and eating the kind of food that made you thinner as you ate it: celery, watery soups, powdered drinks with a picture on the box of a girl whose hand rested on her flat belly. Sometimes, Alice abandoned her diet and ate lots of ice cream, heaping her bowl with mounds of vanilla, strawberry and chocolate and then carrying it off to the sanctuary of her room. Then there were the long baths and the water endlessly running. She spent hours in the bathroom, steam leaking under the locked door and the radio on, playing chart hits. Then more water gushed down pipes and there came the sharp smell of pine disinfectant.

Only Henry guessed what was happening.

'What are you *doing* in there?' he asked once, knocking on the door.

A strained, tight voice replied. 'Nothing. Just washing my hair.'

'You aren't.'

'What else would I be doing?'

He knew but could not say.

There was a pause, then a sigh. 'Oh, go *away*, Henry. Mind your own bloody business.'

And in the end, he did go away and he did mind his own bloody business, because there was no-one he could tell.

'Smile,' said the photographer, when he had grouped them to his satisfaction by a wall in the churchyard. Nearby, lay the peacefully sleeping dead. The sun shone in Henry's eyes, and he pinched them half-shut in the glare. His parents hadn't let him wear sunglasses to the wedding because they said he would look like someone in the Mafia. Meanwhile, Keith's family stood watching in their bad suits and haircuts, which were spiky on top and long at the back, and dyed outlandish colours: piss-yellow blond, Halloween orange, a greenish shade of black. They were the ones who looked like members of the Mafia, the real gangsters, and some of them had sunglasses on. You could see the bulges in their pockets where very likely knives or firearms were concealed, but his mother hadn't noticed that. Meanwhile, Alice, Henry and Chloe stood by the church wall. Alice was skeletal and smelled of smoke and ashes, and she stood on one side. Chloe grinned and stood on the other. Henry stood scowling in the middle.

'Why won't he smile?' his mother said again, tragic in her white hat.

Henry tried once more but failed.

And that was how he'd ruined the wedding photos, and that was why his mother would never forgive him.

Chapter 59

The Sound and the Fury

Henry was drunk in his university interview, which was not the best way to begin. Two men questioned him, one from behind the desk, the other from a position near the window. They were the Good Professor and the Bad Professor. The Bad Professor was gazing out on the courtyard where a woman was standing. He appeared to have already dismissed Henry as useless. The Good Professor had a small smile on his lips.

'So, is it your contention, Mr Truffle,' he asked gently, 'that some poets are more interested in sound than meaning?'

Henry tried to assemble his thoughts. He wasn't sure that he had any contentions. 'Pardon?' he said, hoping this would buy him some time.

The Good Professor, all nose, chin and flashing spectacles, beamed. He repeated his question about poems and the conundrum of meaning versus sound.

'Some poets are more into sound, yes,' Henry said, dimly aware he shouldn't have used the preposition 'into' like that. He did not expand. He was temporarily incapable of expansion.

'I see. Well, you said in your application that you liked Thomas,' the Good Professor went on. 'Now, that confused us a little, I admit.' His colleague gave a curt nod to the window. 'There's more than one literary Thomas you could have meant, of course.'

Henry tried to think who the second Thomas might be. He was

daunted by the 'of course'.

'So, we were wondering exactly which it was?'

Henry smiled blankly. The name John Thomas came to mind, which was how Mellors had referred to his penis in *Lady Chatterley's Lover*. He couldn't say that.

The Good Professor looked down at Henry's form. 'Thomas *is* one of your favoured authors, isn't he? Along with Lawrence and Forster?'

'Dylan,' Henry said, remembering now. He belched softly. Old Dylan had liked a drink, too. He had died of it, which made him literally a dead drunk.

The Good Professor nodded. 'Ah, *Dylan*, yes. Not Edward, then — the World War One poet?

'No,' said Henry. 'Definitely not him.' One must be assertive in one's answers.

The Bad Professor turned, assuming the posture of an academic who didn't suffer fools gladly. 'It says on your application that you admire Thomas' poetry, and "*especially the way he employs sound in his verse*".

'Yes,' said Henry. Mr Muldoon had taken them through a Dylan poem. He recalled Muldoon saying something about writers who'd 'rejected political certainties in favour of the sheer music of words.' It all seemed a long time ago. It might have been poets who'd rejected the music of words for political certainties. He couldn't remember now.

'Perhaps you would care to elucidate, Mr Truffle?'

Henry thought of that song by the Beatles: *Elucidate in the Sky with Diamonds*. Then he remembered that he'd once been on a date with a girl called Lucy, and it hadn't worked out. He smiled and stifled a hiccup. His father had given him a hip flask of vodka for his nerves, and he'd sipped from it on the train all the way down. He should have tried whiskey. Then he remembered he was supposed to be elucidating. That man wouldn't wait forever. Time was of the essence.

'Thomas didn't write to be understood,' he said at last. 'He wrote stuff to be felt. The bards were musicians, basically, weren't they? So, you can't analyse his poems in a normal way. They're sounds and feelings, not thoughts. Language is basically music.'

He thought he'd put this extremely well, but not everyone agreed, for the Bad Professor was frowning.

'And you think you can't analyse a feeling? If so, there go psychology and psychiatry. My colleagues in those departments will be dismayed.' He looked at Henry as if he had personally made those colleagues redundant.

Henry tried to clear his mind. 'No. I mean, yes, you can.'

'So how would analysing a feeling be different from analysing an idea?'

'Good question,' Henry said. His head was thick with the fog of vodka, and no answer came. Meanwhile, the Bad Professor turned away and resumed his study of the world outside the window. 'I'm not sure,' Henry admitted finally.

'Well, Mr Truffle,' resumed the Good Professor. He re-crossed a knee and plucked his trousers so the crease wouldn't be spoiled. 'Your thesis might be helped if you could give us an actual *example*, I think.'

Henry tried to think of one. 'There's that one about a fuse,' he said, eventually.

'*The force that through the green fuse drives the flower*?'

'That's the one,' Henry nodded.

'And what is it about, Mr Truffle? Perhaps you could tell us?'

Henry considered deeply. 'Life?' he hazarded.

The Nasty Professor snorted.

The Nice Professor persisted. 'Isn't it about *time*?'

'Yes,' Henry said, considering this now, because it *was* about time. It was about time he left this interview and went home; it was about time gave up any pretention to being an academic. 'But time is life, I suppose,' he added. He had read that somewhere. On a lolly stick, perhaps; or on a subway wall.

'Indeed, it is not,' said the man at the window.

'And in that poem,' the Good Professor said, ignoring his colleague, 'how does sound manifest itself as more important than time — which is, of course, the poem's more ostensible theme?'

Henry took a breath. 'Because the sounds are...' He hesitated, feeling a ball of vomit crawl up from the pit of his stomach. He swallowed it and felt his throat burn. 'Well, timeless, I suppose?' His eyes watered and he blinked. He was crying in his interview, but at least he hadn't been sick.

The Good Professor nodded, giving him another chance. 'And how can sound be timeless?' He snapped his fingers. 'There, do you see? I made a sound and it's gone. Departed. *Disparu*.'

'I suppose we have the poem,' Henry said, wiping his eyes. 'I mean, Thomas is dead, isn't he? *Il est mort*.' He was matching the Professor's French with his own but wondered if he'd said it right. He remembered his blunder with Karen. *La nuit est jaune*.

'Yes,' said Professor Nice. 'We do indeed have the poem.'

If only Henry had it now, he could bloody well read it. 'But unlike Dylan,' he improvised, 'the poem isn't dead. When I read it, the sounds are still there, like a melody. Like, I don't know, *Auld Lang Syne*. No-one analyses *Auld Lang Syne*, do they? It's in some weird Scotch dialect. They sing it. And that's enough.'

Professor Nasty turned. 'So, you think studying literature is a waste of time? Is *that* your contention? That we should all just sing the poems and chant the novels and not analyse them? In that case my job would go, as would my learned colleague's.'

Henry realised had just fired most of the staff in the humanities department. 'No, I didn't mean that.'

'Then what did you mean?'

Henry frowned. 'I'm not sure.'

There was a sigh and a shuffling of notes.

'Well, I think that's it, Mr Truffle. Thanks for coming down to see us. We'll be in touch.'

Outside, his mother was waiting in the neat square of Georgian buildings. Soft, yellowish stone; a city built of sand that would crumble and dissolve in the rain, which was falling gently, like the realisation of his failure. His mother smiled. She was smart in her red coat, patent-leather shoes, black handbag, and red silk scarf. She'd dressed up as if she was to be interviewed, too. 'So, how did you get on?' she asked.

'I think I messed it up,' he admitted.

'You mean the vodka didn't help?'

'No.'

'Oh, well, that was your father's idea. I told him it wouldn't work. Not in the morning, and on an empty stomach.'

'Yes. No.'

'Well, let's go home. It may have gone better than you think. These things often do. You never know, Henry.'

'No,' he said.

But he did know. He had failed the interview and would not go to that prestigious college.

On the way home he listened to the sound of the train wheels on the track. 'Pomper pomper,' the wheels said, as they went over the points. The train's sound was its meaning, he knew then, and it was talking to him, and it was correct in its assumptions. For those men had been pompous, and he was glad he'd gone to the interview disguised as a drunken Dylan Thomas, and he was damned if he wouldn't become a writer in the future just to spite them. One day he would show them what idiots they were.

Chapter 60

On The Road

Henry received only one university offer, because he'd refused to put himself through the ordeal of another interview. Despite this, he retained the conviction that he was a genius. He believed it in the way he believed in God: that is, sporadically and half-heartedly. It might turn out to be true in the future, so there was no point in discounting it as a possibility. One place, at least, had accepted him, so that was where he was going. It was a university he knew nothing about, in a city he'd never visited, to do a course described in a prospectus he hadn't read. In classical tragedy, the Three Fates had decided everything, spinning, measuring and cutting the thread of the hero's destiny. The protagonist thought he was in control of his life, but it was The Fates who were really in control of him. Well, let them decide his life too. Henry didn't care, and insouciance was a virtue.

Francis hadn't applied to university. His recent grades had been poor, and like Mr Micawber in the novel they'd studied with Ma Bartlett, he was looking about him. He was a citizen of nowhere and everywhere. Having read a book by Sartre, he claimed that life was absurd, anyway. Knowing this, he said, made him free; others weren't free because they were cowards and conformists and members of the *petite bourgeoisie*. On the strength of this, Francis announced that he would take a year off after the drudgery of A-levels. He would get a job on the bin lorries. He would travel and drift about. He would 'go the full Jack Kerouac' — whatever that meant. Henry was deeply envious. He imagined himself in a pair of Levis and with a backpack over his shoulders, hitchhiking down an endless road in America, heading nowhere, which was the best destination to have if you were a Zen Buddhist, which he sort of was. Meanwhile, there were exams to revise for.

Before he knew it, it was study leave, and he was sitting in a deckchair in the full heat of the sun, poring over history and poetry books, and pouring his sweat onto them, for it was very hot in the garden, listening to the ripple of the neighbours' pool and the soughing of the wind in the conker tree, which wasn't a conquer tree, because its green leaves and bark and sticky buds preached the message of ease and surrender, and of letting things go. Just relax, said the tree, as the swing ebbed this way and that, and then the swing said let the wind carry you, it will be all right. He read with one eye closed, due to the glare from the page, and consequently one half of his brain, like a budgie in a cage with a sheet over it, nodded off. After a while, the other half, downing tools in a spirit of solidarity, followed suit.

'Are you asleep, Henry?'

His mother was beside him with a mug of coffee on a tray. 'You have an exam this afternoon. You're supposed to be revising.'

He blinked. 'I *am* revising.'

'With your eyes shut?'

He cleared his throat. 'I was trying to remember what's on this page.' He pointed to his lap, but for some reason his book was lying face-down on the grass.

His mother shook her head. 'Henry, I do think you should be taking your exams a little more seriously. You're not taking an A-level in sunbathing, as far as I'm aware.' She paused. 'I think you're just daydreaming, aren't you? And I think that's Francis' fault. He's a bad influence on you. He's not focusing on his future, so you aren't, either.'

'That's not true.'

She set down the coffee. 'You can't just copy your friends, Henry. You can't just float through life.'

Henry looked around him. The balmy air that hung above the garden was full of drifting seeds and dandelion clocks. The juicy grass was cool under his feet. He heard once more the ripple and whir of the filtration system of their neighbours' swimming pool. 'I'm not floating. I'm working.'

She ran her eyes over his naked torso, the shorts and flip flops, the drink he'd made himself that was now a watery orange slush of melted ice-cubes. 'It doesn't look like it.'

'I'll do all right, you'll see.'

She took a deep breath and quelled whatever it was she wanted to say. 'Very well, Henry. As long as you do your best.'

'Of course.'

She went away.

That afternoon, he went in for his history exam sore with sunburn. He began his answers, writing about the Reformation and Counter-Reformation, but his shirt stuck to him and his tie was too tight. He wrote about Martin Luther and Calvin and the Wars of Religion, then about the atrocities that had resulted from being a Protestant or Catholic at the wrong time or place. Then he paused, sweating once again, for it was as hot in the school hall as it had been in the garden, and there was no air, no voice of the tree or pool or drifting wind-borne seed. His mind wandered. Then some words came back from the poem he'd read just before he fell asleep, something about the mind being an ocean where everyone finds his own resemblance, or a garden that annihilates all that's made, reducing it to a green thought in a green shade.

He shook himself and carried on, trying to concentrate. He wrote about transubstantiation and consubstantiation, and the debates over the communion bread and wine that could lead to a heretic being burned alive. He wrote about the Defenestration of Prague and the breaking of the mediaeval world view and the new fascination with the human form, remembering how he'd admired his own exquisitely muscular brown one in the deckchair that morning. He wrote about Benvenuto Cellini and the new preoccupation with autobiography and the individual self, and he wondered, as he did so, how he might use his own life and put it in a book one day. Then he wrote about the abuses of the mediaeval church, and pardoners selling pigs' bones and claiming they were the bones of Jesus. They were bones that would save your soul, and Henry quoted a bit from *The Pardoner's Tale* to corroborate his point. Then, as the invigilator at the front solemnly announced that they had 'five more minutes', he realised he'd gone wildly off topic, because the question wasn't really asking about that, and he'd just written down everything he knew, but it was too late now.

Chapter 61

String Theory

Now that the exams were over, and now that it was too late to worry about them, the three boys decided they must do something to occupy themselves. Henry and John had wearied of their girlfriends, who, in any case, were on holiday or otherwise engaged, washing their hair, or having second thoughts, or doing holiday jobs and never available. The boys were thrown back on each other's company, and so they played sport, or tried to. It was hard, because everything had lost its intensity, or seemed to require more effort than they were prepared to give. They attributed this to the heat, or post-exam fatigue. Anyway, they pursued the various sports that were their favourite waste of time, and it was mainly tennis that occupied them, which they called 'tenis' to rhyme with 'penis', thinking this funny. Sport was a virile activity, but it was only ironically masculine, in the way everything was ironic now, even themselves.

Henry and John played more often than Francis, because he was committed to existentialism, and that had apparently proved to be more exhausting than he'd expected. In any case, he was rubbish at tennis. So, Henry and John played each other, copying the strokes of the players they'd seen on TV, albeit sardonically. They adopted their mannerisms and affectations: the headbands, sweatbands, sports bags, and towels to drape around their necks when they ate their freckled, sun-warmed bananas. They were sporting dilettantes, and the more trivial something was, the harder they worked at it, especially the look. It was a sort of rule that summer.

They played until their legs grew heavy and drunken and sweat stung their eyes, their shoes brick-red with dust. Henry was using his father's old racquet. It had an unfashionable shape and a thick grip that had gone sticky with the passing decades, but it would do for now. John had a new racquet because John always had a new everything. It didn't matter. Nothing mattered. He and John played rally after rally, not counting points or games or sets, because why bother? You just hit the ball as hard and as low as you could for as long as you could. And in that way, in the hypnotic exchange of balls, you forgot the future. You focused on the ball and your tan and your muscles and the next passing shot, and it became a kind of trance.

As he played on in a kind of waking drowse, Henry remembered playing with his father on holiday when he was very young. His father was wearing his knee-length, war-time shorts, the ones Henry's mother said were an embarrassment and should have been thrown out on VE day. His father didn't care what she thought, because as far as he was concerned, the war had never ended. He had pulled his khaki socks up to his knees and wore ancient grey plimsolls and a white shirt that strained across his belly. His bald head had gone red in the sun. 'Come on,' said his father, his tongue wedged in the corner of his mouth. 'Play seriously.' His father wanted proper rallies, because tennis without rallies wasn't tennis, but Henry would insist on hitting the ball out, or into the net.

Henry applied himself, but the more seriously he tried, the worse he became. A tightness spread though his limbs and made him misjudge his shots. Balls flew sideways, or winged uselessly over his father's head. 'Come on,' his father urged, more impatient now. But Henry couldn't come on, and they wasted time fetching squandered balls from the other courts, apologising to the people who were better than them and in the middle of important-looking sets, where every shot was measured and gracefully spun, lobbed or angled just within the tramlines.

On the adjoining court, his mother had played with Alice and Chloe. Chloe ran about, red-cheeked and russet-haired, swiping at balls and laughing when she missed. His mother was soft and pale in her tennis skirt. She could only serve underarm on account of her bad shoulder, and from the back you could see the twist of her spine, and the way she carried one shoulder higher than the other. He loved his mother more then, because her body was wrong, and he admired her too, because, for her, tennis was just a bit of fun and could never be anything else. He wished he could be like that, but knew he could not, because something competitive and male hectored him when he did poorly.

It was harder to love Alice. She played with a detached competence, enduring the tiresome process, but waiting for something more interesting to happen. Her long plait hung down her back, and she had thin legs, and a racquet that dangled from her grip like a fashion accessory. She didn't seem to care what happened, because tennis was a stupid game that made you hot and sweaty for no good reason. You only played it on holiday because it was expected.

Tennis mattered to his father. Only women thought games were trivial and not worth bothering about, which was why it was important that Henry took it seriously too. So, when Henry hit another ball into the net and gave way to a fit of temper, his father announced, face dark with rage, that he'd had enough. He marched off the court, leaving Henry alone. Henry watched him go. He'd wanted to have brilliant rallies and impress his father with his technique, but he didn't know how, because he didn't have any technique. And now he'd ruined it, and his father had ruined it, and they had ruined it together, because that's what men did.

'It's only a game, Henry,' his mother had said, coming across from the other court and consoling him as they watched the bald old man disappearing into the distance. 'It's just a bit of fun. You're not professionals, you know. There's no need to fly into a rage.'

'I know.'

'Are you all right, mate?'

John was crouched on the other side of the net and waiting for a service that hadn't come.

Henry was staring out across a cricket pitch, where an old man was flattening the square with an enormous, spiked roller. He looked down at his old racket, like something out of the ark. The grip had left sticky marks on his hands. 'Yeah,' he said. 'I'm okay. It's just this piece-of-shit racquet that's the problem.'

John, who had the latest Slazenger with a padded brown leather handle and nylon strings, nodded. 'You should get a new one, then.'

'Yeah,' he said. 'I will.'

'Where did you get that old thing anyway?' John straightened his back, poking his sweaty fringe out of his eyes.

'My dad,' Henry said, as if that explained everything.

Chapter 62

Against the Day

They were the Three Musketeers again and out in Francis' mum's cleaning van. They drove uphill past Henry's house to the place where rich people lived, passing through the tall iron gates that were closed at night. Each house was four times the size of a regular one and contained lives four times better than theirs.

'One day I'll live in a pink house,' said Henry. There was a pretty one set behind a lozenge of green lawn. It was the colour of the icing on a cake, which is what it was, for anyone successful in life.

Francis laughed. 'Pink houses are for fags, mate.' His eyes twinkled. He wasn't being serious. He never was, because seriousness was boring.

It was picture postcard England. They drove on and circled a village green where there was a pair of mediaeval stocks, and a village shop with bottle-glass windows. On either side, stood a post-box and a telephone box, like a pair of Beefeaters standing sentry over a faded idyll. Meanwhile, on the green, young girls in short skirts were running up and down holding long poles like fishing nets. Their limbs were toned and brown, their hair flouncing as they ran. It looked from a distance as if they were Nabokovian nymphs chasing butterflies.

'Shall we give them a surprise?' Francis said. Before they knew what was happening, he had driven onto the green, wheels bumping, the girls scattering, the games mistress blowing madly at her whistle. Francis drove in lazy circles, hanging out of the window and whooping, like a cowboy corralling cattle. Then, when he had the girls were huddled in the middle of the green, he drove off at speed, bumping off the grass and running straight into the path of a stationary police car. Francis jammed on the brakes and came to a halt.

The policeman climbed out and strolled towards them, reaching for the notepad in his top pocket. Francis leaned out of his open window. 'Hello, Officer,' he said, smiling. An existentialist never apologised, and he wasn't about to start. 'Can I help you?' This was a nice touch, and it appeared to throw the policeman for a moment.

'What do you think you're doing?' the policeman asked. He had ginger sideburns that quoted a pale, gormless face.

'I can explain,' said Francis.

The officer took a step back and wrote the number of the licence plate on his pad.

'You see,' said Francis, improvising, 'we've been under a lot of stress lately, that's the problem.'

'Stress?' The policeman looked up.

'Yes, Officer. We've just finished our A-levels, you see. I think we went a bit insane just then. A psychotic episode, you might say. A reaction to all the pressure.'

'We?' The officer peered into the car, realising for the first time that there were accomplices. 'Names?' he asked. They told him — Henry Higgins and John Silver — and he made a note. 'Exams?' he repeated.

'Yes.'

'A-levels, you said?' He pronounced it suspiciously, as if he'd never heard of them.

'Yes.'

He wrote it all down. 'And you were feeling "stressed", you say?'

'Yes. Stressed, that's the word, Officer. It's the pressure, like I said. Exams *are* a lot of pressure, as I'm sure you know. It won't happen again.'

'I should hope not.' The policeman pushed back his helmet. His ginger hair was dark with sweat. They waited while he considered what to do.

Meanwhile, high-pitched cries came from the green. The game of lacrosse had resumed. It seemed that the honey-limbed girls and their mistress were not to be put off by a mere cleaning van driven by a teenage yobbo, one who was now getting his comeuppance.

The officer cleared his throat. 'This is a private green, so I'm not sure if normal laws apply here. I'll have to enquire as to the correct procedure.'

Francis bowed. 'Yes, Officer. We understand that there might be no legal precedent. We're very sorry,' he said.

If there was anything more the officer should do, he couldn't think of it, and the word 'precedent' seemed to have thrown him now. 'Off you go, then. And remember — I'll be watching you.'

Francis bowed his head, starting the engine and driving away at a sedate pace. When Henry looked back, the policeman was still there, standing in the road and staring after them.

It wasn't only in cars and vans that they got up to mischief. Sometimes, Francis borrowed his brother's Kawasaki 125 trial bike — lime-green, high mudguards, thick tyres permanently caked in mud — and drove around at midnight with Henry riding pillion. They followed the narrow beam of the single headlight where fog curled like the tendrils of a plant, Francis bumping up kerbs and onto pavements, slaloming through back alleys that had been blocked with metal barriers to deter anti-social yobbos like them.

They rode to a local park, mist-shrouded and deserted, revving the engine as they climbed the bank from the carpark and skidding onto the ancient lawns, the earth churning and spattering under them, their bodies locked together on the turns, the roar of the engine echoing off the trees. A light came on in a distant clubhouse, but by then they had come slithering off the grass, and there was no squad car awaiting them this time, no quizzical officer with ginger sideburns and a pen and notepad. They roared off, unchallenged and free, Henry clinging to Francis, and the engine's vibrations travelling through them.

Chapter 63

Goodbye to All That

Henry's suitcase still wasn't packed. He'd delayed for as long as he could and he wasn't ready, because he would never be ready. His college had sent a reading list that he'd failed to get through. He was supposed to be studying English literature, and they'd suggested he begin by reading books by people who were self-evidently not English. Ovid. Plato. Sophocles. Melville. Joyce. Maybe the course wasn't what he'd thought? Maybe there was somewhere else he should be going, and someone else he should be being? He'd left it to chance, and chance couldn't be trusted. Francis said none of it mattered anyway, as long as he was 'authentic,' whatever that meant.

Henry yawned. His suitcase yawned. He threw things in, any old how. Then his mother came in and pulled them all out again.

'You can't arrive with your clothes creased,' she said. 'And that isn't the way to fold a shirt. I've shown you countless times.' She showed him again, folding the arms in and dividing the torso in two, then smoothing the material with her hand. 'See?'

She began to re-do his packing. The lid of the case, which was yellow plastic, nodded as she arranged things as if it approved. She was folding him away, he thought; dividing him into segments, so the various parts of him could be squared and transported far away and with a minimum of bother. He remembered being small and helping her to fold sheets in the garden, the two of them coming together as if in a formal dance, the clean sheet, sun-warmed, going into the basket on the lawn, so that when they carried it in there was always the head of a daisy on top, or a sprig of dried grass.

'It wouldn't be an ideal way to start, would it,' said his mother, 'arriving with everything creased and scruffy?'

'No,' he said. 'I suppose not.'

'You have to prepare for things, Henry,' she said, 'not just do them anyhow. You've left everything to the last minute, as usual.'

'I know.'

But Francis said less was more, and he was never on time for anything. He never wore a watch. He said those who worried about time went mad in the end. So, Henry hadn't worried, and hadn't prepared, and hadn't noticed as the days wore away until only one remained.

His mother looked at him. 'Look, I'll finish this. You go and do something else. No sense in mooning about.'

Moonlike, Henry left the room. He was angry with the suitcases that must be packed and the clothes that must be folded. He was angry with his friends for taking different paths, and with his sisters for not understanding, and with his school for not preparing him for this act of going away.

Then he grew pale because he remembered Jacquie's panties. He'd left them in his suitcase, and his mother would find them, and how would he explain them away? When he'd asked, Jacquie had given him a pair to take with him, passing him the neatly laundered underwear in a clear plastic bag so he could take a little of her with him. Well, it was too late to worry about that now. It was too late for everything.

He stood in the hall, saying goodbye to the house, the mirror, his reflection. Suddenly, everything was valedictory in tone, and humdrum objects were newly precious to him. The paintings of horses and noble peasants; the suspended bells his mother called 'the gong,' and rang when it was dinner time. The yin-yang dogs in their bed. The great horse-chestnut tree in the garden with the swing underneath they used to play on.

He returned to his room, because there were too many things to say goodbye to, and his life was in every one.

'There,' his mother said, when the hasps of the case had finally been snapped shut. 'You're all set.' If she'd found the panties, she said nothing about them. 'Now, don't open it, or I'll have to pack it all over again. If you want to take anything else, you'll have to put it in another bag.'

'All right.'

And that was it.

As it was his last day, he must say goodbye to more than the house; formality must be observed. They drove to see Alice and Keith, the latter ushering them in through the plasticky door of fake wood. He and Alice, newlywed, lived in a new house on a new estate.

'So, you're off to university then, Henry?' Keith asked, in his cheery cockney baritone.

'Yes.'

'Well, enjoy yourself, then!'

They shook hands.

'I will.'

'You want a coffee or something?'

'Thanks.'

'Right you are. Have a look at our wedding photos while I make it, mate. There are some great ones.'

'Thanks.'

Henry stood in the tobacco-smelling lounge with its fake wooden cabinets and smoked glass coffee tables and a brown sofa pretending to be leather. He turned the pages of the album that had 'Alice and Keith' on the cover. The photographer had displayed his creativity by putting their faces inside a love-heart, a balloon, a bubble and a wine glass. Henry saw them through a glass, darkly. Shuddering, he closed the book. He saw that in the corner of the room there was a fish tank. It wasn't like Jacquie's fish tank that was full of guppies and gobies. At the bottom of this one stood a plastic figure in a diving suit. He had a helmet that breathed out bubbles, and he looked oddly stranded and helpless.

'Good luck, then,' said Alice. She had come into the room without him noticing and was watching him inspect their belongings. She was very thin in a skirt and light sweater, her feet in a pair of fluffy slippers with faces on the front. Her hair still had the burnt-looking highlights; her manner was cold and brittle, her grin fixed. He didn't ask her if she hated her house and everything in it, because he knew; and she didn't ask him what he thought of it, because she knew.

'Take care,' she said. 'And don't do anything silly.' Her voice was brisk. She was playing the role of an elder sister who knew about life, a life that had burned her and left its mark.

'I won't.'

'Make sure you write,' she said. He'd never written her a letter in his life and wasn't about to start now. 'And keep in touch.'

'I will.'

She planted a cigarette-scented kiss on his cheek. And that was it.

The next morning, he said goodbye to Chloe. She had a new Cairn terrier called Polly. Despite or because of killing the puppy when she was young, Chloe was in love with all things canine. 'Goodbye,' she said, holding the dog up like a puppet and making its paw wave. 'Say goodbye, Polly.'

'Goodbye, Polly,' Henry said.

'No, that's not what I meant. I was talking to the dog.'

'I know.'

She had never understood his sense of humour.

He and Chloe hugged awkwardly then, and the dog got squashed between them. It yelped, and they laughed, because for once it didn't matter.

Goodbye, goodbye.

They set off at last: his father driving, his mother navigating, Henry in the back. You couldn't get lost on so simple a journey, and yet they had — a sign not seen, an exit missed — and all because Arthur was driving too fast, Mum said, because you can't just bark instructions at me like that with the signposts whizzing past every second. His father had clamped his tongue in the corner of his mouth. He had to drive on to another motorway exit so he could turn round and retrace his steps, and soon the air was blue with muttered expletives.

And now it was goodbye to all that.

Henry opened the window. His father was smoking and Henry had to let it out somehow. He blinked in the wind, and it hurt his eye. A window was a wind-eye, the Vikings had said. Once he'd worn a Viking longship around his neck and he'd told a lie to Jacquie Sea-Cucumber about his Norse ancestors, those savage men with horned helmets and drooping moustaches who'd come across the North sea to engage in a little light raping and pillaging. That was then but this was now. And though he had her knickers in his case, he wasn't sure he was really with her any more. Because you couldn't have a person; you could only borrow them. He blinked again. A single wind-tear fell. He thought about where he was going next. He'd seen photos of the university in the prospectus, and it was a place of ugly iterations: concrete and glass, glass and concrete, repeated ad infinitum. It was a campus somewhere near the end of England, where England sputtered out into the sea.

He stared out of the window as the framed landscapes zipped by. Wayside litter. Fields. Plastic caught in trees, waving like bunting. Laybys with vans selling greasy food. More fields, a green quilt thrown over the despoiled bones of Old England. Telegraph poles, the wire leaping nimbly from post to post. He imagined himself sliding on that wire or vaulting from hilltop to tree towards his future. Or walking the wire, his pole outstretched, over an endless green sea.

Acknowledgements

Thanks to Claire Steele and Jill Glenn at Constellations Press for your tireless and patient help in bringing Henry to fruition. I have doubtless been a demanding and tiresome diva at times, but I am grateful for your sensitivity to my requests and for your diligent and perceptive efforts in getting Henry to an acceptable shape and fighting weight. I am deeply indebted to you both.

Thanks too to my wife, Bridget Strugnell, for kindly agreeing to read various mangled versions of the narrative and for always offering helpful and constructive comments when I was tempted to abandon the whole project. Your help has been invaluable. Thanks also to my son, Rowan, who has had to endure many literary conversations about characters and scenarios about which he knows little and probably cares less.

I would also like to thank the 1960s and 70s, which furnish the background for this narrative and which saw the birth of so many extraordinary musical and creative talents in Britain, from The Beatles to David Bowie. These geniuses also created Henry, and he is their progeny.

Constellations Press is a small independent press
committed to publishing works of fiction, memoir and essays.

We publish books that boldly reimagine society and
celebrate our diverse humanity, adding to the
total sum of the world's beauty.

constellationspress.co.uk